MURDER AT
NATIONAL
GEOGRAPHIC

MURDER AT
NATIONAL
GEOGRAPHIC

PAUL MARTIN

Ⅱ
Gemini Originals

Gemini Original Books, Falls Church, Virginia.
Address inquiries to geminioriginalbooks@gmail.com.

Front cover photo iStock.com/michipinter.
Cover design by Moboyo.

ISBN: 979-8-218-51187-6

This novel is dedicated to my former colleagues at National Geographic. Together, we shared some of the Society's golden years, our own treasured version of Camelot. —PM

Impossible Journey: Danger, Death, and Deceit
On the Lewis & Clark Expedition

"Lively, entertaining, and historically compelling." —*Kirkus Reviews*

"Lovers of realistic frontier adventure will feast." —*Publishers Weekly*

Summer of Love: A Music & Murder Mystery

"Murder, music, and a tour of '67 San Francisco power this literary mystery. Martin exhibits a mastery of the city." —*Publishers Weekly*

"A deeply immersing, character-rich plot. A truly enthralling read from start to finish." —*San Francisco Book Review*

Dance of the Millions: A Music & Murder Mystery

"The Cuba of legend re-emerges in all its glamour, seediness and danger. A classic recreation." —Bestselling author James Conaway

"A striking work of historical fiction and political drama with a murder mystery tying it together." —*Publishers Weekly*

Killin' Floor Blues: A Music & Murder Mystery

"This rich, atmospheric thriller follows musicologist detectives into the heart of the blues. The music jumps off the page." —*Publishers Weekly*

"Martin's admiration for the talented, mostly self-taught musicians shows through. An honest page-turner." —*Historical Novels Review*

Lost in Saigon

"A smart blend of vivid observations, profound political views, and sensational romantic quests in the face of war." —*Chicago Book Review*

"Martin has probably forgotten more than I ever learned during my own tour of duty in the City of Sorrows." —Author Nicholas Cain

Far Haven

"A time-traveling showstopper [featuring] a bleak, dystopian future where dissidents are exiled to the past." —*Manhattan Book Review*

"Full of memorable characters. A frightening look at the past and an even more terrifying glance into the future." —*Los Angeles Book Review*

Chapter 1

Quito, Ecuador, June 1964

Riley sauntered down Avenida Sucre to the sound of honking taxis, clattering trolleys, and clip-clopping horse-drawn carriages. The handsome six-foot-two American shared the sidewalk with throngs of plump Amerindian women in ornate embroidered blouses, fleet-footed urchins with mischievous smiles, easygoing bohemians in jaunty fedoras, and slim señoritas whose dark eyes lingered tantalizingly on him. All around, jabbering hawkers bargained with gabby customers over bouquets of technicolor flowers, bins of equally vivid fruit and vegetables, and spicy, aromatic foods of all descriptions, a scene out of an old-time travel poster.

This was Riley's first visit to Quito, a city that had never entered his mind until a few weeks ago. If anyone had asked him what Quito was famous for, he'd have guessed absolutely nothing. He'd have been wrong. For one thing, Quito was the oldest capital city in South America, founded in 1534. It was also the second highest capital in the world, after La Paz, Bolivia.

Quito sprawled across the sides of a narrow valley 9,350 feet high in the Andes, in north-central Ecuador. It was home to nearly four hundred thousand people, their tile-roofed row houses and apartment buildings painted in every color of the rainbow. The city's mountain setting and proximity to the equator blessed it with balmy days and cool nights—ideal weather, Riley thought, although he'd purposely avoided the eight-month-long rainy season.

Quito wasn't as cosmopolitan as Caracas, Riley's last base of operations, but it was civilized enough that he didn't have to rough it. He liked clean hotel rooms, good restaurants, and

1

exciting nightlife, and Quito had enough of all those things to keep him happy. Riley had never found much to commend gritty backwater outposts, with their tumbledown hovels and scruffy inhabitants. No, cities were definitely Riley's style.

The tall American paused on the corner of García Moreno to flick the ash from his Ecuador Sumatra panatela. Smoothing his unruly black hair and adjusting his aviator sunglasses, he gazed at the picture-postcard buildings in the historic heart of Quito. The gaudiest church in the city, La Compañía de Jesús, rose to his right like a gingerbread castle. There were enough colonial-era churches and monasteries in Quito to keep a tourist slack-jawed for days, but Riley wasn't here to take in the sights.

Since he'd been in the capital, he'd hit most of the outdoor markets and curio shops selling native crafts. He'd gotten lost more than once prowling the maze of narrow streets and cobblestone squares. He was working his way up to the better shops, where he had a greater chance of finding what he was looking for—authentic artifacts from South America's indigenous Jivaro tribe, the wild, warlike headhunters who lived in the remote Amazon rainforest of southeastern Ecuador and northern Peru, a forbidding realm where casual travelers never ventured.

On Avenida Simón Bolívar, Riley stopped in front of a craft and curio shop recommended to him by an English expat he'd bumped into one night in his hotel bar. A garrulous fellow with rheumy eyes and a white tropical suit, the man had winked and touched the side of his nose, assuring Riley that he'd find the genuine articles at "old man García's place." Riley bought the Limey another shot of aguardiente in thanks and made his escape before the gent's boozy breath melted the buttons on his new Abercrombie & Fitch safari jacket.

A little brass bell on the shop door tinkled as Riley stepped inside. The shop was a murky cavern crammed with every sort of souvenir that Ecuador produced—the country's famous but misnamed Panama hats, serapes and blankets, bags of locally

2

grown coffee, leather goods, wood carvings, and musical instruments—typical wares he'd already seen in abundance. Riley picked up a few items and looked them over, disappointment registering on his face. As he was about to chalk up the drunken Brit's advice as bogus and make his exit, an aged man with a limp shuffled from the back room.

"Good afternoon, señor," the man said, beaming a cheery welcome. "May I help you find something? We recently received some very nice alpaca scarves. I'm sure that your lady friends would love them."

Riley frowned and shook his head. "I'm not looking for souvenirs," he said. "I was told you might have some authentic Jivaro artifacts. Museum quality."

The dealer scrutinized his customer. "What you seek is hard to come by, señor. It can be quite expensive." The dealer's face took on a different aspect. Instead of a welcoming shopkeeper he looked like a man who'd happily slit someone's throat in a dark alley.

"The cost doesn't necessarily present a problem," Riley said, "within reason."

The dealer nodded. "Please step this way then. I may have what you're looking for." He turned and limped toward the back room.

Riley followed the old man into a stockroom piled high with merchandise. Most of it was the kind he'd seen out front. Before he could register his displeasure, the dealer opened a door at the rear of the stockroom. He flicked on a light and beckoned to Riley. "In here, señor."

The small chamber Riley entered held racks of long thin blowguns and quivers of needlelike darts, bows and arrows, bright feathered headdresses, bead necklaces, wooden flutes, and other unusual items. In a case at the end of the room was a display of shrunken heads. Their dark, wizened little faces were the handiwork of the Jivaros, the only South American tribe never conquered by the Spanish or any rival tribes and still fiercely independent.

3

Riley stood in silent amazement. "Is this stuff for real?" he asked. "I've heard there's plenty of fake Jivaro artifacts on the market."

The dealer drew himself up to his full height. "Señor, you insult me. I've been in business for over thirty years, long enough to know the difference between authentic goods and tourist reproductions. If you like, I can give you the names of several distinguished local collectors who've trusted my judgment."

Riley waved him off. "That won't be necessary." He could imagine the type of collectors the man was talking about— chiselers who wouldn't hesitate to buy stolen antiquities from grave robbers. He walked over to the case of shrunken heads. "How much for these bad boys?"

"In U.S. dollars, one thousand each."

"And the blowguns and darts?"

"Five hundred for the pair."

"Are these poison darts?"

"Indeed. They are tipped with curare. I would not advise you to test them by pricking your finger. You'd be dead before you reached the front door."

Riley pointed to three of the shrunken heads. "I'll take Larry, Curly, and Moe."

"I beg your pardon?"

"Just a joke. I'll also take two of the blowguns and quivers of darts, and a couple of bows and some arrows." He perused the other items and ended up selecting a substantial quantity. "Total all this up and give me a bill. I don't walk around with as much cash as this will require, so I'll be back tomorrow with the money."

"That will be fine."

"And I'll need complete documentation as to where each of these articles came from—specific regions and any other information that establishes their authenticity."

"Naturally. I demand that sort of information from any trader bringing me artifacts."

The dealer made notations about everything Riley had selected, then he led the way back to the showroom to calculate the cost. He looked up as he finished making out the sales slip. "May I have your name, señor?"

Riley smiled. "That won't be necessary."

The dealer handed the slip to Riley, who gave it a quick inspection. "Okay then," he said. "I'll see you tomorrow morning. Say ten o'clock?"

"Very good. I should mention that you will likely incur additional expenses shipping these items out of the country. Our postal and customs agents aren't unduly greedy, but they have to live. They routinely charge for 'special wavers' to ship parcels without checking the contents."

"It's to be expected," Riley said.

The next day, Riley saw his purchases safely packed. After he'd paid the necessary bribes, his acquisitions were handed over to the shippers. He then turned to the least pleasant but necessary part of his trip. It began with a meeting with freelance photographer Jake Plummer, a skinny blond Texan with a fondness for dark rum and exotic women. Plummer had been biding his time in Quito by shooting architectural shots for another client. Riley and Plummer were soon on their way to the little town of Baeza east of Quito. The back of their rented Land Rover was full of camping gear and photographic equipment, plus a pair of Jivaro headdresses Riley had retained. Both men muttered curses during the seventy-mile drive on increasingly abysmal dirt roads.

Baeza offered convenient access to the indigenous Quijos Quichua villages scattered along the nearby Coca River, a stretch of muddy brown water meandering through the western fringe of the Amazon rainforest. The area suited Riley's needs, a lush jungle wilderness that could be almost anywhere. Riley was willing to put up without the amenities of Quito for a few days, although the steamy climate was about all he could take. He was drenched with sweat just sitting still. Then there were the intermittent downpours that never let him forget he was in a tropical environment and which ramped up the ferocious humidity when the sun came back out.

They found accommodations in Baeza at a place billing itself as the Maravillosa, the Spanish word for "marvelous," though there was little to be seen that met that description. The building sagged like a tired old man who wanted to sit down. The "dining room" was a wishful exaggeration, and the empanadas they were served for dinner could have been filled with anything from horse meat to minced shoe leather. Riley was glad that he always carried an ample stash of stomach medicine.

Riley's bedroom at the Maravillosa left him questioning the wisdom of crawling between the sheets. He feared what else might be crawling there. He decided he would spread his bedroll on the floor and avoid finding out. The boy who showed him the room grinned as if making an apology. The bathroom down the hall was a thing of wonder.

Their first day in Baeza, Riley and Plummer explored the sights. The town was said to be a center of commerce dealing in agriculture and livestock. It certainly had that aroma. A number of shops supplied the basic needs of the townsfolk— clothing, food, guns, liquor. There was also a single cantina with guitar music trickling out the open door. While Plummer communed with the local luminaries inside, Riley continued his investigations. The dusty streets seemed to be populated principally by free-range chickens, mongrel dogs, and gawking, gap-toothed children garbed in a colorful assortment of rags. The chickens ignored him, but the dogs and kids formed a yammering train that followed him everywhere. He felt like the Pied Piper of Hamelin. He concluded that he liked everything about the town except being in it.

That evening, Riley settled into his room with the file on the Amazon rainforest that he'd photocopied from the *Encyclopaedia Britannica*. He needed to brush up on what they might be encountering so he could avoid any unphotogenic displays of terror or disgust. Over in a back room of the cantina, Jake

Plummer was going toe to toe with a Baezan floozy named Carmen. It was a fairly even contest.

Riley and Plummer spent the next two days visiting indigenous villages around Baeza. They settled on a collection of thatch-roofed shanties perched on a bend of the Coca River amidst thick rainforest vegetation. Riley parked the Land Rover at the edge of the village and Plummer hopped out to track down the village headman. Making inquiries with a combination of Texas Spanglish and improvised sign language, Plummer located the village chief, a squat, somber old fellow wearing what appeared to be a grass hula skirt. After a brief conference, Plummer returned to the Land Rover.

"The boss man says it's all right if we camp here for a few days," Plummer told Riley. "And he's willing to let us hire his people as guides."

"Perfect," Riley said. "We can dress them in the Jivaro gear I brought along for a few shots with me in the picture. The rest of the time they'll look like ordinary guides and bearers."

The next morning, Riley and Plummer set out on the Coca River in two canoes, with a guide in each vessel to do the paddling. They hugged the bank so that Plummer's photos included the dense jungle in the background, making any identification of their precise location impossible. Riley sat in the front of his canoe with the determined expression of an adventurer headed deep into little-known parts of the Amazon. He wore his shabbiest khaki shirt and pants, everything suitably stained and soaked with sweat. A beat-up Panama hat added to the image of a seasoned backcountry traveler.

High overhead, black-and-white Andean condors circled in the blue arc of sky like aerial undertakers. Jade green parrots burst from the forest and skimmed across the swirling brown river. Six-inch-wide blue morpho butterflies wafted along the edge of the jungle like iridescent pennants. Frisky giant otters slid from the banks, and a pod of curious pink river dolphins nosed around their canoes like creatures from the mind of a surrealist. Riley never gave the spectacular wildlife a second thought. He was too busy mopping his brow and pulling on his canteen in the steam bath heat.

After a long lunch break and siesta back at the village, the foursome headed into the nearby jungle on one of the local hunting trails. Plummer captured shots of Riley hacking at the tangled vegetation with a machete. The two guides were laden with heavy packs containing everything needed to survive in the wild, including several bottles of the country's ubiquitous Cervecería Nacional Pilsener.

The rainforest was a dripping green hell in Riley's opinion, made even less appealing by the stench of rotting plants and muck. Sunlight hardly penetrated the dense forest canopy. The light at ground level had a sickly gray tinge. High in the trees, monkeys kept up a chattering, howling racket. Small birds of every hue flitted about, creating a noisy open-air aviary. Riley could hear unseen critters crashing through the undergrowth. He hoped they wouldn't stumble on a hungry jaguar, or that a damned twenty-foot anaconda didn't drop on his head. The guides carried bows and arrows, but those didn't look very reassuring.

Later that afternoon, they set up an authentic-looking jungle campsite, complete with a canvas wall tent. Riley sat beside a small campfire drinking beer out of a tin mug while Plummer captured images of an intrepid explorer taking his ease at the end of a long, grueling day. Riley couldn't imagine living like this for a week, let alone all your life. He gazed at the two guides, who were gnawing on something suspicious they'd pulled from their packs. Poor dumb bastards, Riley said to himself. When Plummer had all the shots he needed, they broke camp and headed back to the village.

On their last day, Riley dressed their guides in the bright feathered Jivaro headdresses he'd bought in Quito. Plummer captured a few carefully arranged group shots that showed Riley interacting with the make-believe Jivaros, then the two Americans stowed their gear and Riley gave their guides and the headman generous tips. The villagers insisted on sharing a meal with their guests before they departed. Shabbily dressed women set out the food on a table-size banana leaf, and everyone sat on the ground to eat. The humble banquet consisted of baked plantains, corn, rice, and beans, along with a selection of dubious meats that Riley avoided.

"We've got what we came for," Riley said to Plummer after they'd eaten. "Let's get out of this godforsaken place before moss starts growing on our testicles."

The two men made the drive back to Quito in silence, Plummer taking snorts from a half-pint of local rotgut. Riley pulled up in front of Plummer's second-rate hotel and turned to the photographer. "You know what to do now. The guides to Jivaro country have already been paid. All you have to do is meet them down in Macas. If they get curious about what you're up to, give them the usual story—that you're adding stock shots to your portfolio. Not a word about anything else. The less they know the better."

Riley gave Plummer a stern look. "And make sure you get all the shots on the list, especially the Indians hunting with blowguns and conducting their religious ceremonies, with plenty of shrunken heads on display. It would be great if you can get some shots of jaguars and other wildlife, and a few shots of young females would be nice, preferably bare-chested. And remember, I want every photo you take accurately annotated. I don't want any more mistakes cropping up like they did last time."

Plummer scowled. "How much longer are we going to continue this arrangement? It's getting tiresome."

"As long as I say so," Riley replied. "After all, you wouldn't want word getting out about your little escapade in Mexico. If it did, you'd have a hard time living it down. Besides, you have no reason to complain. You're being very well paid, so suck it up, boyo."

Plummer unloaded his gear from the back of the Land Rover and slammed the tailgate shut. He trudged into the hotel without another word, at least none that Riley could hear.

Riley headed back to his own hotel, the luxurious old Plaza Grande, where he intended to take a long, hot shower. Ramona was due back in town, and Riley was looking forward to seeing her again. Ramona was a vivacious Ecuadorian airline stewardess he'd met on the flight to Quito. She'd graciously offered to acquaint him with some of the more interesting sights in her country's capital. The sights she'd chosen to show him were among the most memorable he'd ever seen, even though the two of them never left his hotel room.

Chapter 2

Washington, D.C., March 1965

An attractive young woman in a charcoal gray business suit stepped up to the lectern at the front of the library in DAR Constitution Hall, the popular Washington performance center a stone's throw from the White House. The woman's dark suit set off her long blond hair, which framed an oval face animated by deep blue eyes. She revealed a dazzling smile as she looked around the room, which was filled to capacity for the Wednesday evening lecture. The young woman nodded to *Washington Post* reporter Joel Hampton, who was seated in the first row. She'd invited Hampton to tonight's event, assuring him it would be worth his time.

"Good evening, ladies and gentlemen," the young woman began, her honeyed drawl giving away her Southern roots. "My name is Pamela Johnson, and I'm the head of the public affairs office at the National Geographic Society. I'd like to welcome all of you to this evening's program, which promises to be both educational and entertaining. Tonight's speaker is part of a long tradition at National Geographic. Ever since its founding in 1888, the Society has been bringing renowned scientists and explorers to Washington to speak to the public about their work. Over the years, eminent figures such as John Wesley Powell, Gifford Pinchot, and Roald Amundsen have thrilled audiences with tales of their adventures.

"This evening, you have the opportunity to hear a rising star among the contributors to *National Geographic* magazine. Two years ago, his first article recounted his thrilling adventures in the wilds of Venezuela. That story, "Treasures of the Orinoco," set a high standard for the author, but we believe he's matched his previous effort with his follow-up article, which

11

will be featured on the cover of our May issue. In addition, the story will be accompanied by an exciting exhibit in our Explorers Hall museum.

"Though some of you may not know of this young adventurer, I'm sure his name will soon be familiar to all our readers. He's here tonight to regale us with an account of his second trek into the wilderness lands of South America, this time the Amazon rainforest of southeastern Ecuador. It was there that he encountered the isolated indigenous people known as the Jivaros, a group whose traditionally warlike culture includes a startling custom that gives the name to our speaker's upcoming article and to tonight's lecture: 'Headhunters of the Amazon.'"

The young woman turned and extended an arm toward the door to her left. "Ladies and gentlemen, please welcome Mr. Xander Riley."

As the audience applauded, Riley bounded into the room and stood beside the lectern, acknowledging the applause with a casual wave. "Thanks for the great introduction, Pamela," he said. "I hope I can live up to the billing."

Miss Johnson laughed and retreated to the side of the room, leaving the tall, handsome Riley in the spotlight he loved. In keeping with the image of an explorer, Riley wore his safari jacket, which he removed and laid aside, a gesture intended to create an atmosphere of intimacy.

"Before I describe my travels in Ecuador, I'd like to ask if anyone in the audience has ever seen the movie *Jivaro*. It was released in 1954 by Paramount Pictures."

A scattering of hands went up around the room.

"So, a few of you have seen it," Riley said. "Well, I have to tell you to forget everything you saw. The movie was pure Hollywood fantasy. The main characters went in search of a horde of Jivaro gold, which was ludicrous. Even more ridiculous, the story is set in Brazil, far from the real Jivaro territory in southeastern Ecuador and northern Peru. I'm guessing they chose to film in Brazil because it was easier to access. The movie's advertising poster reveals what sort of hokum *Jivaro* really is.

The poster shows a shirtless Fernando Lamas posed with a gun in his hand while a half-naked Rhonda Fleming swoons at his feet. The whole thing was an absolute fabrication."

Riley began pacing about in front of the lectern, displaying the restless energy of a man of action. The DAR library was small enough that Riley's deep voice carried to the back of the room, which had a balcony on three sides, corner opera boxes, and a surrounding maze of book stacks. Riley was pleased to see by people's expressions that they were filled with expectation, and he intended to deliver. His presentation wouldn't be a stiff reading of a script while standing behind the lectern. He'd be recounting his adventures as though they were all gathered round a crackling fire in the midst of the Amazon wilderness.

Riley stopped his pacing and leveled a serious gaze at the audience. "What I'm going to tell you tonight is the real story of the Jivaros."

He moved to a table behind the lectern, where he picked up something. The audience couldn't see what he held, since his back was to them. Suddenly, Riley turned and thrust his arms straight out. Dangling from each hand was a shrunken head, suspended from a leather thong. The mouths of the gruesome little heads had been sewn shut and their eyelids were closed, as if to keep them from speaking or seeing. Some of the women in the first row gasped and recoiled from the ghastly sight.

"This is what the Jivaro people are known for. Not gold, but the mutilation of their enemies by removing their heads and preserving them as trophies. The Jivaros believe that the heads of their enemies give them power. After they've slain an enemy, the Jivaros remove the skin from the skull and shrink it by boiling, then they pack the skin with hot sand to shrink it further. By the time they've finished, the head is the size of an orange, but the features and any tattoos are still recognizable. A Jivaro warrior can look at a shrunken head and say to himself, 'That's old So-and-So that I did in last year, the swine.'"
Laughter rippled through the audience.

"A lot of so-called experts say the Jivaros have given up headhunting and that they now foist off monkey heads as the real thing. I can tell you that if you go deep enough into the jungle on the eastern side of the Andes, you'll find Jivaros who still adhere to their ancient ways, especially the Shuar, the most bloodthirsty of the Jivaros."

Riley raised one of the shrunken heads. "This chap met his fate at the hands of the Shuar." Riley studied the tiny grimacing face. "I call him Hubert because he reminds me of an old friend of mine. Hubert cost me a bottle of Tullamore Dew. It was touch and go whether my own head would end up in one of their huts next to Hubert's, but after a few drinks with the Shuar chief, we became buddies."

Riley returned the shrunken heads to the table behind the lectern, which held other Jivaro artifacts the explorer had supposedly brought back from his journey into the wilderness. He selected a long thin tube decorated with strange designs and twirled it like a cheerleader's baton. "In fact, the chief gave me this blowgun as a present. I've been practicing a bit with it. Would anyone like to see how good I've become?"

The audience shouted encouragement. "Okay, but you might want to duck," Riley said with a devilish grin. He picked up a slender reed dart from the table and brandished it for all to see. "These are tipped with curare, which I'm sure you know is highly poisonous." With that, Riley shoved the dart into the blowgun and lifted the tube to his mouth. He hesitated, lowering the blowgun. "You there in the back," he called to a young man standing on the balcony at the rear of the room. "You'd better move a few feet to your left."

The audience turned to discover that a target with the image of a snarling jungle cat had been hung below the clock in the middle of the rear balcony. The next thing anyone knew, Riley's dart had pierced a red circle drawn over the jungle cat's heart. The audience turned back to the front of the room, where Riley stood with the blowgun at his side. "As you can see, I've gotten pretty good with this little item."

Riley laid the blowgun on the table as the audience erupted in applause. He signaled his thanks with another casual wave. Never had any of his spectators seen such a bravura performance at the usually staid National Geographic lectures. Xander Riley was living up to his reputation for unpredictable derring-do.

"Just so you know, there was no curare on that particular dart," Riley said when the crowd quieted down. "By the way," he added, "I didn't tell anyone at National Geographic that I'd be giving that demonstration." He held a hand to the side of his mouth as if sharing a secret. "They'd never have let me do it if they'd known."

Riley had the audience in the palm of his hand. People listened eagerly, many of them leaning forward in their seats awaiting his next revelation.

"Let me tell you about curare," he said. "It's a neurotoxic alkaloid that the Jivaros extract from certain plants by boiling the bark, which produces a dark paste that they apply to their arrowheads and the tips of darts. An odd thing about curare is that it's harmless if you swallow it. It's only poisonous if it enters the body through a wound, which introduces the curare into the bloodstream. When that happens, the neurotoxin paralyzes the victim's muscles and they die of asphyxiation.

"I've watched Jivaro hunters bring down game with their blowguns. They can knock a monkey out of a tree with ease. The poor monkey loses control of its muscles and falls to the ground, where it dies in a remarkably short time. The same thing applies if their target is another human being. A person shot with a poison dart or arrow has no chance of survival."

Riley saw that his tale was having the desired effect. People blanched at his description of the powerful poison. Men glanced at their wives and solemnly shook their heads.

"And curare isn't the only poison in the rainforest. There are deadly vipers in Ecuador, such as the fer-de-lance. Those fellows grow to four feet or longer, but for some reason, the venom of the smaller ones is faster acting. What makes the fer-de-lance so dangerous is that their coloration renders them almost impossible to see against the jungle floor, and they're very aggressive. One of my guides was bitten on the leg by a fer-de-lance, and if we hadn't treated him quickly he'd probably have died. Personally, I hate snakes of any kind." A murmur of agreement ran through the audience.

"The Jivaros have some interesting healing ceremonies," Riley continued. "They cook up a hallucinogenic brew called *ayahuasca,* which the patient drinks, and of course the shaman knocks back some as well. The brew is said to put them in contact with the spirits. They've been using the concoction for centuries, so it must suit their needs."

Riley kept spinning yarns of hardships and heroics for another 45 minutes. At the end of his program, he opened the floor for questions. The first came from a large lady wearing a lampshade hat that must have annoyed the person seated behind her. "Did you encounter any rainforest predators—say jaguars or boa constrictors?"

Riley chuckled. "A jaguar literally scared the pee out of me once. I got up to answer nature's call one night while we were camped along a tributary of the Marañón River, the headwaters of the Amazon River. I'd barely strayed beyond the light of the campfire when I heard something breathing heavily in the undergrowth. I flicked on my flashlight and shined it into the eyes of a jaguar not four feet away. Fortunately, the jaguar was as startled as I was, and it bolted deeper into the forest."

Seated at the rear of the audience, 48-year-old Joan Smollett bristled with pique over Riley's use of the word "pee." Umbrage was a familiar attitude for the angular, acerbic head of the editorial research department at National Geographic. Mrs. Smollett cast a gimlet eye toward Riley. She knew that the dashing, dark-haired Irishman was becoming a favorite of the editors of *National Geographic* magazine, but she saw Riley in a different light, since she was the one assigned to vet the man's sensational accounts of his exploits in far-off lands.

The finicky, dark-haired fact-checker bemoaned the damage that Riley routinely inflicted on the English language. The man seemed unaware of certain finer points of grammar that Mrs. Smollett vigorously defended, even though some of her dictums had been ignored by writers since the passing of the horse and buggy. Riley, for example, split his infinitives with abandon and ended his sentences with prepositions left and right. Mrs. Smollett also knew that the womanizing cad was just as likely to end his sentences with a *proposition.* Riley had cut a wide swath through the tender ranks of female staff members at National Geographic, another unforgivable transgression in the opinion of the moralistic Mrs. Smollett, although the young ladies involved never expressed any regrets.

Mrs. Smollett had come to tonight's lecture out of a sense of duty, since she'd begun reviewing Riley's upcoming article and wanted to hear whatever he might say. As she'd listened to his tale of adventure, she'd been offended by his account of sharing a bottle of liquor with an indigenous person, something no representative of National Geographic should ever consider doing. And his reckless display with the Jivaro blowgun was an even worse offense. She intended to relay her concerns to her higher-ups as soon as possible.

Mrs. Smollett searched the audience for signs of anyone who shared her outrage. She was disappointed to realize that everyone appeared to be having a grand time.

"Plebeians," she muttered to herself.

A portly, bankerish gentleman at the rear of the room raised his pudgy hand. "Mr. Riley, I'm curious about your background," he said. "Just what led you to a life of adventure?"

"I'm afraid my own story is rather pedestrian," Riley replied. "I never knew my parents, but my mother left a note when she abandoned me as a newborn baby on the steps of a Catholic church in New York City. The note said my ancestors were from Ireland, and the family name was O'Reilly, which they anglicized to Riley when they came to America. Growing up in an orphanage, I was too poor to live the proverbial 'life

17

of Riley.' I had to make my own way in the world. I worked at several low-paying, uninspiring jobs before I decided to dedicate my life to exploring and writing about the world's hinterlands. I have to say it's been working out well."

A starry-eyed young woman in the third row timidly held up her hand. Riley had been studying her all evening. "Aren't you ever terrified when you're out there in those wild places?" she asked. "Just thinking about headhunters gives me the chills."

Riley gave her the confident smile of a soldier of fortune. "The only worry I've ever had is that my guides might lead me into the wilderness, rob me blind, and leave me there. You can't always be sure about the honesty of some of the people you meet in out-of-the-way locations. I've dealt with some iffy characters. That's why I always pay my guides extravagantly, giving them half up front and the rest when we're safe and sound back in civilization. That's worked so far." Riley tapped the wooden lectern for good luck.

On that note, Pamela Johnson rejoined the speaker beside the lectern. "Ladies and gentlemen, let's thank Mr. Riley for his terrific presentation." After an interval of applause, Miss Johnson held up a hand. "And I'd like to thank each of you for coming out tonight. National Geographic appreciates your support. We hope you continue to read our flagship magazine and attend our special events. And don't forget to purchase advance tickets to Mr. Riley's upcoming exhibit in Explorers Hall. You won't be disappointed.

"Finally, if you've enjoyed tonight's lecture as much as I have, I remind you that Mr. Riley will be repeating his lecture here at Constitution Hall next Wednesday night. If you have any friends you think might like to hear Mr. Riley's talk, please pass the word along. Good night, and please drive safely on your way home."

Once the audience had filed out of the hall, Miss Johnson helped Riley pack up his artifacts and carry them outside, where they put everything in the trunk of her Plymouth Valiant. "I'll keep all of this right here until you've finished your remaining lecture," she said. "Save you from having to lug it around. After that, I'll take it back to headquarters and we'll store it with the rest of your collection until our museum curator is ready to assemble your show in Explorers Hall."

Riley patted her on the back as she closed the trunk lid. "You're a doll, Pam."

She gave him a beguiling smile. "We aim to please."

From Constitution Hall, Miss Johnson drove to Alexandria, Virginia, where she parked near Gadsby's Tavern, a swank colonial inn that had been serving hearty traditional fare since 1770. The woody, softly lit interior looked almost as it must have when George Washington and Thomas Jefferson were gallivanting around town.

After Riley and Miss Johnson dined on steak and salad, they drove to a nearby apartment building. Inside, Miss Johnson slipped out of her business suit and into a black silk negligee. She and Riley sipped an expensive Cabernet Sauvignon while Sergio Mendes and Brasil '65 set a relaxing mood with their dreamy samba "So Nice." It wasn't long before the couple sambaed their way into the young lady's bedroom. Later, as the two cuddled in cozy contentment, Miss Johnson gently laughed.

"What's so funny?" Riley asked.

"I was thinking about your talk tonight," she said with her mellow drawl. "That trick you did with the blowgun was a corker, although I was relieved that you used a nonpoisonous dart."

Riley fondled a lock of her long blond hair. "Pam darlin'," he said, "I'm glad what I told the audience sounded convincing, but the truth is, I don't have any nonpoisonous darts."

Chapter 3

Thursday

For the past three-quarters of a century, the National Geographic Society had been America's preeminent nonprofit institution dedicated to informing people about the world and all that's in it. Every month, the engrossing articles and stunning photographs in *National Geographic* magazine broadened humanity's knowledge of history, natural history, geology, archeology, anthropology, oceanography, and other fields of learning.

Of all the many fascinating articles published in the magazine, stories of groundbreaking expeditions were among the most popular. In 1909, Robert E. Peary wrote about his trek across the Arctic ice to become the first person to reach the North Pole. Two years later, archeologist Hiram Bingham discovered Machu Picchu, the lost city of the Incas that had lain silent in the Peruvian Andes for three centuries. Bingham led three joint National Geographic–Yale University expeditions to study the magnificent ruins, and the article that he wrote about his discovery filled the entire April 1913 issue of *National Geographic*.

In 1926 and 1930, Richard E. Byrd contributed articles about his trailblazing flights over the North and South Poles. In the 1950s, Jacques Cousteau thrilled readers with accounts of his exploration of the world beneath the sea using the recently introduced Aqua-Lung, the underwater breathing apparatus that gave humans the freedom to swim with the fish. National Geographic's doughty staff member Luis Marden photographed many of Cousteau's underwater adventures, and Marden became a legend himself after his discovery of the wreck of the H.M.S. *Bounty* in 1957 in the South Pacific waters off Pitcairn Island.

The names of these and other writers and photographers who contributed to the Society's journal read like an honor roll of the world's foremost scientists and explorers. What those men and women brought to the pages of *National Geographic* could not be found in any other periodical. From its earliest days up to the present, the National Geographic Society represented adventure, discovery, and wonder. It was a legacy Xander Riley wanted to be associated with, if not actually part of. He could do without trooping to the ends of the earth and freezing his butt off or getting eaten by sharks.

Riley lingered on the corner of 17th and M Streets NW, sipping his tall mocha latte. He stood beneath the clock tower of the Charles Sumner School, a decorative brick structure built in 1872 for the education of black Washingtonians. The springtime air was like an elixir, and the magnolias were in full glory in front of National Geographic's headquarters, on the opposite corner across M Street. Dedicated just last year, the elegant, severely modern ten-story building of white marble and glass was a grand upgrade from Hubbard Hall, the Society's original headquarters, which opened in 1903 on 16th Street, on the other side of the block.

Riley approached the new building, shaking his head in amazement. Carved into the marble above the entrance were the words "National Geographic Society." Every adventure writer and photographer worth his salt dreamed of seeing his work published by the hallowed organization, and now Riley had gained entrance to that magical empire. *National Geographic* magazine was definitely the most prestigious periodical he could think of, and it didn't hurt that it paid its contributors top dollar or that its expense accounts were virtually bottomless.

Yes, Riley was on top of the world. His lecture last night had been a smashing success, he'd gotten in some sweet lovin', and now the boss of National Geographic wanted to shake his hand. Word of his performance at Constitution Hall had quickly reached the ear of Melville Bell Grosvenor, the Society's president and editor-in-chief. Riley had received a phone call earlier this morning asking him to stop by Mr. Grosvenor's office at 10 a.m. As Riley sprang up the steps in front of the headquarters building, he silently congratulated himself. He'd proven just how far a man could go with a vivid imagination, a flair for the dramatic, and a complete set of the *Encyclopaedia Britannica*.

Walking through the bronze-framed glass doors into the first-floor reception area, Riley found himself jostled by the usual crowd of tourists and rowdy school groups that roamed Explorers Hall. The first thing that caught visitors' eyes was an 11-foot-tall world globe sitting in a pool of water amidst splashing fountains. Kids and adults alike stood staring as the orb slowly rotated, simulating Earth's tilted axis. The big revolving ornament could transfix a person for minutes on end, an inexpensive and educational high.

The walls of the museum were covered with examples of National Geographic's acclaimed photography—shots of natural wonders and exotic animals, and evocative portraits of people and places around the world. Glass cases held historical artifacts and other reminders of the expeditions underwritten by National Geographic. Riley considered that his own carefully acquired artifacts would soon be on display here. The museum curator had given him a hint of what the exhibit would look like, an eerily lit recreation of a Jivaro settlement illustrating the headhunting tribe's way of life. Nothing so elemental—and, frankly, so disturbing—had appeared in Explorers Hall in years, the curator assured him.

Riley stopped at the reception desk to get his visitor pass. He winked at the slinky brunette working this morning. "Hello, Angela," Riley crooned. "When are you going to make me the happiest man in the world by having dinner with me?"

The receptionist suppressed a smile as she handed him his clip-on pass. "I'm not sure," she said. "I'll have to check with my husband first."

Riley laughed good-naturedly and walked past the security guard to the hallway of elevators. He pressed the up button and hummed the Beatles recent hit "Can't Buy Me Love" while waiting for the next available car. When the doors swung open, a posse of staff members surged inside. The men wore coats and ties, and the women were all well-dressed. Outfitted in his safari jacket and cargo pants, Riley felt like he'd invaded a posh British boarding school.

Passengers scrambled off as the elevator rose from floor to floor, with researchers, text editors, photo editors, bean counters, and other personnel distributed according to clout. Riley was alone by the time the car reached the tenth floor, where he stepped out into the plush, expansive spaces occupied by the biggest of National Geographic bigwigs.

Mabel Mayweather, Melville Bell Grosvenor's longtime secretary, was a spindly gray-haired lady who looked like she could bite a tenpenny nail in two. Seated at her desk outside Mr. Grosvenor's office like a guard at Buckingham Palace, she greeted Riley with a curt nod and asked him to have a seat, informing him that Mr. Grosvenor would be with him shortly.

Being invited to a one-on-one meeting with MBG, as he was referred to by staff members, was a rare privilege. Relatively few of the Society's hundreds of employees had ever had the experience, and even fewer freelancers. And here Riley was, waiting to be lauded for his first public appearance on behalf of National Geographic. Not bad for a lowly orphan boy.

When Riley heard the intercom buzz on Mrs. Mayweather's desk, he adjusted his shirt collar, readying himself for his official admittance to the big time. He'd have to get used to moving in such exalted circles, he told himself.

The door to Grosvenor's office opened and a young man in a dark suit walked out. His shoulders slumped, and his head hung down. He looked like he'd been flogged. The poor sucker must have screwed up, Riley told himself.

"Mr. Grosvenor will see you now," Mrs. Mayweather announced, impaling Riley with a caustic look. The woman could have wrung a confession from the most hard-boiled criminal with that expression.

Riley entered the inner sanctum, where the bespectacled, 63-year-old Melville Bell Grosvenor sat behind his huge walnut desk reading some papers. After a prolonged silence, he looked over the top of his glasses and motioned Riley toward a chair in front of his desk. The skinny old dude sure wouldn't win any smiling contests, Riley thought.

Riley sat down and Grosvenor resumed his reading. Riley glanced around the enormous office, which was full of memorabilia from landmark stories published in *National Geographic*. Riley noticed a framed photograph of a pretty young woman on the credenza behind Grosvenor's desk. He had no way of knowing that the photograph was of MBG's mother, Elsie Bell Grosvenor, the daughter of inventor and educator Alexander Graham Bell, National Geographic's second president. The photo had been taken in 1901, the year MBG was born.

Riley concluded that whoever the young woman was, she was something of a vixen. She was seated in the photograph, wearing a lacy, fluffy white dress and an old-fashioned hat decorated with a white plume. What struck Riley was her expression. She stared straight at the camera with her head tilted slightly downward, giving her eyes a veiled, sultry look, and she was chewing coquettishly on the ring finger of her left hand. All Riley knew about the woman was that he would have liked to have met her.

Riley had boned up on the lineage of the Grosvenor family. He knew that MBG's father, Gilbert H. Grosvenor, had been the magazine's first full-time editor, and that one of MBG's sons, Gilbert M. Grosvenor, was working somewhere around the building, a likely heir to the kingdom. Riley had devoted most of his attention to the background of MBG himself, a man born to serve National Geographic. When he was five months old, a relative had guided his tiny hand to help lay the cornerstone of Hubbard Hall. As a youngster, he was tutored by his father in writing and photography. He went to work at National Geographic in 1924, long before Riley was a gleam in his unnamed daddy's eye.

An avid outdoorsman brimming with intellectual curiosity, Melville Grosvenor had been named president and editor-in-chief in 1957 and had since racked up several milestone achievements. One of the most notable came in 1959, when he livened up the traditionally all-type cover of the magazine with color photographs—despite the objections of some of the editors, including his son. Over the past eight years, Grosvenor had more than doubled the magazine's circulation, from two million subscribers to nearly five million, and he'd increased funding for the Society's research grants.

More recently, Grosvenor had been the guiding spirit behind the upcoming National Geographic television specials, which would bring live coverage of scientists and explorers into living rooms across the country. The shining new headquarters building was a testament to Melville Grosvenor's leadership. Few had contributed as much to the Society's success, and now the great man wanted to bestow his blessing on the modest, virtuous Xander Riley.

Grosvenor laid his papers aside and looked up. Riley's chest began to swell with pride. Grosvenor stood and gazed out the window, then he turned and fixed Riley with a serious expression, considering how best to frame his compliments.

"Just what did you think you were playing at last night?" Grosvenor snapped. "Mrs. Smollett informed me about your foolhardy exhibition with the blowgun. If that had gone wrong and someone had been injured, it could have cost us a fortune in damages."

Riley's mouth fell open. Holy crap, this wasn't what he'd been expecting. Where was the camaraderie, the cordial pat on the back?

Grosvenor was normally outgoing and approachable and as placid as a millpond, but now his face had turned red and his eyes were slits. He began pacing back and forth.

"I've seen some boneheaded stunts in my time, but nothing like this. And on top of putting our supporters at risk of bodily harm, you blithely described having shared a bottle of whiskey with an indigenous man, a breach of every anthropological guideline for not corrupting primitive societies. If word of that indiscretion gets around, the Society will be embarrassed no end."

Riley's chest deflated noticeably, and he began sliding down in his chair. He tried out a halfhearted smile, which seemed to anger Grosvenor even more.

"You've got a lot to learn about the important responsibilities that come with representing the National Geographic Society," Grosvenor sputtered. "You can be sure we'll be scrubbing your article of any potentially damaging anecdotes, and I may well cancel your remaining lecture because of your thoughtlessly insensitive blunders."

Riley saw that it was time to grovel. "I apologize for everything, Mr. Grosvenor, and I give you my word that I'll be more circumspect in the future. However, I would ask that you hold off on cancelling my final lecture before we see tomorrow's *Washington Post*. "I've heard through the grapevine that my 'Headhunters of the Amazon' talk is going to receive a positive review."

Grosvenor sat back down and toyed with a two-million-year-old fossil bone that Louis Leakey had discovered while searching for evidence of our humanoid ancestors in East Africa. "There'd better be no mention of any blowgun theatrics or drinking bouts."

"I doubt if the reporter will include the story about my sharing a drink with the Jivaro headhunter, although the blowgun demonstration will more than likely get a word or two. The only risky part of that was shooting the dart over the heads of the audience. Next week, I can set up the target at the side of the room up front, so there'd be no risk whatsoever."

Grosvenor appeared to give that some thought. Encouraged, Riley charged ahead. "You've got to admit, a good review of the lecture could mean that the exhibit in Explorers Hall will do well, which would bring in a substantial amount in ticket sales."

"Let's hope that's what happens," Grosvenor said, "but if you've frightened off the public with your rash actions, your standing with the Society will suffer accordingly."

With his knuckles rapped and his servile display of contrition in the books, Riley decided it was time to pan for a little gold. After all, how many times would he have the ear of National Geographic's top man?

"Not to change the subject, sir, but I'd like to say how much I'm looking forward to the Society's first television special this fall."

A tiny smile flickered across Grosvenor's craggy face. "Yes, we're quite proud of it. We're hoping it will be well received. The subject is certainly a good one. 'Americans on Everest.' What could be more appealing to our members?"

Riley didn't give a hoot about mountain climbing. It struck him as one of the world's most useless pursuits, nothing more than a colossal ego trip. He'd once read a famous mountaineer's explanation of why he wanted to climb Mount Everest. "Because it's there," the man said. That struck Riley as the most chuckleheaded rationale for doing something he'd ever heard. Sewage lagoons were "there" as well, but only a blithering idiot would go swimming in one simply because it existed. And besides, if a mountain climber made it to the top, all he'd find were rocks and snow. You could get a better view from the window of an airliner, plus you could take it all in while sipping a cold gin and tonic with a warm blanket on your lap.

"I can't think of anything more exciting," Riley said.

Grosvenor picked up some of the papers on his desk, a sign that the interview was over, but Riley still had a self-serving round in his arsenal that he desperately wanted to fire.

"Have you ever considered running regular television programming?" he asked. "Some folks say that it's the wave of the future."

What Riley was hoping was that TV might be the wave of his future. He could easily see himself standing in iconic locations around the globe and reciting facts from a script someone else had prepared. And the gig would be safe, too. After all, how dangerous could a place be if an entire television crew could access it?

Grosvenor scoffed. "An occasional timely special is enough. The journal is what makes us who we are. It's what people have known and loved for the past 77 years, and I'm confident that will still be true 77 years from now. In case you don't know, young man, our mission is to increase and diffuse geographic knowledge while promoting the conservation of the world's cultural, historical, and natural resources—and nothing does that better than the combination of the printed word and illuminating photographs.

"Of course, we also want to entertain our members, but not by churning out a constant stream of television ephemera. We aren't in show business, you know. People revere the journal. That's why bookshelves and attics all across America are filled with our back issues. People can't bear to part with them. You can't say that about most TV programs, which come and go in a matter of minutes and are as quickly forgotten."

Grosvenor was getting worked up again. "I'll tell you this. If people ever stop reading *National Geographic* and all of America's other fine magazines and newspapers, it will herald the beginning of the end of this country. A nation cannot sustain itself without a well-informed citizenry, and simply staring at a glowing screen won't do the job."

Riley couldn't alter that attitude, and experience had taught him that it was always best to go along with the convictions of the powers that be—until they were replaced by the equally cocksure convictions of a new honcho.

"I'm glad to hear you say that, sir," Riley said with the oily sincerity of a car salesman. "I'm a print man myself, and I couldn't agree with you more. Most of the TV programs out there do seem to be little more than pablum for the masses."

"Yes, well, just you remember what I've said about those antics of yours at last night's lecture."

28

"No worries there, sir."

Grosvenor flicked a hand to indicate that Riley was dismissed. "Hidebound old fogey," Riley said to himself on the way out. As he passed Mrs. Mayweather's desk, he gave her his most engaging smile, but she ignored him. Getting on the woman's good side was like trying to pet an angry Rottweiler. Oh well, he thought, he wouldn't likely be dealing with the old biddy on a regular basis, so to hell with her. He started humming "Can't Buy Me Love" again.

Chapter 4

Thursday

Joan Smollett was wearing a puffy teal blue satin sack dress, a style that had been popular a decade earlier. She sipped her unsweetened cranberry juice and looked around the Holiday Inn lounge with a feeling of annoyance. Her thirtieth annual high school class reunion had kicked off this evening with a cocktail party in her hometown of Falls Church, Virginia, a half-hour drive west of Washington. After graduating as her class valedictorian and rising to the head of editorial research at National Geographic, Smollett had come to believe that she merited first position among her classmates. Although it still pained her, she'd finally admitted to herself that others had forged careers equal to her own.

There was, for instance, her National Geographic colleague Pythagoras Bib. Bib, who'd been president of their senior class, held the notable post of National Geographic chief of protocol. He was a tall, handsome figure with dark wavy hair, like the brooding English actor Ronald Colman when he was young. Suave and worldly, Bib was a man of unusual interests. At Georgetown University, he'd studied psychology, one of the most unmarketable academic subjects known to mankind in the opinion of Smollett. She'd graduated from the University of Virginia with a double major in history and geography, with honors naturally.

A bachelor and man-about-town, Bib spoke several languages, and he often escorted visiting female dignitaries to Washington social events on behalf of the Society. He also drafted letters of introduction used by writers and photographers on assignment in foreign countries, documents written in such grandiloquent language that they never failed to impress

30

their recipients. Joan Smollett had never had occasion to work with Bib, but she always greeted him courteously whenever they met. She'd been around National Geographic long enough to know it was wise to curry favor with any person assigned to the president's staff.

Pythagoras Bib had a fraternal twin brother with a similarly strange given name—Archimedes. At present, the two men were standing across the lounge, chatting with classmates. Archimedes didn't share his brother's good looks. Shorter than Pythagoras and slightly stooped, Archimedes more closely resembled Rumpelstiltskin than a movie star. His once luxuriant brown hair had started dwindling while he was in his thirties, and his long, narrow nose supported a pair of heavy black-framed bifocals, which he unconsciously pushed back in place whenever they crept downhill. Smollett understood that Archimedes held some senior position with the Washington Metropolitan Police and that he'd lost his wife a few years back. In school, she'd rarely spoken to him, calculating that he could add nothing to her luster.

Smollett sat at a corner cocktail table with her husband, Jeffrey, a silent, colorless man who'd taken on the appearance of a whipped spaniel after years of browbeating at the hands of his wife. Even his posture reflected his submissive attitude, his shoulders hunching forward in defeat. He sat staring into space with a vacuous expression, pretending to listen as his wife pigeonholed her classmates, few of whom took the time to stop by and say hello.

"Oh no," Smollett snarled, "there's that godawful philistine Bill Price."

The owner of Price Pharmaceuticals in Baltimore, William Price was another classmate whose achievements equaled—or surpassed—Joan Smollett's. Starting with next to nothing, he'd made himself the richest member of their class, although the snooty Mrs. Smollett still held his humble roots against him. Price's father had run a neighborhood grocery store in Falls Church.

"I'll bet the lout's been throwing around hundred-dollar bills to impress people," Smollett said. "He's living proof that you can't buy refinement."

Price caught sight of Smollett. He'd despised the woman ever since she made fun of his pronunciation in their Spanish class. A powerfully built man, he ambled across the lounge like an awkward bear, a tall drink in his hand—not the first of the evening. For some reason, Price wore an enigmatic smile.

"Hola, Joan. ¿Cómo estás? Espero que estés disfrutando de la fiesta." Price spoke fluent Spanish, without a trace of an American accent.

Smollett looked at him in astonishment. Her unused high school Spanish had faded away over the years. She had no idea that Price had asked how she was and told her he hoped she was enjoying the party.

"Um, hello, Bill," Smollett stuttered, clearly embarrassed.

"Oh, maybe you didn't catch what I said," Price noted. "I assumed you'd have kept up your Spanish. You were once so proficient, with such a lovely accent. I've gotten much better with the language myself. But then I had to. You see, my company does millions of dollars' worth of business every year in Latin America."

Smollett wanted to scratch the man's eyes out. Price, on the other hand, was delighted by her discomfort. He noticed that Smollett was wearing an imitation pearl choker—and he hoped that it would.

"It just goes to show that you never know which classes you take in school will become important later in life," Price said.

Having taunted Smollett with his linguistic accomplishments and wealth, Price was ready to head back to the bar for another drink. "Maybe we can grab a dance later on," he said, knowing both of them would sooner die than dance together. He recalled the emaciated woman's high school nickname—Bony Joanie.

"What a repulsive parvenu," Smollett said as she watched Price walk away. Jeffrey Smollett nodded in silence.

Joan intended to enjoy the rest of the evening in her own peculiar way. As Jeffrey fixated on the lounge's wallpaper, she continued her critical monologue, dredging up old stories about how she'd one-upped various classmates in high school and pointing out their current shortcomings. It was her favorite form of entertainment. She'd have gotten along with Teddy Roosevelt's daughter Alice Roosevelt Longworth, who once remarked, "If you haven't got anything nice to say about anybody, come sit next to me."

Archimedes Bib needed to find a place to sit. The homely, widowed homicide investigator had been on his feet all day. He took a seat at the bar and ordered a tonic and lime. He was surprised that so many members of their high school class had turned out for their reunion. The Class of 1935 had been small—under fifty students, but around half of them had shown up for the Thursday evening mixer, the first night of a weekend packed with get-togethers. Over the course of their several past reunions, Bib had observed his classmates' gradual changes from youthfulness to middle age. They'd soon become card-carrying members of AARP and be asking for their senior discounts.

"I'll be darned. If it ain't old Archie Bib." The speaker slapped Bib on the back a little too roughly. "How you doin' pal? Still chasing the bad guys?"

Bib forced a tepid smile, despite nearly choking on his drink. "Hello, Tim," he said. Tim Wilson, a beefy insurance salesman, had been something of a class clown back in the day. Bib doubted that the fellow had worn out any of his schoolbooks. "Yes, I'm still with the D.C. police department."

"Once a cop, always a cop, eh?" the big man said. "When we were in school, I always figured you'd end up as a teacher. You were such a bookworm. Never went out for sports"—the big man laughed—"or chased the gals."

"I guess I was a bit of a nerd."

"Shoot, you were *the* nerd. You and your brother were the only ones in our class who could actually *speak* Latin."

"We can thank our parents for that. Every Wednesday night, we were only allowed to speak Latin at the dinner table. You quickly learn how to say 'pass the potatoes, please' when you're hungry."

Tim raised his glass in a salute. "Good seein' you again," he said as he wandered off.

Bib thought of his late parents, paired in life with names that had started a thousand conversations—Mary and Joseph. How ironic it was that neither of them had been religious. Their adoration was for the ancient Greek masters of math and philosophy, which was why the Bib brothers ended up with millstones around their necks. Fortunately, "Archie" had been an easy substitute for Archimedes, but poor Pythagoras had to make do with the nonsensical nickname "Py," which he told people was Armenian for "man of wisdom." Their curious surname also had intriguing roots. "Bib" was a Slavic word for a grower of beans or a tall thin man. Archie considered himself the grower of beans, his beans being clues to the crimes he investigated. Py was the tall thin man.

Out on the small dance floor, couples were swaying to Jackie DeShannon's "What the World Needs Now." From the way some of them were canoodling, it might have been 1950 instead of 1965, but then 48 wasn't too old for passion, Bib told himself. Picasso was still chasing women in his eighties. Bib took a sip of his drink. As Tim Wilson alluded to, Bib's own amorous pursuits had been limited, and they were truly over now, despite his brother's periodic offers to introduce him to one of the many agreeable ladies who seemed to orbit him.

While Bib was musing on the vagaries of love, a remarkably well-preserved brunette slid onto the barstool next to him. "Hello, Archie," she purred. Helen Brooks had been a flamboyant, titillating cheerleader thirty years ago and the sexual fantasy of every male in their class. Every male with the possible exception of Archimedes Bib. He'd known that she was as far out of his reach as the North Star, so there'd been no use in thinking about her.

What was most surprising about Helen Brooks was that she was as clever as she was desirable. She'd written for the school newspaper and had gone on to establish herself as a successful writer of romance novels in New York City. Bib had read one of her books and wondered how much of it was based on her own life. She'd never been reserved. She'd been the first girl in their class to wear a two-piece swimsuit, a primary topic of conversation for an entire summer.

"How's life treating you these days?" Helen asked. She lifted the olive from her martini and rubbed it teasingly against her lower lip.

"Hello, Helen. I'm fine, thanks. I read a review of your latest book in the *Post*. It seems you haven't lost any of your steam."

The woman tossed back her long dark hair and let go with a girlish giggle. "It's always easy to steam it up on the page."

"Um, I suppose so." Bib quickly changed the subject. "I don't think I've ever told you how much I admire your ambitiousness. You're the only one in our class brave enough to take on New York. All that energy in the Big Apple must be what keeps you looking so young."

"Some days I feel as old as Methuselah," she said. "Have you ever stopped to consider all we've been through? I mean our age group. The Depression, World War II, the Korean War, the assassination of President Kennedy, and now this mess in Vietnam."

"Thankfully, it hasn't all been traumatic," Bib said. "We've also sent men into space, and it shouldn't be long before we land someone on the moon."

"Yes, that's something to be proud of. And you've done well for yourself. One of the few of us who was able to get through college during the bleak 1930s."

"That would never have happened if my parents hadn't been working at Georgetown University. I guess you knew that my mother taught math and my father taught philosophy. Faculty brats got a sizable discount on tuition."

"You went to law school, too, didn't you?" Helen asked.

"I started law school after college, but I was never so bored in my life. I wasn't cut out to be a lawyer. Most people think attorneys all spend their time in courtrooms, working on exciting cases. The truth is, nine out of ten lawyers do nothing but shuffle paper. The Second World War saved me from that fate. I got into military intelligence. That's why I decided to go into law enforcement after the war." Bib fished a business card from his inside coat pocket and handed it to the woman.

"Inspector A. Bib, Washington Metropolitan Police," she read aloud. She tapped the card on her chin, then she dropped it into her clutch. "Very impressive. Maybe I'll put you in my next book."

Bib's record as a senior homicide investigator actually was impressive. What he lacked in appearance he made up for with perceptiveness and perseverance. No wrongdoer ever wanted Archimedes Bib on his trail. The man was as relentless as a bloodhound, and he seldom failed to track down his quarry, although whenever he identified a culprit he never shouted "Eureka" like his namesake reportedly did when he discovered the principle of buoyancy by sitting in his bathtub.

Bib shuddered at the thought of being included in one of Helen's bodice-rippers. "As long as you don't put me in any bedroom scenes."

The woman laughed. "All right. Strictly police business."

Just then Doris Day's sedate recording of "Fly Me to the Moon" starting playing. "Let's dance," Helen said.

Bib looked startled. "Me, dance? I haven't been on the dance floor in years."

Helen grabbed his hand and tugged him from his stool. "C'mon. It'll do you good."

"But what about my reputation?" Bib said as she led him to the floor. "I'm supposed to be a taciturn defender of the law. Being seen tripping the light fantastic may shock people."

"Always so serious, aren't you? But I've always suspected those still waters run deep."

"Sometimes they're nothing more than still waters."

Helen snuggled close. "You aren't a bad dancer, Archie."

"As long as it's not the Twist. I'd throw my back out if I ever tried that."

While they danced, Helen provided insightful commentary on the classmates around them, delivered with a novelist's eye for detail. "There's Brenda Clark and her husband Tom. Hard to fathom that our class homecoming queen would end up marrying a minister. It's even harder to believe that Tom would become a preacher. He was a skirt-chaser in school." Helen gave Bib a naughty look, like Shirley Temple confessing to having taken the last piece of candy. "Tom and I had a brief fling, you know, back in the Stone Age."

Bib couldn't resist. "Maybe that was what persuaded him to take up the ministry."

Helen giggled again and punched him lightly on the shoulder. "You dog."

Helen's breezy manner suddenly changed. She gazed toward a corner of the room where a good-looking man sat by himself in a wheelchair. "There's Dick Radford. What a tragedy," she said, "becoming a starter on the University of Virginia football team and then suffering a crippling spinal cord injury in his second season."

Helen glanced at the couple next to them on the dance floor and gave them the captivating smile that graced the back covers of her books. "Hello there," she said to Sara Henderson, a plump, dowdy woman in an unbecoming orange dress. Her partner was Mick Stuart, a stocky, haggard man in a dark suit that he must have purchased in readiness for his funeral. The unglamorous pair waved and spun off across the floor, as if too cowed to chat.

"Poor Sara always was a shrinking violet," Helen said, "but she was smart. Mick, on the other hand, wasn't much of a student. Bit of a tough from the wrong side of town. Outside of school, he liked to strut his stuff, a real cock of the walk."

"What does Mick do for a living?" Bib inquired, trying to hold up his end of the conversation.

"I've heard he manages an auto supply store. You've got to give the fellow credit for succeeding even in that small way, considering his background." Helen stared at the couple a moment longer. "What those two are doing together is beyond me. They're like oil and water."

Bib shrugged. "Like they say, love makes you whole."

When Doris Day finished beseeching her lover to fly her to the moon, Bib started to lead Helen back to the bar. She patted him on the shoulder. "Thanks for the dance, Archie." She looked off across the room. "There's Sue Montgomery over there, and I'm dying to hear how she's been doing since her emancipation. You know she finally divorced Andy. It's a wonder that drunken bum of a house painter hasn't fallen off a ladder and broken his neck by now."

Bib was relieved to see Helen head off to mingle with the others. She was too high-energy for him to keep up with. He didn't need his still waters being roiled. He returned to his seat and ordered another tonic and lime as the Righteous Brothers' haunting "You'll Never Walk Alone" began playing. Bib liked their songs, although he wasn't too keen on some of the other modern music. The Beatles were okay. They were clever, but you could keep the Rolling Stones, who were too raucous. Their music set him on edge, and he liked—he needed—to be soothed. Listening to quiet background music while he read a good book was his preference. He was a fan of Lawrence Welk, and unlike most people, he enjoyed elevator music.

Bib stifled a yawn. He needed to get some sleep after the grueling week he'd spent trying to track down the thug that had robbed and killed a congressman who was walking his dog at night on Capitol Hill. A half dozen other murders had occurred in the past week in Washington, but as always, the priority of the Metropolitan Police Department was on solving crimes involving the high and mighty. It was a fact Bib had lived with for twenty years, and he still didn't like it. Every life was precious. His current case was one of those he hated, since senseless, unpremeditated murders often left little evidence.

He decided to call it a night. He hadn't spoken with half of the people at this evening's reception, but there was plenty of time to remedy that. Tomorrow night, a dinner party would be held at the elegant Westwood Country Club in nearby Vienna, Virginia, with his multitalented brother acting as master of ceremonies. Saturday morning, a breakfast for the guys was scheduled at JV's Restaurant, a Falls Church landmark for the past twenty years, and the last event of the weekend would take place later that morning with everyone heading down to the Tidal Basin to see the cherry trees in bloom.

Bib didn't know if he could take all that conviviality, but he vowed to try. For a man who dealt with the seamy side of life every day, it was the therapy he needed. He said goodnight to his brother and walked outside into the cool March air, climbing into an unmarked black Ford sedan belonging to the police department. The drive back across the Potomac to his home in Georgetown, the historic residential and commercial area in northwest Washington, was a quiet, peaceful interlude.

Bib looked forward to the fresh pot of coffee his live-in Jamaican housekeeper, the eternally smiling Amara Brown, would have waiting for him on the kitchen counter. By this time of night, Amara would have said her prayers and tucked herself into bed like the good Christian she was. Amara meant "grace" in the Igbo language of Nigeria, and the description fit. Bib had never seen the woman lose her temper or heard her speak a harsh word about anyone. He needed that, too.

Chapter 5

Friday

Xander Riley slid onto a corner of Pamela Johnson's desk, placing a sugar-free chai tea latte before the attractive young public affairs officer. He took a sip from his own tall mocha latte. "Guess who was in a private meeting yesterday with your vaunted president and editor-in-chief?"

"You were with MBG?" Johnson said in surprise. "What on earth for?"

"Oh, Pam, surely you know what life at the top is like," Riley chuckled. "Actually, the old boy gave me a pretty stern tongue-lashing over my target practice with the blowgun the other night. He even threatened to cancel my final lecture." Riley winked confidently. "But I calmed him down, and I scored a few brownie points as well. I think he was impressed with yours truly."

Johnson sniggered. "Yeah, sure. Mr. Grosvenor is easily impressed." She gave Riley an inquisitive look. "So what exactly did he say?"

"He said it was dangerous for me to use a blowgun in front of a live audience, that I might have injured someone, which could have resulted in a lawsuit that would drain some of the dough from your overflowing coffers."

"And you well could have hurt someone," Johnson said. "You might have killed them if that dart you used really had curare on it."

"Pam, Pam. Have a little faith. I knew what I was doing."

"You're one lucky son of a gun," Johnson said with a shake of her head. "You take more chances than anyone I know, yet you keep coming up roses. Someday your luck may run out, Xander. Especially if you keep pushing things."

Riley lifted the woman's chin. "Now what would life be like without taking chances, Pam darlin'?" He caressed her long blond hair. "You know, you've taken a few chances yourself since we met."

Johnson blushed. She stared into Riley's dark eyes as if hypnotized, then she brushed his hand away. "How did you get Mr. Grosvenor to calm down?"

"I asked him to wait until the review of my talk at Constitution Hall appeared in the *Post* before he cancelled next week's lecture. I mentioned that a little bird had told me the review would likely be positive. And I pointed out that a good review could mean more people might want to see the exhibit in Explorers Hall. Money, money, money. After your tip that your friend at the *Post* enjoyed my talk, I thought it was safe to toss that bone to Grosvenor."

"Joel Hampton and I go way back."

Riley unfolded the copy of the morning *Washington Post* he'd bought at the M Street coffee shop near the headquarters building. He laid the paper on Johnson's desk. The arts section was on top, with the headline of Joel Hampton's article circled. "Take a gander at that," Riley said, tapping the page.

Johnson scanned the article, a smile slowly spreading across her face. She read the story out loud. "On Wednesday evening, National Geographic adventure writer Xander Riley gave one of the most interesting and exciting lectures this reporter has attended in some time. The genteel crowd in Constitution Hall was rockin' as Riley related hair-raising tales of his adventures among the headhunters of Ecuador, and he backed up his tales with a demonstration of his skill with one of the blowguns the indigenous Jivaro people use to bring down their prey—both animal and human.

"Another highlight of the evening was the pair of shrunken heads Riley brought back from Ecuador, grim little fellows that prove the Jivaros remain one of South America's most warlike tribes. More of Riley's Jivaro artifacts will be on display in National Geographic's Explorers Hall museum this May, when the adventure writer's article will be featured as the cover story in *National Geographic* magazine. This reporter will be at the head of the line to see what's sure to be a worthwhile exhibit. Advance tickets are now on sale."

Johnson put the paper down. "Boy, I'll have to thank Joel. He really laid it on thick. I couldn't have written a better press release myself."

Johnson pursed her lips. "Let's see if John Q. Public was as impressed with your lecture as Joel was. She picked up the phone and punched in some numbers.

"Who're you calling?" Riley asked.

"My good friend Susanna Baker down in the Explorers Hall ticket office."

After a few rings, the young PR woman perked up. "Hello, Sue," she said with her soft Southern drawl. "Pam Johnson here. Could you tell me how the ticket sales are going for the May 'Headhunters of the Amazon' exhibit?"

Johnson listened to the person on the other end. "All right," she said. "I'll hold while you check." Johnson twiddled with the phone cord while she waited. Suddenly, her eyes widened. "Is that right? That's encouraging. Thanks for checking, Sue. Let's get together for lunch one of these days. Bye now."

Johnson hung up and smiled at Riley. "She said that sales for the exhibit jumped significantly yesterday. And this morning, the telephones haven't stopped ringing, with nearly every caller wanting tickets."

"I wonder why sales jumped yesterday," Riley said in an innocent tone. "Could it possibly be that I dazzled folks at Wednesday's lecture?"

"All right, you arrogant peacock. So they liked your talk and want to see the exhibit."

"Um...and do you suppose that the *Post* raving about my presentation might be spurring ticket sales even more? How scrumptious that would be."

"Get the heck out of my office before I have you thrown out," Johnson said with a laugh.

Riley got up off her desk and sauntered toward the door. "I do have to run, Pam dear. I've got an appointment with one of the most enchanting persons at National Geographic."

"Who's that?"

"Dear, sweet Joan Smollett—the busybody who blabbed to Grosvenor about my blowgun trick. She wants to see me before she passes on her research comments to the lucky chap who'll be editing my story."

"Have fun, then. I'm sure meeting with Mrs. Smollett will make your day."

Riley blew the young woman a kiss. In the hallway outside her fourth-floor office, he punched the up button on the elevator. He hummed Roger Miller's "King of the Road" while he waited. When the doors opened, he hopped aboard and hit the button for the sixth floor. Melville Grosvenor was standing at the rear of the elevator.

"Good morning, Mr. Grosvenor," Riley said. "I just heard the good news that tickets for the 'Headhunters of the Amazon' exhibit are selling like hotcakes."

Grosvenor gave him a wan smile. "That's to your advantage then," he noted.

Riley brandished his copy of the *Post.* "That's not all the good news. There's a review of my lecture in this morning's paper, and it's extremely flattering."

"I'll be certain to read it."

Riley nodded politely to the slender gentleman when the elevator stopped at the sixth floor. He stepped out and made his way to Joan Smollett's office, where he tapped on the open door. Mrs. Smollett looked up with the grim expression of a prosecuting attorney.

"Ah, Mr. Riley," she said. "Please come in."

Riley took a seat in the chair beside Smollett's desk. "How are you this morning, Joan?"

"I've had better starts to my day," Smollett replied tersely. She reached for a folder in her desktop organizer. Opening the folder, she glanced at its contents and sighed.

43

"There are a few points in your article I feel we should discuss, Mr. Riley."

"Please, call me Xander, Joan. I don't see why we should be so formal."

"I prefer formality, Mr. Riley, and I would ask that you address me as Mrs. Smollett."

"Okay. Mrs. Smollett it is."

Smollett picked up Riley's manuscript and scrutinized the first page. "Let's begin with the smaller issues, shall we?"

"Um, why not?"

Smollett peered over the top of her reading glasses at the prisoner in the dock. "Here on page one you state how 'adverse' you are to modern incursions into the tribal lands of the indigenous people of South America, your current area of interest. The most backward high schooler would know that the word you were groping for was 'averse,' meaning opposed to. 'Adverse,' of course, means having a harmful effect. And while that's obviously not what you meant, your mistake did, ironically, have an 'adverse' effect on the sentence in question."

Smollett's expression was that of an irascible hyena slowly circling its prey. Riley lounged in his chair. He wasn't fazed by the woman's voluminous petty comments on his manuscripts. Last time, he jotted a note above the title saying, "Just fix whatever needs fixing, Joanie." This time, he feigned a thoughtful attitude and said, "Good catch, Mrs. Smollett. I can't tell you how much I appreciate your attention to detail."

Smollett's reply consisted of a cheerless grunt. She continued paging through Riley's manuscript, singling out various minor flaws. Riley attempted to keep smiling throughout the ordeal, but a smile never came within five yards of Smollett's face. She was just getting started.

"I'm afraid that on top of your compositional oversights, you have a hard time keeping your facts straight," she said. "The rigorous fact-checking process at National Geographic exists so that writers are kept from coming off as blundering fools, but you test the limits of that process."

Smollett tapped the manuscript with her pencil. "Here, for example. I'm curious as to why you say you camped along the Napo River. According to my research, the Napo River is in northeastern Ecuador, and your story, I'm led to believe, is centered in southeastern Ecuador." She removed her glasses and gave him a piercing look. "You seem to have a somewhat loose grasp of the lay of the land, Mr. Riley. I recall that you made several similar mistakes in your previous article, 'Treasures of the Orinoco.'"

"Good heavens, I'm an adventurer, not a bloody cartographer. I don't walk around all day long with a map and a compass in my hand."

"There's always the sun," Smollett said, her voice dripping with sarcasm. "You know that it rises in the east and sets in the west fairly regularly."

"I'll try to remember. That might come in handy."

Smollett put her glasses back on and proceeded with the prosecution. "And down here you talk about visiting Jivaro villages, but from what I've read, Jivaros don't live in villages as such. They live in communities of related families, which are separate from other related communal groups. I would have thought you'd have learned that during your visit."

Riley felt it was time to fight back. "Anyone would describe those communities as villages."

"But we are not just anyone, Mr. Riley. We are the National Geographic Society, and we get things right."

Riley abandoned any pretense of friendliness. He stared daggers at the stick-thin researcher.

"Also," Smollett continued, "you say that Jivaros have no contact with outsiders, but that's not true either. Jivaros living along the edge of their territory routinely trade with outsiders. They, in turn, trade with more isolated groups of Jivaros, so that trade goods eventually reach those living in the remotest regions. How you could be unaware of this suggests that you haven't done your homework. Sometimes, one might almost wonder if you've even been to the places you write about."

That barb hit home. Riley rose in indignation and hovered over the woman. "That is a slanderous accusation. If you ever repeat it to anyone you'll find yourself facing serious consequences."

"Oh my, Mr. Riley, I seemed to have touched a sore spot. My apologies."

Smollett restored Riley's article to its folder and filed it away. "I think that covers everything. I'll make the necessary fixes and pass this along to your editor. Good day, Mr. Riley."

Riley did his best to affect a conciliatory tone. "Sorry I blew up there, Mrs. Smollett. I want you to know that I really do appreciate the great effort you put into making sure everything is correct."

The woman merely nodded, as silent and inscrutable as the Sphinx.

Riley cursed under his breath as he walked away from Smollett's office. He needed to calm down, to get this horrible creature out of his head. And he knew a fine way to do that.

Riley had had his eye on young Rachel Mathers from the first time he saw her. When he sold his article on the Orinoco to National Geographic, he'd had to visit the payroll office and fill out some forms. The pert, 24-year-old Miss Mathers had been the secretary who'd assisted him. He'd made a number of mistakes while filling out the forms simply because he couldn't stop gaping at the young woman's exceptional physique, which zigged and zagged in all the right places. Her thick auburn hair hung past her shoulders, like Rita Hayworth's. A sprinkling of freckles across her nose set off her flawless ivory complexion, and her eyes were the lightest shade of amber Riley had ever seen, the color of Scotch and water. Yes, Miss Mathers was quite a package. She rated high on Riley's list of trophies to acquire.

Riley strolled from the ground floor of headquarters over to the 16th Street Administration Building, a structure built next to Hubbard Hall in 1912. He threaded the building's maze of hallways until he came to the payroll office, where Rachel Mathers was absorbed in her work at her corner desk. Riley stood at the counter near the entrance until Miss Mathers looked up. She smiled when she saw him and came over to the counter.

"Hello, Mr. Riley," she said in her little-girl voice. "How may I help you?"

"Nothing would help me more than if you'd come have lunch with me."

Miss Mathers's mouth dropped open. "Excuse me?"

"C'mon, let's go have lunch. We can pop across the street to the Jefferson Hotel."

Miss Mathers didn't know what to say. The prospect of having lunch with the dashing Xander Riley was a treat that had never crossed her mind. He belonged to the pantheon of stars who made National Geographic famous. And here he was, asking her out to lunch.

Miss Mathers looked over her shoulder. "I guess I could slip away. Let me tell my supervisor I'll be going out today. I usually bring a sandwich for lunch." She was embarrassed to admit this, her creamy face flushing pink.

Minutes later, the couple entered the luxurious Jefferson Hotel, on the corner of 16th and M Streets across from the National Geographic complex. After they were shown to a table in a dim nook, Riley ratcheted up his charm offensive. "Now the first thing we need to get straight is that you're to call me Xander, and I'll call you Rachel, if that's all right."

The young girl blushed again. "That would be fine." She looked around the room, which had the clubby, wood and leather atmosphere befitting one of Washington's favorite lunch sites for movers and shakers. "I've never been here before," she said. "It's too rich for my blood."

"You can put that out of your mind, because everything is on me. Order anything you like."

Once they'd ordered, Rachel gave Riley a halting smile. "I attended your lecture this week. It was amazing."

"I'm glad you enjoyed it. You know, I'm currently planning my next trip. I'm thinking of exploring a part of the world other than South America. I've always been fascinated by Mesopotamia, a region that conjures up images of wonderful adventures, real Arabian Nights stuff. You know, of course, that the name Mesopotamia comes from the Greek word for the land between the Tigris and Euphrates Rivers. It's where the ancient civilizations of the Sumerians, Akkadians, Assyrians, and Babylonians flourished. Today, the area takes in most of Iraq and parts of Turkey, Syria, and Kuwait."

Riley had been boning up on the subject in his *Encyclopaedia Britannica.*

Rachel's eyes lit up. "It sounds exciting. You're lucky to be able to visit those places."

"It is a privilege," Riley intoned, "but it can come with certain...challenges."

"You mean danger? Your descriptions of the headhunters you visited gave me the willies."

"Sometimes there's danger," Riley said in his most devil-may-care manner. "But that comes with the territory. In Mesopotamia, for instance, you have to brave the nomadic thieves and killers that infest the desolate Syrian Desert in western Iraq. But there are so many discoveries to be made there that it would be worth it."

Riley thought about the fine hotels and ample shops of Baghdad, where he could score all the historical swag he'd need for a dandy article. Jake Plummer would probably bitch about having to stumble around in the desert to get the necessary photographs, but he could be brought to heel.

After lunch, Riley led Rachel by the hand through the bowels of the Administration Building.

"Where are you taking me, Xander?" the girl asked nervously.

"Into the ancient catacombs of the Society, where only the brave dare go."

In truth, they were making their way through the building's basement storeroom, where old or unneeded office equipment was stockpiled. Ranks of filing cabinets, desks, sofas, and chairs were crammed together in a shadowy warren where a person could easily get lost. Desk lamps with flexible necks stared down at them like watchful swans from atop tall metal cabinets.

"I didn't know this place existed," Rachel said. "How did you find it?"

"I'm an explorer."

Deep into the maze of office equipment, they came to a spot where the tightly packed odds and ends had been rearranged to create a small alcove, allowing access to a comfortable sofa covered with dark blue fabric. The faint glow cast by the few overhead lights gave the little space a soft, romantic touch.

"This is it," Riley said, "my private refuge."

Riley sat on the sofa and motioned for Rachel to join him. The young secretary hesitated then eased onto the sofa with a wary look. "Aren't you worried that someone might find us? We could get in trouble."

"No one ever comes down here except for the occasional porter," Riley assured her. "I heard they once discovered a homeless family that had been living here for months. I sometimes come here to get away from the nitpickers and curmudgeons. It's the best hidey-hole I've found for a quiet snooze."

Rachel sat with her hands in her lap. She kept glancing around as if she feared there might be spies lurking about.

Riley took her chin in his hand and turned her face so that he could peer into her amber eyes, which reminded him of the eyes in a Barbie doll—sparkling with a sort of innocent allure. He leaned forward and kissed the girl on the lips. She accepted that first kiss with trepidation, but then her emotions took over and she returned the kiss with growing fervor. Riley had that effect on women.

Chapter 6

Friday

William Price was still feeling good about his handling of the obnoxious Joan Smollett at last night's cocktail party. When he put her in her place with his greeting in Spanish, her eyes had bugged out like two boiled onions. She couldn't bear being caught short in any field of knowledge. The great Joan Smollett, class valedictorian and la-di-da know-it-all. What a dreadful woman. He wasn't through with her by a long shot, but this afternoon it was time to turn his attention to other classmates who deserved a dose of humiliation. There were four in particular who'd gotten on his wrong side in school, and payback time was here.

Price was parked in front of the Falls Church Western Auto store, but instead of seeing the distinctive round red sign above the door, Price saw a bright orange Rexall sign in his mind's eye. He was thinking about a Saturday night in his freshman year of high school, an evening when he'd emerged from the downtown Falls Church Rexall after enjoying a chocolate malt at the drugstore's soda fountain. Outside the store, Mick Stuart and two of his lowlife friends from the edge of town were hanging around, ogling girls and making crude remarks.

When Stuart saw Price, he decided to put on a show for his cronies. He walked up to Price and grabbed him by his shirt-front. "Whatcha doin', punk?" he sneered.

Price was so startled that he didn't know how to react. He was no brawler, so instead of punching Stuart in the face, he lamely replied, "Get your hands off me."

Having won the battle of intimidation, Stuart let go of Price's shirt. "Sure thing, punk. Now run along home to your mommy." He turned and smirked at his buddies.

Bill Price had never forgotten—or forgiven—that assault, although Mick Stuart had probably forgotten about it the next day, since it was just one of many examples of his high school bullying. If black leather motorcycle jackets had been the fashion for hooligans back in 1931, Stuart would have worn one.

Price shook off that disturbing memory and climbed from his car, a shiny new flaming red Ferrari 250. The burly entrepreneur entered the Western Auto store and walked back to the sales counter, where Mick Stuart was waiting on someone. When the customer completed his purchase, Price stepped up to the counter.

"Hey, Mick my man," Price said in a boisterous voice.

Stuart was dumbfounded to see his former classmate. "Uh, hello, Bill. I thought that was you I saw at the party last night. I don't remember you ever coming to any of our previous reunions."

"This one is special. Thirty years. How time flies. You and I haven't had a chance to chew the fat in ages."

"What would we have to talk about? We never palled around together."

"Old times, Mick. Old times."

Mick Stuart was a different person from the delinquent he'd once been. At 48, he had a half-paid-off mortgage, a bum knee, and a dodgy heart. His life had taken a turn for the better when he married quiet, unassuming Sara Henderson right after high school. He found a steady job at the local Phillips 66 service station, and while the pay was decent, the hours were terrible. Stuart drew all the night and weekend shifts. Sara's complaints about him being away from home so much had prompted him to change jobs several times. He ended up at Western Auto, a job he'd held for fifteen years, and he was proud to have risen to store manager.

"Is there anything I can do for you?" Stuart asked. "Do you need a part for your car?"

"I doubt if you stock parts for my Ferrari." He pointed to the racy looking vehicle out front.

"You're right. You'd have to go into Washington to find gear for a pricey foreign rig like that."

"Then I suppose you wouldn't stock parts for a Mercedes 600 either," Price said. "That's my wife's car. She couldn't make it to the reunion. She's off at some fancy spa in Palm Springs. You know how it is with these bathing beauties. Always making a fuss over themselves. She was Miss Maryland in 1960." Price winked. "She's still only 28."

"That's nice," Stuart said in a flat tone.

"How's Sara doing?"

"She's fine. Our two kids kept her busy when they were young, but now she has more time to do things she likes. She volunteers at the hospital three days a week."

"That's admirable," Price said. "I wish my wife would do something like that. About all she's good at is spending my money. She's got enough expensive jewelry to fill a pirate's treasure chest."

Stuart stared into Price's grinning face. For the first time in years, he felt like smacking someone.

Price glanced around the store, which was deathly quiet. It was empty except for the two of them and a pimply teenager who was looking at the floor mats. "Don't you have any help?" Price asked.

"I have a man that comes in on Saturdays."

"You've got it made. Last time my accountant gave me a list of my employees I had over two hundred."

"What is it you do exactly?" Stuart asked. "Sara told me you have some sort of medical business up in Baltimore."

"I own one of the largest pharmaceutical companies in Maryland. Of course, I've got plenty of managers and middle men to take care of the day-to-day chores, so I can concentrate on the big picture. Gives me plenty of time to goof off, too."

The pimply teenager had made his mind up about the floor mats and was now standing behind Price.

"I'd like to visit," Stuart said, "but as you can see, I've got customers to wait on."

"Sure, sure," Price said. "Are you going to the reunion dinner tonight?"

"If it were up to me, I'd skip it, but Sara said that she'd like to go."

"Then I'll see you there."

"Okay," Stuart said hesitantly, hoping their paths would never cross again in his lifetime.

"Nice chatting with you," Price said over his shoulder as he breezed out the door. He paused on the sidewalk, soaking in the glorious feeling of having rubbed Mick Stuart's nose in the mediocrity of his life by flaunting the staggering success of his own—the classmate Stuart had once bullied. Damn, payback felt good.

Hopping in his Ferrari, Price drove to an upscale residential area on the east side of Falls Church. He stopped before a large brick home with a wheelchair ramp out front. Listening to the Ferrari's engine ticking as it cooled, Price recalled the unforgivable infraction committed by the classmate who lived here. The incident occurred during Price's sophomore year, when he tried out for the football team. Price remembered every detail of the hot afternoon when the team met for a weightlifting session in the field house behind the high school.

Price had never lifted weights, and when his turn came to hoist the hundred-pound barbell, he could barely get it above his knees. The football coach, a not-too-bright ex-jock who taught his history class by reading to them directly from their textbook, goaded him on. Price had struggled mightily, but to no avail. He couldn't get the barbell over his head. That's when the team's star running back, Dick Radford, let go with a horselaugh that still echoed in Price's memory. "C'mon, Hercules, you can do it," Radford shouted.

Price had dropped the barbell with a clang and headed for the showers. His interest in making the team was over. A few days later, Price ran into Radford in the hallway at school. Radford asked Price why he'd missed the last couple of practices. When Price told him he'd decided to give up football to concentrate on his studies, Radford said he should stick with the program, that he showed a lot of potential. Yeah, Price had said to himself—potential for providing amusement for Dick Radford. Price had felt like turning the tables on Radford and laughing in his face over his absurd suggestion.

Price climbed from his Ferrari and walked toward the house, thinking about how Dick Radford's life had started out with such promise. As the captain of the football team, Radford had his pick of the girls and was the envy of nearly every guy in his class. Tutors assigned by the school helped him keep up his grades, and when he went off to the University of Virginia on a football scholarship, everyone expected great things of him.

A record crowd had turned out for the biggest game of the 1936 season, when Virginia played its archenemy, Virginia Tech. As the starting running back, Dick Radford performed up to expectations—until the third quarter. After a vicious hit by a Hokie linebacker, Radford never got up. He lay inert on the field, paralyzed from the waist down. The young football hero would never walk again. Radford had dropped out of college and gone into real estate, eventually opening his own firm in Falls Church. He never married, and he saw enough divorces among his friends to convince him that the sacred rite of marriage was more myth than reality.

Today, Radford had slept in. After finishing the elaborate process of getting ready for work—simply taking a shower and getting dressed was a challenge—Radford ate a late lunch. He'd just loaded the dishwasher when his doorbell rang. He wheeled himself into the front hallway and peered through the peephole he'd had installed at a level he was able to access. He was surprised to see who was standing outside. He opened the door and backed up his wheelchair.

"Look who's here," he said. "Bill Price. Fancy you visiting. Come on in."

"I hope I'm not intruding," Price said. "I thought I'd drop by to say hello since we never got a chance to chat last night. It's been awhile, hasn't it?"

"You bet it has." Radford wheeled into the living room, indicating a comfortable side chair. "Take a load off."

"How've you been?" Price inquired as he settled in.

Radford gave him a rueful smile. "About as well as could be, I suppose." He smacked the side of his wheelchair. "I don't get around like I used to."

"No more end runs, huh?"

"That was in another lifetime," Radford replied softly. He tried to strike a cheerful note. "Can I get you a cup of java? I just brewed a fresh batch."

"Thanks. That would hit the spot."

Radford wheeled into the kitchen and poured his guest a steaming cup of coffee. "I hear you're a big-time businessman now," he said when he returned to the living room. "What do you do with yourself when you're not making all those pricey little pills?"

"Oh gosh, I've got several outside interests. Golf for one thing. It's taken me years, but I finally got my handicap under ten. I played Pebble Beach last year, and I get down to Pinehurst fairly often. I've got my name on the list to play St. Andrews next year. Yessir, there's nothing like golf. Getting out in the fresh morning air and stretching your legs."

A strained look appeared on Radford's face.

"Gee, I'm sorry, Dick. Didn't mean to remind you of your accident."

"That's okay. I'm used to such things. So what else do you like to do?" He was struggling to find something to talk about with a man he'd never been friends with.

"I love hunting—big game, naturally. Last year I bagged a monster elk out in Wyoming, and this summer I'm headed to an island off southern Alaska. I'm hoping to come home with my biggest trophy ever—a Kodiak bear. Man, those things are scary. You've got to be on your guard constantly when you're tramping through the wilderness. If a Kodiak gets the drop on you, it's lights out. But then, that's what makes the challenge so thrilling."

55

"I never took you for an outdoorsman, Bill. Excuse me for saying it, but in school you were pretty much of a wimp."

Price roared with laughter. "You hit the nail on the head there, Dick. I used to struggle to lift a fifty-pound sack of potatoes at my dad's grocery store. But you might have noticed that I've bulked up a smidgen. I've got a home gym you wouldn't believe, and a personal trainer to keep me going. I can bench press 250 pounds. Not bad for an old duffer. I guess no one will be kicking sand in my face."

Radford's own body had withered away since his football injury. He was a shadow of the powerful athlete he'd once been. Price took immense pleasure in seeing Radford's face crumple as he described his own physical prowess. What a delicious form of revenge. He could still see the mocking grin on Radford's face when he'd ragged him about not being able to lift that hundred-pound barbell. He wondered how many reps Radford could do now.

Radford glanced at his watch. "I hate to say it, but I'm way overdue at the office."

"I'll get out of your hair then," Price said, having accomplished what he'd set out to do. "Will I see you at the reunion dinner tonight?"

"You bet. It's always great to see old friends."

"It really is," Price said with a false smile.

He was still smiling as he drove away. In the heart of Falls Church, he parked alongside a squarish, unadorned brick building. Like everyone else who'd ever lived here, Price knew this was the most historic structure in town. Built in colonial times, it was a church—The Falls Church. Named for the nearby Little Falls of the Potomac River, the church had given its name to the town that grew up around it. Price recalled how proud townsfolk were that George Washington had once been a church warden. During the Civil War, the church had served as a Union hospital and stable. Since then, it had been in use as an Episcopalian house of worship, looking much as it did when it first opened its doors two centuries earlier.

Reverend Tom Clark and his wife Brenda were the current stewards of the venerable church. Tom Clark's call to the Episcopal priesthood had been a shock to everyone who knew him. To transform from a frivolous playboy into a man of the cloth was quite a turnabout. Tom had been a rake all through high school, partying as much as possible, but when the light struck him, it struck him hard. He must have sown his last wild oats, for he reinvented himself as a person who put the needs of others before his own. Everyone in his small congregation thought the world of Reverend Tom.

Brenda Clark's transformation was no less startling. Once a self-infatuated tease, she'd left a string of broken hearts in her wake in high school. Most of the other girls in her class were cattishly jealous of her, and a few had despised her, but now many of those same women were happy to support Brenda in her tireless work on behalf of the church. From baptisms and bake sales to counseling services and choir practice, Brenda did all she could to help her husband fulfill his endless duties.

One of the broken hearts Brenda left in her wake belonged to William Price. The couple had started dating in their junior year, but after Brenda was elected homecoming queen in their senior year, she fell for the handsome homecoming king Tom Clark. Brenda had unceremoniously dumped Bill Price, leaving him at the top of the list of those who despised her.

On this quiet Friday afternoon, Tom and Brenda were preparing for weekend services when an unexpected visitor arrived. Price lumbered down the center aisle of the empty church toward the sanctuary, where Tom was laying out communion wafers and wine on the altar in readiness for the celebration of the Eucharist.

Tom looked up from his work. "Will miracles never cease?" he said. "I don't believe I've ever known a bigger skeptic, yet here you are in our humble little house of worship. Have you come to pray for forgiveness for a life of impiety?"

Price threw back his head and issued a laugh that echoed throughout the church. "I stand guilty as charged," he said.

"And while my sins may be great, I'm not here to seek forgiveness. I stopped by to say hello and see if you and Brenda would care to share a glass of wine." Price held up a bottle of premium Bordeaux, a 1945 Petrus Pomerol Merlot. "I'm partial to this vintage. I've got several cases of it in my wine cellar at home. I guarantee it'll beat your communion wine."

Price stepped up to the sanctuary and held out the bottle. Tom put on his reading glasses and examined the label. He whistled softly. "Look at this, dear," he said to Brenda. "I've never even seen a bottle from this famous winery." He turned to Price. "This must have cost a fortune."

Price waved his concern aside. "A couple of hundred bucks."

Brenda gasped. She put her arm in her husband's. They made a handsome couple, he with a distinguished touch of gray at the temples and she with the lingering appeal that she'd traded upon so often in her youth.

"You must be doing very well," Brenda said. "Perhaps you'd care to make a donation to the church." She pointed to the collection box in front of the sanctuary.

"I am doing well," Price said. "My company's sales topped twenty million dollars last year." He let that statement sink in. "And I will happily make a donation to your church. But first, let's have a drink. I brought along some cups."

He lined up three white paper cups on the altar and poured a generous amount of the fruity, dark red wine into each of them, then he handed both Tom and Brenda a cup. Lifting his own cup, Price offered a toast. "To old friends."

Tom and Brenda looked at one another with bafflement. Given the history among the three of them, they found it odd that Bill Price would consider himself an old friend. With a shrug, Tom lifted his cup. "To old friends."

They all three drank, savoring the costly vintage.

"This is definitely the best wine I've ever tasted," Tom said.

"It is yummy," Brenda agreed.

Price studied the woman closely. She still had an unaffected, wholesome beauty that needed no artificial embellishments.

Her radiant smile was as pure as sunlight. It seemed to confirm that life was good and everything would be all right. But had life turned out well for Brenda, Price wondered. She was the wife of a small-time pastor in an archaic small-town church. How happy could she be? He hoped not very.

Price gave Brenda an inscrutable look. "I guess yours was a match made in heaven."

Price removed a crisp hundred-dollar bill from his wallet. He waved the bill for Tom and Brenda to see then stuffed it into the collection box. He told a few more self-congratulatory anecdotes before he said goodbye, leaving the rest of the expensive wine he'd brought displayed on the altar, a reminder of the things Tom and Brenda could never afford.

Outside the church, Price gazed at the old building. He was satisfied that he'd settled his debts with the classmates he'd visited this afternoon. Frankly, he regarded their transgressions as second tier, dealing only with physical and emotional slights. But Joan Smollett was different. She'd insulted his intelligence, and he could never let that stand. More would have to be done before those scales were balanced.

Chapter 7

Friday

Blues Alley was the place to be on a Friday night. Recently opened in a refurbished 18th-century brick carriage house in the heart of Georgetown, the smoky supper club was packed with doctors, lawyers, streetwalkers, fast-talkers, and every other strain of jazz-loving hipster. The lucky folks sitting at the café tables up front were so close to the musicians they could reach out and shake their hands.

At center stage, Dizzy Gillespie was frolicking through his twenty-year-old standard "Groovin' High," a song that put the *bop* in bebop. With his pufferfish cheeks and bent trumpet, Gillespie looked like he was a bit dizzy, but it was the right kind of giddiness, and it was contagious. Heads were bobbing and shoulders shaking all over the small, dimly lit nightclub. The scene could have been taking place in a basement speakeasy in the Roaring Twenties.

Seated in a back corner, Xander Riley and Jake Plummer had polished off the last of their blackened catfish and Cajun chicken, two of the Southern specialties of the house. Plummer was taking hits from his flask of Barbancourt, a mellow dark rum that was Haiti's most famous export, aside from misery. Right now, Plummer looked like some of that misery was rubbing off on him.

"What do you mean *our* cover could be blown?" Plummer said. "*You're* the one who's a phony, not me. I'm only going along with your scam because you've got me in a bind."

Riley frowned at his reluctant partner.

"To tell you the truth," Plummer continued, "I don't care if you are found out. In fact, I'd welcome it. It would get me out from under this crappy arrangement."

"Don't get carried away, my fickle friend. If my little game comes crashing down, I might let everyone know why you played along."

"Damn you," Plummer said.

"C'mon now, Jake. I'm just jerking you around. You know I wouldn't rat you out. You and I make a great team."

"Sure," Plummer groused. "Like Abbott and Costello."

"They were the best comedy duo ever."

"Except for the fact that they hated each other." The photographer squinted at Riley. "So who are you worried about spilling the beans?"

Riley's expression turned grim. "A sour old crone at National Geographic who thinks she's God's gift to journalism. She's pestered me on both of my articles about all sorts of little things, but this time she got all high and mighty about me not getting my facts straight. She the same as accused me of making stuff up. If she mentions that to anyone, things could unravel fast."

"What are you gonna do about it?"

"I'm not certain," Riley said in a despondent tone. He stared into the middle distance. "But I need to think of some way to muzzle the old bag."

The two of them sat in a silent funk for several minutes while Dizzy Gillespie whizzed through another of his classics, the breakneck virtuoso piece "Salt Peanuts."

"Have you ever traveled to Iraq?" Riley asked Plummer out of the blue.

"Hell no, and I never intend to. As far as I'm concerned, the entire Middle East is a worthless dust bowl. I hate hot, dry climates. I don't even like Arizona."

Riley saw that some attitude adjustment might be called for.

Plummer took another healthy swig of Barbancourt, wiping his mouth with the back of his hand. He didn't like the look on Riley's face. There was no telling what ridiculous scheme the silly bastard might come up with next. "Why are you asking me about Iraq anyway?"

"Oh, nothing. Just thinking out loud."

Over in Vienna, Virginia, William Price was also thinking out loud. The beefy businessman gave a derisive snort. "Who's she supposed to be—Little Bo Peep?"

Price was gazing toward the entrance to the ballroom at the Westwood Country Club, where the Class of 1935's reunion dinner party was just getting underway. The tables around the chandelier-lit room were draped with formal white cloths and set with gleaming china, sparkling crystal, and fresh flowers. Joan Smollett stood framed in the doorway. She was dressed in a fluffy pink ball gown and wore a tall silver paper crown. In her right hand, she had a long thin scepter topped by a tin-foil star. She seemed to be waiting for someone to compliment her on her wonderfulness.

Margery Kendall, a classmate who worked as a sales clerk in a Falls Church dress shop, recognized Smollett's character. "I believe she's supposed to be Glinda, the Good Witch of the North, from *The Wizard of Oz* movie. I think she looks nice."

Price wrinkled up his nose. "The Wicked Witch of the West would have been more appropriate."

Jeffrey Smollett stood at his wife's side, outfitted as the Wizard of Oz himself, although he'd have made a better Cowardly Lion. Costumes were the theme of tonight's party, the high point of the class's reunion events. Margery Kendall had come as Price's companion for the evening. She was dressed as the plucky cartoon character Little Orphan Annie, complete with a curly red wig. Price was dressed as a tuxedoed Daddy Warbucks, Annie's filthy rich patron. Price had chosen the costumes himself.

The most historically correct costume was worn by the evening's master of ceremonies, senior class president Pythagoras Bib. He came dressed as the original Pythagoras, draped in the white tunic the ancient Greek philosopher was usually depicted in and wearing a long false beard. Part of the fun for everyone was guessing who their fellow classmates were portraying. Most people thought that Py had come dressed for a toga party.

Py took his seat at the head table and signaled for the waiters to begin serving dinner. At Py's side was his date for the evening, Barbara Thatcher, a slender, statuesque brunette who made a convincing Persephone, the ancient Greek goddess of springtime and rebirth. Barbara owned the popular Georgetown flower shop Bouquet Boutique. Py had rented the apartment above her shop for several years. He shared his apartment with a fluffy white Pomeranian named Snickers, a pint-sized dog that his brother Archie could barely tolerate. Snickers had a piercing high-pitched bark and an annoying habit of getting underfoot. Archie worried that one day he might inadvertently step on the tiny thing and squash it.

Py had grown close to his lady friend Barbara. She wasn't the only woman he squired around Washington, but she held the top spot, for the simple reason that she always had something interesting to say. As a student of psychology, Py had been fascinated to hear Barbara explain how her customers' selection of flowers revealed their personalities. Though Py wasn't a practicing psychologist, he'd written articles on the subject for general readers, which led to his being invited to join the Cosmos Club, an exclusive Washington social organization for writers, artists, scientists, and other men of accomplishment.

Py was also a published poet, and he sometimes dressed the part. He might have been the lone man in Washington to sport a cravat and a boutonnière. Strangers often underestimated him, regarding him as a dandy. A Georgetown mugger once made that mistake while Py was taking Snickers for a late-night walk. The mugger ended up in the hospital with a dislocated shoulder and abrasions from having landed face-first on the sidewalk. The mugger would definitely have chosen a different victim if he'd known that Py held a black belt in jujitsu and had won a number of medals for bravery as an Army demolitions expert in World War II.

Unfortunately, Py's brother wasn't able to make it to tonight's dinner. Archie had been looking forward to it, but a new lead had opened up on the Capitol Hill murder case he'd been investigating. As any cop would attest, duty always came before pleasure. During his lengthy career, Archie had missed so many dinner parties, days off, and baseball games on TV that he'd stopped counting. He'd even missed the weddings of two of his best friends on the force, although they understood the reason for his absence.

Archie was hoping to make it to the two final reunion get-togethers on Saturday morning—the breakfast in Falls Church and the trip to the Tidal Basin to see the cherry trees—but that would depend on how things went with his investigation. At least Py would be able to fill him in on anything he missed. What Archie would miss out on tonight was the fun of seeing a group of middle-aged friends making fools of themselves by dressing up like little kids on Halloween.

After the partygoers finished their meal of chicken cordon bleu followed by Virginia's famous peanut butter pie, Py stood up and tapped his wine glass with his table knife. "Ladies and gentlemen, may I have your attention. I assume there are some ladies and gentlemen present."

"Shucks, Py," yelled the jovial insurance salesman Tim Wilson, "the ladies and gentlemen all left. Ain't no one here now but us Falls Churchians, or whatever we're called."

"I thought the crowd had thinned out," Py said with a smile. He held up the school yearbook from 1935. "I was thumbing through our yearbook last night, and as I looked at the photos of the kids we used to be, I was reminded that we had some fine-looking girls and boys in our class. Despite being on the brink of the Big 5-0, we're still looking pretty good. A few of you don't look much different than you did at our senior prom, especially Helen Brooks. What's your secret, Helen?"

"Clean living," she called out.

"I also couldn't help thinking about some of the classmates we've lost. Tragically, Mary Ann Powell died in a car accident the year after we graduated, and Terry Melham and Vince Murray were killed in the war. I'm happy to see that Terry and

Vince's wives are with us tonight. Carol, Patty, we all want you to know that Terry and Vince are still very much alive in our hearts. Py's remark brought several shouts of "Hear, hear."

"What struck me most about our class," he continued, "was that, with a few exceptions, we all got along great. I think that's a product of growing up in a small town, even though Falls Church is no longer quite so small. When we were young, we stuck together, supported each other. Maybe it was the Depression, but whatever it was, something forged a bond among us. And I'm glad to say I can see that bond still exists."

Py laid the yearbook aside. "Now, before I get too maudlin, I think it's time to reward the ingenuity that went into creating the costumes we're wearing. If you'll bear with me for a few more minutes before the band comes on, I'd like to hand out some prizes in recognition of tonight's most memorable outfits. And we should thank my lovely guest Barbara Thatcher for providing tonight's awards and for helping me pick the winners. The $25 gift certificates are good at her Georgetown flower shop."

Py led a round of applause then consulted his notes. "In the category of Best Cartoon Characters, I'd like Margery Kendall and Bill Price to come forward." The audience cheered as Margery and Bill made their way to the head table. Py gestured toward the couple. "Standing before you are Little Orphan Annie and Daddy Warbucks. To prove their identity, I'll ask Annie to say a few words."

Margery tittered like a little girl and chirped two of Annie's catchphrases. "Gee whiskers," she said, goggling at the crowd in imitation of Annie's enormous vacant eyes. "Leapin' lizards!"

Py handed them their gift certificates before announcing the next category. "And for Best Television Characters, the winners are Pete and Ingrid Emerson, our adorable Mouseketeers." The couple stood up and waved, their Mickey Mouse hats on their heads and their white pullover sweaters emblazoned with the names Bobby and Annette, two of the original *Mickey Mouse Club* stars.

After handing Pete and Ingrid their gift certificates, Py announced the winners for Best Literary Characters, Tim Wilson and his wife Vicky. The two were decked out in matching forest green tights, green medieval tunics, and feathered green archer's caps. "I've got to admit," Py said, "I thought Tim and Vicky had both come as Robin Hood, but Vicky told me she's actually Peter Pan. I guess she is too small to make a believable Robin Hood."

The next awards were for Best Movie Characters. "The winners are Joan and Jeffrey Smollett," Py said. "They're dressed as Glinda, the Good Witch of the North, and the Wizard of Oz, although they could pass for the Cherry Blossom Queen and a doorman at the Mayflower Hotel."

Joan Smollett made a production out of her walk to the head table, bowing and waving her scepter like Glinda did in the movie. Jeffrey skulked along in her wake like the sinister hunchback Igor from the horror movies. "Thank you so much, Py," Joan trilled as she accepted the gift certificates from her distinguished National Geographic coworker. "We'll stop by and select some nice flowers as soon as possible. I'm sure that Miss Thatcher's shop is delightful."

Over at his table, Bill Price pretended to retch into his glass.

"Tonight's final prizes go to the Best Superhero Characters," Py said. "We have several fine candidates, but I think you'll all agree that no one does justice to their costumes quite like Batman James Timberlake and Wonder Woman Helen Brooks." Timberlake, a bald, pudgy family doctor, offered his hand to Helen, who was bulging from her scanty outfit just as she'd bulged from her scandalous two-piece bathing suit years ago. Some of the men wolf-whistled as Helen performed a slinky walk toward the head table alongside Timberlake.

"Perhaps Wonder Woman could demonstrate her Lasso of Truth," Py remarked. "We all know how she used to lasso guys in school. She seldom missed her intended target, although some of you fellows may be shy about revealing the truth in front of your wives."

Helen took her gift certificate and stuffed it into her low-cut top, then she went through the motions of binding Py with a magical rope. "Well, folks," he said, "that about wraps things up. Not only because I can no longer move, but also because I've run out of gift certificates. The music will begin in a few minutes, so let's all enjoy the rest of the evening."

While the waiters cleared the tables and the three-piece combo began setting up, Joan Smollett approached Py. "Sorry to bother you," she said, "but could I have a word in private?"

He gave her a curious look. "Of course."

They stepped over to a quiet corner. Smollett checked to see that no one was close enough to overhear them. She had a serious expression. "I'm dealing with a delicate issue at work," she said, "and I was hoping you might give me some advice about how to handle it."

Py was nonplussed. He and Smollett had never exchanged anything more than polite greetings on the job. It seemed un-likely that she'd suddenly be asking for his counsel about a work issue. Smollett did need advice, and while she could have turned to any number of staff members at National Geographic, she knew that tonight offered an opportunity to consult the exalted Pythagoras Bib on a personal level.

"What's this concerned with?" Py asked.

"Oh, I don't think I should go into it here. I was wondering if we could possibly meet at the office on Monday, if you can spare the time."

"Certainly. Call my secretary and she'll fit you in." Py stud-ied Smollett. "I hope you're not having health problems."

"No, no. Nothing like that. It's something I've never been faced with before."

"You've got me excited to hear about it."

"I may be getting keyed up over nothing, but I'd like your opinion about what I should do."

"I'm always happy to hand out advice, like Lucy in *Peanuts*. Five cents per customer. I hope my advice is worth more than hers usually is."

Smollett laughed and thanked him. "I'll see you on Monday then," she said before returning to her table, where her husband was entertaining the other guests with his imitation of a moldering corpse.

Py took his seat beside Barbara Thatcher. "That was strange," he said. "That woman is the head of research at National Geographic. I've never worked with her on any of her projects, yet now she's asking me for advice."

Barbara placed her hand on Py's. "She's probably secretly in love with you."

"Good Lord, I hope not."

Just then the band began playing "I Left My Heart in San Francisco." Py led Barbara to the dance floor, where they joined a menagerie of colorful characters. Batman was dancing with the flapper Sue Montgomery, and Robin Hood had found a new partner in Wonder Woman. Meanwhile, pirate Dave Sims, owner of a Falls Church plumbing company, was swooping about with Little Orphan Annie in his arms.

While Daddy Warbucks's companion was enjoying herself on the dance floor, Bill Price made the rounds of the tables, chatting with the short list of classmates he regarded as friends. Price was on his fourth Black Russian, and his step wasn't too steady. As he came to the table where Joan Smollett was sitting, he seemed to trip. Pitching forward, he spilled his drink on Smollett's pink ball gown.

Smollett let out a shriek that was heard all over the room. Everyone turned to stare, including the master of ceremonies. Could a party of 48-year-olds be getting out of hand?

"You great hulking oaf," Smollett yelled. "You did that on purpose."

Price grabbed a table napkin and made a halfhearted effort to mop up the damage. "Golly, Joan, you know I'd never do anything like that."

"Get your filthy paws off me," Smollett snapped. She snatched the napkin from Price's hand and dabbed at her gown, a dress she'd rented for the evening.

"If you're going to get all huffy, I'll leave you to it," Price said. Wobbling back to his own table, Price wore a tight smile. He was hoping the Black Russian would stain Smollett's dress. The scales were nearly balanced.

Down in Georgetown, someone else was considering how to deal with Joan Smollett. Xander Riley was thinking of buying a voodoo doll in her image and sticking pins in it.

Chapter 8

Saturday

Archimedes Bib was contemplating murder as he drove from his home in Washington to the Saturday reunion breakfast in Falls Church. He wasn't thinking of committing a murder but of solving one. His investigation in the Capitol Hill murder case had begun to pay dividends, thanks to the killer's greed. In addition to stealing Congressman Bill Blake's wallet, the thug had taken the victim's gold Rolex, a gift from a member of the flock of lobbyists that circled the U.S. Capitol like birds of prey.

According to the congressman's wife, the watch bore an inscription on the back, the incriminating message "With our sincere thanks." Those words would identify the watch when the killer got around to pawning it, as he surely would. Bib's men had alerted every pawnshop in D.C. to be on the lookout for a gold Rolex with that inscription, so it was only a matter of time before the police had a direct link to the murderer.

At the moment, Bib needed to forget about killers and concentrate on negotiating the streets of Falls Church. He always welcomed the opportunity to return to his hometown, a community of some ten thousand where the peace was seldom disturbed by big city woes. Washington, D.C., had its charms—the imposing houses of government, the Smithsonian museums, the many leafy parks and fantastic array of restaurants—but it also had the usual crime, clutter, and congestion.

Anytime Bib needed to decompress, nothing beat spending an afternoon in the relaxing byways of Falls Church. His parents' old home, a two-story white Victorian, sat in a quiet neighborhood in the heart of town. When Bib was growing up, children could play in the streets without fear of being run down by motorists. Though times had changed, Falls Church still looked much as it had decades earlier, and Bib hoped it would stay that way.

During the war, Bib had gotten a taste of Europe and seen some of the world's wonders, including the Eiffel Tower and the Sistine Chapel. Foreign travel was a rarity for a small-town kid, but no matter where he'd been or where he might go, his heart would always be in Falls Church. It was where his wife and parents were buried, and where he would one day rest. Most of his high school classmates had never strayed far from their immediate environs, but they were none the worse for it, and if they had a hankering for big city thrills, they could always find them a few miles to the east on the other side of the Potomac.

Driving southwest on Washington Street, Bib passed the State Theatre, opened in 1936 and still entertaining townsfolk with the latest movies. Sitting in that darkened theater on a long-ago summer evening, he'd shared his first kiss with his future wife, Phyllis McGuire. He even remembered the movie playing that night—*Gunga Din*, a semi-silly feature based on the tales of Kipling and starring Cary Grant, Douglas Fairbanks, Jr., Victor McLaglen, Sam Jaffee, and Joan Fontaine. Bib recalled that a member of the audience had shushed them when he and Phyllis laughed at an inappropriate place in the film. They'd laughed a lot back then.

Three blocks northwest of the State Theatre was the Falls Church Public Library, a brick building across the street from the historic Cherry Hill farmhouse, which dated to the mid-1800s. The town library was always as quiet as a tomb, and the shadowy stacks of books had a faintly romantic aspect. At least Bib had felt that way when he was spending time with Phyllis studying for their college exams. He remembered looking up words in a huge old dictionary that must have weighed ten pounds. He'd found it hard to believe there were so many words for love.

Why the beautiful Phyllis McGuire had agreed to marry him was one of the greatest mysteries Bib had ever encountered.

71

They'd wed right after college and enjoyed a blissful two years together before the war came along. A few months before Bib joined the Army, they were blessed with a baby girl. Phyllis had been gone for nearly ten years now, and Bib still felt a hollowness in his chest whenever he thought of her, but at least he had his daughter to comfort him, his buoyant, dependable Sylvia. She'd been fourteen when her mother died and had grown up fast, becoming the woman of the house when her father was bereft.

Married and living in far-off California now, Sylvia was as loving and beautiful as her mother had been. She called every Saturday night to check on her father. Bib was still rattling around in the Georgetown townhouse that Phyllis's wealthy parents had given them as a wedding present when they settled in Washington. Only Bib's Jamaican housekeeper kept him from going crazy in the spacious dwelling that had once rung with a child's laughter and his wife's angelic voice as she accompanied herself on the piano.

Bib's mother had also played the piano, and she and Phyllis occasionally performed duets during those brief years when the family was whole. Mary Bib had likened music to mathematics, for their mutual elegant precision. Despite how much he tried, Bib had never gotten past a few elementary scales. His father had shared his musical ineptitude, consoling his son with a wink and the remark, "Let's leave music to the womenfolk. You and I can sit back and enjoy it." If Bib had known how fleeting those treasured moments would be, he'd have asked his wife and mother to play for them every night.

Bib hadn't taken a drink of liquor since the month-long binge that had followed his wife's death from breast cancer. He'd hit rock bottom, and it was only the intervention of his teenage daughter and the considerateness of his boss at the Metropolitan Police Department that kept him from wrecking his life and losing his job. He could have ended up as a homeless drunk roaming the streets of Washington, like so many other lost souls.

Bib recalled the night he took his final drink. His daughter had confronted him about his behavior, asking him what her mother would say if she could see him now. Bib had stared at the half-empty bottle of J&B Scotch sitting on the kitchen table. He poured the rest of the liquor into the sink and hugged his daughter with all his might, both of them weeping on each other's shoulders. Recently, Sylvia had telephoned from California and urged him to come out for his first grandchild's first birthday party. The sight of one-year-old Charles Archibald Kemp grinning at his granddad with his chubby little arms outstretched had reminded Bib that, despite the inevitable losses, life was still worth living.

On the corner of Washington and Broad Street, the town's main commercial thoroughfare, Bib passed Brown's Hardware, a mom-and-pop emporium that had been in business since before he was born. He remembered visiting the store with his father on Saturday mornings in search of some doodad needed for a home repair. For a young boy, roaming the aisles of tools, bolts, nails, light fixtures, cans of paint, and a hundred other wondrous items was like wandering through Aladdin's cave.

Bib branched off Washington onto Annandale Road, passing mixed neighborhoods of apartment buildings and commercial properties. At Arlington Boulevard, he turned into the parking lot of the tiny plaza where JV's Restaurant had been welcoming patrons since 1947. Originally a family café, JV's had later added a bar and a stage for live music. Bib was grateful there were no shows during breakfast. Trying to hold a conversation in the crowded restaurant was difficult enough without a group of starstruck locals holding forth.

Big band music had been popular when Bib and his wife were newlyweds. They'd both found the music as soothing as a warm bath. He recalled Phyllis's favorite recording, Vera Lynn's "We'll Meet Again." She'd played and sung that song for him before he went off to Europe at the start of the war. He'd hummed the tune whenever he thought of his girl back home—the beautiful colleen who'd inexplicably fallen in love with a homely loner with a cockamamie first name.

Inside JV's, every inch of wall space was covered with photographs and random memorabilia. The place resembled an eccentric collector's jam-packed recreation room. In a back corner, some of the tables had been pushed together to accommodate a large party. Tim Wilson waved and called out. "Hey, Archie, I saved you a seat."

Bib settled in between the genial insurance salesman and family doctor James Timberlake. Wilson slapped Bib on the back. "We missed you last night at the dinner party. You should have seen the costumes."

"I was actually there," Bib said, rolling his shoulders from Wilson's stinging blow.

"But I never saw you."

"That's because I came as the Invisible Man."

Wilson scrunched up his face in concentration. "Hmm."

James Timberlake chuckled. The physician was tucking into a plate of corned beef hash and poached eggs. He glanced at Bib. "Don't tell any of my patients you saw me eating this. I'd never hear the end of it."

Bib greeted his other classmates, the gang of friendly souls he'd grown up with. He'd already eaten—he'd forgotten to tell Amara about the breakfast get-together and she'd fixed one of her tasty Jamaican porridges—so he only ordered orange juice and coffee.

Dr. Timberlake finished the last morsel of his unhealthy meal. He shoved the plate away and sighed. "I'm betting our Invisible Man here was out chasing some crook last night."

Bib smiled. "You got it."

"What sort of case are you working on?" Timberlake asked.

"Congressman Blake's murder on Capitol Hill."

"Oh yeah, I read about that in the *Post*," Timberlake said. "It made me wonder why he was out late at night walking a dog. That seems risky over in D.C."

"People get complacent," Bib said.

"I've always been fascinated by how detectives go about investigating a murder," Timberlake commented. "I've read enough Agatha Christie novels to know how fictional detectives work—simply figure out who stands to gain the most from putting rich Uncle Reggie out of the way—but what's it like in the real world?"

"You don't want me to bore you with shop talk," Bib said.

Several others in the group spoke up. "Come on, Archie," plumber Dave Sims said, "we'd like to hear about your job. I'll bet it's more interesting than fixing a leaky faucet."

"All right, if you don't mind being reminded of how low human beings can sink." Bib paused in thought. "A colleague of mine likens a murder investigation to exploring a large, unfamiliar office building, which he calls Murder Enterprises. Inside the building, each floor is dedicated to a different type of homicide, and a detective has to determine which floor he should spend his time on. There's a floor for spur-of-the-moment killings—say those committed during a robbery, like my present case, or in an instant of blind rage resulting from an argument. I once had a case where a husband killed his wife for changing the TV channel. Of course, that was just the spark that set off an old stick of dynamite."

Bib's classmates were instantly hooked on his story.

"Most of the other floors in the building are devoted to premeditated murders. There's the floor for murders done for financial gain, like those James mentioned. Another floor is dedicated to revenge killings. Personally, I find those crimes the most irksome of all. I've known killers who obsessed over some petty offense for years, long after everyone else involved had forgotten about it. That kind of hatred is always a step away from homicide."

Tim Wilson shuddered. "Crikey. You get into some weird stuff, Archie."

"Yep, and murders related to love and sex are some of the weirdest. They're also some of the seamiest crimes I've had to contend with, and they can have any one of several motives,

75

including jealousy, pride, betrayal, and unreciprocated feelings. Those seem like inexplicable reasons for murder to me, but romance can bring out the worst in us. It can literally drive people crazy."

"But aren't all killers crazy?" Dave Sims asked.

"That's a debate I avoid. My job is to catch murderers, period. After that, the courts have to decide if they're mentally competent. I will say that killers who pick their victims at random, with no motive other than their own twisted logic, certainly strike me as insane. And without any connection to their victims, random killers can be the hardest to track down, unless they commit multiple murders. In that case, patterns usually emerge that lead us to the killers."

Bib took a sip of coffee. "There's one other floor in the Murder Enterprises building, the one dedicated to murders committed over hidden secrets. You'd be surprised how innocuous some of the supposedly dark secrets are that have spurred killings. I had a case where a man committed murder to keep someone from revealing that he'd stolen five dollars from a church collection plate as a teenager. If he had fessed up about the theft and made restitution, the issue would have gone away in two seconds."

Building contractor Peter Emerson spoke up. "I bet most of us have some secret we'd be embarrassed to have others find out about."

"Probably so," Bib replied, "but there's something strange about people who are willing to kill to keep their secrets from becoming known. I've consulted Py now and then when I need help negotiating the maze of the human psyche. That's more up his alley."

"Say," Sims said, "where is Py this morning?"

"He slept in. He said he was tired after last night's party."

"I'll bet it was the party *after* the party that tired him out," Wilson quipped. "His date was a real looker."

"Archie, you've only told us about the different kinds of murders," Dr. Timberlake said. "How do you go about solving them? I'm sure you don't sit in your easy chair and employ your 'little grey cells' like Hercule Poirot."

"There's a fair amount of sitting and mulling over the case, but of course you have to gather the evidence first. And that takes a lot of plodding around, investigating the scene of the crime and talking to witnesses, like every cop does in books and on television. There's a reason why policemen are called flat-feet. And just like every fictional cop, we have to establish that a suspect had the motive, the means, and the opportunity to commit the crime if we hope to get a conviction—although real cops seldom get helpful tips from kindhearted hookers or miraculously find vital clues tossed in a dumpster like they do on television."

Bib glanced at his watch. "Speaking of plodding, I need to get back to D.C. We're waiting for an important piece of information that could break the Capitol Hill case."

"Think you'll make it down to the Tidal Basin to see the cherry trees?" Timberlake asked.

"I definitely intend to swing by if work permits. But I know Py will be there."

Bib stood up and laid some money on the table for his juice and coffee. "I guess I should say goodbye, in case I get tied up. It's always great to see you fellows."

After a round of handshaking, Bib headed out to his unmarked police car and called his office on the two-way radio. His call was routed to his sergeant, Matthew Dowden.

"Sir, you'd better get back as soon as you can," Dowden said. "The congressman's Rolex was pawned, and we have an ID on the man who brought it in."

Inside JV's Restaurant, James Timberlake ordered another cup of coffee. "You know, come to think of it, my job is a little like old Archie's—examining clues to solve the mystery of what makes people sick."

"Yeah, doc," Tim Wilson said, "except unlike Archie's murder victims, your patients can all talk to you. At least they can when they walk in."

By ten o'clock, Bib and his sergeant were prowling Southeast Washington in search of a character who went by the quaint nickname of Crowbar. He was reputedly a bushy-haired beanpole with a bad attitude and no visible means of support, even though he was always flush with cash.

At that same hour, some twenty members of the Class of 1935 were prowling the Washington Tidal Basin in search of the best view of the capital's glorious cherry blossoms. Helen Brooks was wearing a bright yellow halter-top sundress, one of the benefits of springtime from the male perspective.

Joan Smollett wore a white empire waist dress, with a wide-brimmed white sun hat. She looked like she was ready for the Easter Parade. Smollett was fortunate there wasn't a breeze, which might have sent her hat sailing over the Potomac like a flying saucer.

Most of the other women were dressed in slacks, which were more practical for strolling among the groves of trees. The men all wore chinos and polo shirts, their standard weekend outfits for the golf course. Py Bib's Panama hat set him apart. Py wasn't escorting his friend Barbara today, since Saturday was the busiest day of the week for her Georgetown flower shop.

"Isn't it fantastic," Helen said to Py. She whirled with her arms outstretched, reveling in the sight of avalanches of snowy white and pale pink blossoms.

In 1912, three thousand Japanese cherry trees were planted at the Tidal Basin and other parts of Potomac Park. A gift to America from Japan, the cherry trees transformed the capital into a fairyland each spring, attracting thousands of tourists. Locals were just as taken by the spectacle. During the week, groups of office workers picnicked on outspread blankets all around the grounds of the Tidal Basin, enjoying the brief moment when their gray workaday city became a kingdom of flowery wonder.

"First Lady Helen Taft is often given the credit for having the cherry trees planted," Py said to Helen, "but the idea was originally suggested by travel writer Eliza Scidmore. After visiting Japan, she kept urging Washington officials to beautify the capital with ornamental cherry trees. Her plan succeeded when Mrs. Taft got involved."

"Sounds like the old familiar story," Helen said. "You've got to have someone important endorse an idea in order to make it happen."

"Eliza Scidmore was an important person herself," Py said. "She wrote several books about her travels, and she worked for the National Geographic Society in its early days, contributing articles and photographs. She also lectured here, and she became the first female member of the board. She's even got a glacier named after her in Alaska. I'll bet that you and Eliza would have hit it off. Two talented ladies who never took no for an answer."

"I remember the time you said no."

Py winced. "We all make mistakes."

She gave him a puppy dog look.

"Moving on," Py said, "did you notice the incident at the dinner party when Bill Price spilled his drink on Joan Smollett's dress?"

"How could I not notice? She screamed like a stuck pig."

Py nodded to where Price and Smollett were standing, a few feet away. "I think maybe Bill is making a peace offering."

Price was holding out a small package wrapped in brown paper. "It does look like he's trying to patch things up," Helen whispered. They could just hear what Price was saying.

"I want to apologize again for that accident the other night," he told Smollett. "I hope my drink didn't stain that lovely dress."

Smollett eyed him suspiciously. "It's at the cleaners now."

"To prove how sorry I am, I bought you this little gift. It's not much, but I hope it shows you how I really feel."

Smollett hesitated in taking the package. Her lip curled as if he was offering her a plate of rotten fruit. Smollett glanced at her husband, who was lost in his own thoughts, staring at the cherry blossoms like a child.

"Please accept this, Joan," Price urged, extending the package toward her.

Smollett took the gift with reluctance. "It feels like a book," she said.

"Right you are. No one can fool you."

"Well…thank you," she said grudgingly.

Price turned away with the smile of a con man who'd just stumped a rube.

Chapter 9

Sunday

Leisure wasn't a priority for Archie Bib. He found it gave him too much time to dwell on the past. A quiet weekend at home left him casting about for odd jobs to prevent his mind from drifting into dark corners. In warm weather, he spent most of his weekends in the backyard, tending to his wife's beloved flower garden, and he sometimes shared afternoon tea with his neighbor lady, a 90-year-old font of wisdom said to be the last living direct descendant of Abraham Lincoln.

On this sunny Sunday morning, Bib diverted his mind by going over the Capitol Hill murder case. Yesterday, he and Sergeant Dowden had combed the streets of Southeast D.C. in search of tips that might lead them to the man who called himself Crowbar. They'd followed the man's trail to Anacostia. In one of the poorer neighborhoods, they found Mister Crowbar playing pool at his favorite hangout. The arrest had gone smoothly thanks to Sergeant Dowden, who, at six foot three and a solid 225 pounds, got little resistance from the skinny suspect.

A search of Crowbar's fleabag apartment had turned up a wad of cash and a .45 automatic, the same caliber of weapon used to kill Congressman Blake. If ballistics determined that the gun had fired the fatal bullet, the case would be sewn up. Crowbar would need a crowbar if he ever hoped to escape the accommodation he'd likely be occupying for the next several decades. When Sergeant Dowden took Crowbar to his cell at police headquarters, the man didn't seem fazed. He was no stranger to police lockups.

Bib collected his coffee cup and the *Washington Post* comics section from the kitchen table and took them out to the patio.

He sat staring at the tulips Phyllis had planted the year they moved into the townhouse. Every spring, the rainbow blossoms of the tulips competed for best in show with banks of yellow and white daffodils. Phyllis had also planted their own cherry tree in a back corner of the yard. The drooping branches of the weeping cherry tree were laden with delicate blossoms. Bib could never decide precisely what color the flowers were. Sometimes they looked pink and other times lavender. The one thing he was certain of was that the tree was aptly named, for more than once he'd wept just looking at it.

Years ago, his housekeeper had talked him into attending a Sunday church service with her at the Nineteenth Street Baptist Church, saying that it might help him cope with his wife's death. The oldest black Baptist church in Washington, the unpretentious brick building at 19th and I Streets NW had been ringing with exuberant hymns and shouts of "Amen" and "Hallelujah" since 1871. Bib enjoyed the service, but as the only white person in the congregation, he'd been a definite curiosity. A pigtailed pixie in the pew in front of him had gawked at him repeatedly, until Amara told her to turn around.

After Amara returned from this morning's church service and changed out of her Sunday best, she would fix Bib a light lunch, a routine that hadn't varied for as long as the effervescent Jamaican lady had been with him. Bib didn't want to spoil his appetite for Sunday evening, when he and his brother always got together for dinner to discuss the previous week and life in general. Along with his daughter's Saturday night telephone calls, the Sunday dinners with Py constituted Bib's lifeline.

Bib finally took his eyes off the floral display that brought back so many memories. He sipped his coffee then checked his newspaper to see what Blondie and Dagwood were up to.

Over near Dupont Circle, Joan Smollett was fussing around the apartment she shared with her husband. She'd chosen the apartment because it was handy to National Geographic, even though Jeffrey had to take an inconvenient twenty-minute bus ride across town to his job at the National Bank of Washington. Smollett was in a hurry to dispense with breakfast so she could clean up and get ready to go in to her office. She snatched Jeffrey's half-eaten bowl of oatmeal from the table and carried it to the kitchen sink. Jeffrey didn't utter a word of protest.

Smollett often spent Sunday afternoons at her office. Except for tourist-filled Explorers Hall, the building was deserted and blessedly quiet. Without the distractions of the daily workplace, Smollett could get almost as much done on a Sunday as she could in an entire week. This Sunday was especially important, since she wanted to put things in order ahead of what promised to be a busy Monday. Also, though she'd never admitted it to herself, she enjoyed her time away from Jeffrey. Her job was all that mattered. He never commented on her absences.

Bib finished the lunch Amara had prepared and went back outside to weed his wife's wildflower garden. From spring through fall, a procession of Virginia bluebells, wild bleeding heart, bee balm, Turk's cap lilies, cardinal flowers, purple coneflowers, and other beauties poked through the soil and unfurled their multicolored blossoms.

Bib's mind had shifted into neutral as he grubbed in the loamy soil. Amara had to call out twice to get his attention. Bib looked up to see his housekeeper beckoning him. She had a purple scarf tied around her head and wore a long, loose cotton dress printed with a swirling design, the type of garb she would have worn had she been going to the market back home in Montego Bay.

"You got a telephone call, Mister Archie," she said with her melodious island accent.

"Who is it?"

"That man from your office who always sound like he got a frog in his throat."

Bib grunted to his feet, dusted off his knees, and tromped into the kitchen. Washing his hands in the sink, he reconciled himself to the likelihood that his day off had come to an end.

"Bib," he said into the phone.

The voice on the other end was brusque. "Better come on in, Inspector," Matthew Dowden said.

"What's up?"

"There's been a murder at National Geographic."

Three Metropolitan Police cars were parked on 17th Street in front of National Geographic headquarters, although the department honored the Society's request that it park its ambulance in the lot between headquarters and Hubbard Hall. Visitors in Explorers Hall would be startled enough to see policemen marching inside. They didn't need to see an ambulance with a flashing light sitting in the street.

The offices of National Geographic were silent as Inspector Bib and Sergeant Dowden strode down the sixth-floor corridor. The walls were lined with enlarged photographs taken from the magazine. Bib noticed a panoramic image of the Grand Canyon he'd seen before.

He was a devotee of *National Geographic,* and not just because his brother worked there. Growing up, he and Py had access to the famous yellow-border publication, along with the *New Yorker, Saturday Review, Time,* and a half dozen other magazines. Bib's parents also subscribed to the *Washington Post* and *New York Times.* His family was no doubt one of the most well-informed in Falls Church. As kids, he and Py had learned much about the female anatomy by peeking at the photos of topless native women in *National Geographic.* It was a surreptitious endeavor engaged in by males of all ages—in pursuit of knowledge, of course.

Bib saw some of the forensics team going in and out of the office where the victim had been found. Standing off to the side were three civilians Bib didn't recognize. One was a tall black man wearing the uniform of the Society's security force.

Another was dressed as a janitor, and the third member of the group was an attractive young blond woman. Bib approached the party and introduced himself.

"Good afternoon. I'm Inspector Bib and this is Sergeant Dowden. We'll be leading the investigation. May I have your names please?"

The tall black man held out his hand. "I'm Karl Jackson, chief of security here at National Geographic." He indicated the janitor. "This is Bill Foster. He found the body."

"And I'm Pamela Johnson," the pretty blonde spoke up. "I'm the head of the public affairs office, so I'll be the Society's spokesperson with the media. Thus far, nothing has been announced, although the *Post* and *Star* will be besieging us before long. Naturally, this sort of thing has never happened before at National Geographic, so the interest will be intense."

"I'm sure," Bib said. "I should mention right now that I have a tie to National Geographic. Not only am I a lifelong reader, but my brother Pythagoras is your chief of protocol."

"I wondered about that when you introduced yourself," Miss Johnson said. "There couldn't be too many people in Washington named Bib."

The Inspector gave her a restrained smile. He turned toward the open door of the office. "I'd like you to give me a quick background sketch of the victim and the circumstances of how the body was discovered."

"Why don't I tell you who she is," Miss Johnson said, "then Mr. Foster can let you know how he discovered her...body." The young woman held a hand to her mouth and marshaled her thoughts. "Her name is Joan Smollett, and she's..."

"*Joan Smollett?*" Bib interrupted. He peered inside the office. Smollett was seated in her chair, her upper body lying on her desk, with her arms splayed out to the side and her face turned toward the doorway. "I know this woman," Bib said. "My brother and I went to high school with her in Falls Church. What's more, we were with her over the past few days during our thirtieth annual class reunion. I saw her at a cocktail party

Thursday night, and my brother saw her just yesterday when our class visited the Tidal Basin to see the cherry trees."

Bib shook his head in bewilderment. "This is incredible. Joan Smollett...dead."

"Did you know her well?" Miss Johnson asked.

"Not really. In school, she seemed a little scary."

Bib suddenly regretted his frank admission. He gathered himself and resumed the no-nonsense attitude of a police officer going about his job. "I'm generally aware of the type of work she did here, so let's skip to how her body was discovered."

Chief Jackson nudged the janitor. "Go ahead, Bill, tell him how you found her."

The whey-faced janitor had been lingering in the background. Bib noticed that the man's ears lay flat against the sides of head, giving him a strange, windswept look, like a skydiver plummeting to earth head first. The man cleared his throat.

"I was doing my usual round of vacuuming the hall carpets when I looked into Mrs. Smollett's office, since the light was on. From the way she was spread out on her desk, I thought she'd fallen asleep. I said hello, and when she didn't reply I took a closer look. That's when I saw her expression. Scared the bejesus out of me. I called the security office and Chief Jackson came up. He called the police."

"Before you ask," Chief Jackson said, "we didn't touch anything. I didn't have to check Mrs. Smollett's pulse. One glance told me she was gone."

"How did you know she'd been killed?" Bib asked. "She might have had a heart attack."

"I saw the stab wound on her neck," Jackson said.

Inside the office, the pathologist called to Bib. "Come take a look, Inspector."

Bib stepped over to the desk. The pathologist pointed to the side of the victim's neck, where a small spot of blood was just barely visible.

"Could have been an icepick," the pathologist said. "The odd thing is, the victim is contorted like she'd had some sort of seizure. We'll review her medical history to see if she was prone to those, although a seizure might have been triggered by whatever made this puncture."

Bib was struck by Smollett's expression, one of extreme surprise. Her eyes were stretched open as far as possible, as if she'd been staring at her killer in shock. "You have a fix on the time of death?"

"I'd put it between 12:30 and 1:30 this afternoon."

"I'm assuming the general public doesn't have access to the upper floors of the building," Bib said to Chief Jackson.

"They're not supposed to come upstairs unless they're on official business and have a visitor pass. Only the first-floor museum is open to tourists, but a prowler could have slipped up here if the guard on duty in the reception area was busy helping someone. An intruder could take the stairs and not call attention to himself by attempting to use the elevators."

"Plenty of fingerprints," a forensics technician remarked.

Pamela Johnson was standing in the doorway. "They're bound to be," she said. "I'm sure dozens of staff members have been in here over the past few weeks. You'll probably find my fingerprints here, too."

"That's what makes my job so interesting," the tech said. "By the way, Inspector, the woman's purse has been rifled and her wallet is missing."

"Damn," Chief Jackson muttered. "A thief."

"Maybe," Bib said. "What's that sticking out of the corner of her mouth?" he asked the forensics technician. "Looks like the edge of a piece of paper."

"Jiminy, how'd I miss that?" The tech took a pair of tweezers from his tool kit and eased the wadded-up paper from the victim's mouth, then he spread it out to see what it was.

"Well I'll be," he said. "It's a page from a dictionary."

Bib donned rubber gloves and took the paper from the tech. He saw it was a page with words starting with the letter "L."

He flipped the paper over. "This is curious. The word 'library' has been circled." He showed the page to the pathologist.

"I'm glad you're the one who has to figure that out," the man said.

After the forensics team finished its work and the police photographer had taken all the usual shots, they loaded the body on a gurney and zipped the black body bag closed. Pamela Johnson was sniffling as they worked.

"Are there security cameras on the first floor?" Bib asked Chief Jackson.

"Yes, but we've checked, and we didn't find any footage of an unauthorized person entering the stairwell. Maybe they spotted our cameras and came up with a way to dodge them, but I don't know how they'd pull that off."

Bib glanced around the office to make certain nothing important had been overlooked. "Do you have any idea what she was working on recently?" he asked Miss Johnson.

"Our researchers typically handle several projects at any one time, anything from fact-checking manuscripts to going over the galleys and page proofs of stories that have already been vetted and edited."

"It might help if I had a list of her current assignments."

"I'll get that for you." She held out a slip of paper. "Here's her husband's home address and phone number. Poor Jeffrey will be devasted by this."

Bib took the paper with reluctance. Informing the next of kin about a loved one's death was one of the worst parts of his job. "It looks like this is all we can do today," he said. "We'll be back to interview Mrs. Smollett's coworkers in the next day or two. Miss Johnson, would you mind being our contact at the Society? We'll need someone to direct us to any staff members we should speak with, people who worked closely with Mrs. Smollett or anyone she was particularly friendly with."

"I'd be happy to. Whatever I can do to help catch the monster who did this."

"Thanks. You folks can go now."

When the three National Geographic staffers left, Bib turned to Sergeant Dowden. "What's your take, Matt?"

"It could be a robbery, like the security fellow said, but that strikes me as shaky. How would a thief even know there'd be anyone here to rob on a Sunday afternoon?"

"Good point." Bib sat in Smollett's chair. "No signs of a struggle. From my recollection of Joan Smollett, she wouldn't have meekly sat here and let herself be robbed. The effrontery of such a thing happening to her in her own office would have enraged her. She'd probably have gotten up and given the person a clout on the jaw."

Bib was preparing to leave when he saw a handsome leather-bound book lying on Smollett's desk. He picked it up and turned to the title page. It was a copy of *Don Quixote*, the 17th-century novel by Miguel de Cervantes. The text was in Spanish. Bib noticed the book had a handwritten inscription on the flyleaf, also in Spanish. Though he couldn't read the inscription, he saw that it had been signed by William Price. He took the book with him.

On the way out the door, he handed Dowden the note that Miss Johnson had given him. "Let's go see if Jeffrey Smollett is at home."

The Smolletts' apartment was in an older three-story brick building on P Street NW. Bib and Dowden stood by the entrance watching dog owners walk past with their pets. Couples strolled by hand in hand, and mothers were leading toddlers toward Stead Park, a playground a block to the east. The quiet, tree-lined street was almost like one you'd see in a small town—right in the heart of a big city. Bib wouldn't have been too surprised to see an old-style tractor parade roll by. With Dupont Circle's shops, cafés, and buskers a block away and Episcopal and Methodist churches both within easy walking distance, the neighborhood seemed like a nice place to live.

Bib buzzed Jeffrey Smollett on the intercom beside the front door. He introduced himself and told Jeffrey that he and his sergeant needed to speak with him. When the lock on the door clicked open, they stepped inside. The entryway of the old building gleamed with marble floors and a brass chandelier. Bib and Sergeant Dowden climbed the stairs to apartment number 300.

"Excuse the mess," Jeffrey said as he answered Bib's knock and motioned them inside. There was no mess that Bib could see. The living room's hardwood floors were spotless, and the few pieces of furniture—a sofa, side chair, and coffee table—couldn't have been tidier.

"Please, have a seat," Jeffrey said, indicating the sofa. He settled on the side chair.

"You may not remember me," Bib began, "but I was at the class reunion cocktail party on Thursday night. I was there with my brother. We both went to high school with your wife."

"I don't know many of Joan's friends," Jeffrey said.

"That's okay. This isn't a social call." Bib paused. "I'm afraid I have some bad news."

"Bad news? What sort of bad news?" Jeffrey Smollett spoke in a vague, dreamy voice, as if he wasn't quite in touch with reality.

"I'm sorry to have to tell you this, but your wife has been killed."

There was a long silence. Finally, Jeffrey spoke again. His voice was even wispier than before. "Joan's dead?"

"Yes."

"What happened? Was she run down by a car?"

"No. Someone killed her in her office. She was murdered."

Another long silence.

"Are you all right, Mr. Smollett?"

"Yes. I...I can't believe this. Why would anyone want to harm Joan?"

"That's what I intend to find out. I'm in charge of the investigation, and I promise you I won't stop digging until I've discovered who did this."

Another period of silence.

90

"Do you have children, Mr. Smollett, or any other immediate family members you can call on for support?"

"No children. My family is all back in Iowa, and Joan's parents are dead. She didn't have any brothers or sisters."

"I see. Please accept my condolences. I remember Joan was an impressive student. At the top of our class."

"Yes, Joan was smart."

"Normally, we ask the next of kin to identify the victim, but since I knew her personally that won't be necessary. Three of her coworkers also established a positive identification. However, you're welcome to come down to police headquarters and see Joan, if you'd like."

"I don't think I'd be up to that. I'll see her one last time at her funeral."

"I understand. We will need to ask you a few questions to help with our investigation. Do you think you'll feel strong enough for us to stop by again tomorrow morning?"

"Of course. I'll call my office and let them know I won't be in for a few days."

"All right then. I'll telephone tomorrow before we come."

Bib and Sergeant Dowden said their goodbyes and left Jeffrey Smollett to his thoughts, whatever they might be.

"Strange guy," Bib said as they walked back down the stairs.

Chapter 10

Sunday

Any day of the week was special at Duke Zeibert's, the Washington restaurant where VIPs in politics, sports, business, and entertainment gathered to gab, cut deals, be seen—and eat. The place was always as crowded as an oriental bazaar, and the person at the next table might be the FBI's autocratic director J. Edgar Hoover, or Canada-born mogul Jack Kent Cooke, a man who collected sports franchises like some people collect matchbooks. Reporters could usually find a juicy lead somewhere in the room, whether it involved a wayward congressman, a designing actress, or a busted high roller.

Diners of a lower order simply soaked up the atmosphere while soaking up their three martinis and stockpiling stories about celebrity sightings to impress their coworkers. One thing every patron could expect was a friendly greeting from Duke Zeibert himself, a bald, portly, mustachioed gentleman who served kings and commoners with equal aplomb.

Located at 17th and L Streets, a block south of National Geographic headquarters, Duke Zeibert's was one of Pythagoras Bib's favorite restaurants. Tonight, he and his brother had agreed to meet there for their Sunday evening get-together. Archie was waiting in front of the restaurant when Py strolled up, looking very much the man-about-town in a natty blue blazer, gray slacks, and paisley ascot. Py's impeccable attire always made Archie feel like a poor relation. He was wearing an ill-fitting suit he'd bought on sale at Sears twenty years ago.

The brothers stood beneath the restaurant's showy, streamlined black and white sign, which was emblazoned with Duke Zeibert's name in two-foot-tall letters. The sign floated above a long planter of greenery and the building's red fieldstone exterior. In case anyone was uncertain as to which eatery they were about to enter, the burgundy and white circus awning over the doorway also bore Duke Zeibert's name. Inside, the brothers were greeted by the owner, who gave Py a bear hug and Archie a hearty handshake.

"It's about time you two visited us again," Zeibert said. "I thought maybe you'd found some other joint you liked better."

"How could we possibly do that?" Py asked. "The one chop-house that would be anywhere near as interesting would be Rick's Café in Casablanca—and only if Bogie was still there."

Zeibert let go a rumbling laugh that shook his ample belly. "You won't find any baked camel or fricasseed goat on the menu tonight, but we got some brisket that'll warm the cockles of your heart."

Zeibert ushered the brothers to a table up front, in the area reserved for guests of distinction. One wall was covered with giant caricatures of Zeibert dressed for every sport imaginable. He wasn't fit enough to play any of them but golf, although he wagered freely on them all. As they sat down, Archie told himself it paid to have a distinguished brother. He knew that if he'd been by himself he'd have been seated in the back of the restaurant, a section known as Siberia. Two tables over, Ben Bradlee, the managing editor of the *Washington Post,* was having dinner with his boss Katharine Graham, and across the room, oddsmaker Jimmy "The Greek" Snyder was jawing with union leader Jimmy Hoffa.

After Py ordered a glass of wine and Archie a tonic and lime, the brothers began catching up on their week. "I heard about your visit to National Geographic this afternoon," Py said.

"News travels fast. This one's a shocker. It's the first case I've ever had where I knew the victim personally."

"So what happened? How was Joan killed?"

"We found her sprawled on her desk, with a spot of blood on her neck. The pathologist thought the wound might have been made with an ice pick. We'll find out when the medical examiner does the autopsy."

"Was it a robbery?"

"Could have been. Her wallet was taken, but Matt Dowden and I both find it hard to accept that a thief would target National Geographic on a Sunday, when the place is all but empty."

"That wouldn't make much sense, but if you rule out robbery, where does that leave you?"

"It leaves me looking for a more convincing motive, and I'm almost certain that I'm going to find it among the people Joan knew."

"What makes you think that?"

"The expression on her face for one thing. I've seen some revealing looks on the faces of the dead. Usually it's relief or relaxation, but occasionally I've seen fear or horror or even a smile. The look frozen on Joan's face was one of total surprise, as if she couldn't believe she was being attacked by the person who murdered her. And there's another reason to think that Joan knew her killer. Whoever did it stuffed a piece of paper in her mouth."

"A piece of paper? Anything written on it?"

"No. It was much quirkier. It was a page torn from a dictionary, with the word 'library' circled. That's not something a common thief would do. Only someone who was trying to deliver a final message, and a twisted one at that."

"You should know that I was supposed to meet with Joan tomorrow at work," Py said.

"Is that right? What about?"

"I have no idea. She came up to me at the dinner party on Friday night and asked if we could get together to discuss some issue about her work. She didn't say what it was. Just that she wanted my advice."

"Had she ever done that before?"

"Never. I rarely saw her, and then only to say hello. She began working at National Geographic around the same time I did, and she must have been good at her job or they wouldn't have made her the head of the research department."

Just then the waiter brought their drinks and took their orders. They went with the brisket, which came with an array of sides that always included the restaurant's trademark onion rolls and sour pickles.

Archie had brought along the copy of *Don Quixote* that he'd found in Smollett's office. "This was on Joan's desk. It's from Bill Price."

"How do you know?"

"He signed the inscription, which is in Spanish. The book's in Spanish as well."

Py examined the costly leather-bound volume. "This must be what I saw him give her at the Tidal Basin. I thought he was making a peace offering for having spilled a drink on her dress at the dinner party."

"He spilled a drink on her?"

"Yes, and you should have heard her yell. She accused him of doing it intentionally. The incident did seem suspicious. However it happened, it was clear there was no love lost between those two."

Py opened the book and studied the inscription. "Now this is peculiar."

"What did he write?"

Py translated Price's words. "To the insufferable Joan Smollett, a woman who mistakenly thinks she knows everything."

"That's pretty harsh."

"Joan must have really ticked him off somehow. I recall he had a bad temper."

"He did. I remember the day he came to school with a broken hand. He said he hurt it in an accident, but it got around that he'd smashed his hand against a wall in anger." Archie took a sip of his drink. "All right, professor, tell me this. Can someone's personality change over time?"

"That gets into the old debate about nature versus nurture, meaning the relative influences of heredity and environmental factors on a person's character. For example, is a hothead like Bill shaped by his genes or by his surroundings? Psychologists agree that both factors are at work, although it's difficult to determine which is more influential in a given individual. Say a man with anger issues marries a calm, soothing woman and changes his ways. That would point to an environmental influence. If the man doesn't change, that would seem to indicate his personality is deeply ingrained in his genes."

"Then Bill Price could still be smashing his hand against walls?"

"It's always possible."

"Didn't Joan take Spanish in high school?" Archie asked.

"She did. We were in the same class, but unless she kept it up, she probably wouldn't have been able to read what Price wrote. Bill may have known that, and maybe Joan took the book to work to have one of the Society's translators tell her what the inscription says."

"If she couldn't read Spanish, why would Price give her a book in that language?"

"He may have done it out of spite, as a way of rubbing her nose in her limitation."

Archie was thoroughly perplexed by Price's shenanigans. "Aside from the language question, do you have any idea why Price would give her a copy of this particular book?"

"The character Don Quixote had delusions of grandeur. Not to speak ill of the dead, but Joan was always high on herself in school. Perhaps Price was implying she was like the dotty Spanish nobleman. He tilted at windmills believing he was a great hero, a knight errant."

"This is all interesting," Archie said, "but I doubt if it has anything to do with Joan's death."

"Oh, I wouldn't think so. Just a nasty prank."

"I'll be interviewing Joan's family and associates this week. I'm starting with Jeffrey Smollett tomorrow morning, along with the people at the bank where he worked. After that I'll tackle Joan's coworkers. Maybe I'll find out what she wanted to speak to you about. I wonder if it concerned some type of friction between Joan and someone she worked with."

"Could be, although with her dominant nature, I'd have thought she could handle any sort of problem with a co-worker. I know she kept her husband in line."

The waiter brought their dinners, and the brothers dug in.

"That Jeffrey Smollett is an odd duck," Archie said after a couple of bites. "You know how badly I took it when Phyllis died, but this fellow barely reacted to the news of his wife's death."

"That doesn't surprise me. From what I've seen of him, he seems withdrawn, and he and Joan didn't display much affection for one another."

"Do you mind telling me how much life insurance the National Geographic Society provides its employees?"

"We get two and a half times our annual salary."

"I'm in the wrong profession," Archie said.

"But surely you don't think..."

"There are plenty of motives for murder besides money, but you've got to establish if anyone benefits financially from the victim's death. And in this case, the only one who does appears to be Jeffrey. Two and a half years of salary wouldn't put a person on easy street, but it could be enough to persuade a disgruntled husband that he'd be better off if his wife was dead. People have been doing away with their spouses for money since money was invented."

Before they finished their meal, Duke Zeibert came by to check on them. He sat down and told a couple of funny stories, then he continued on his rounds, stopping by every table to make his guests feel welcome. It was a major reason his restaurant was so popular.

"I liked Duke's anecdote about the barflies who pay the bartender to say they aren't here when their wives call," Archie said. "It made me think of the article you wrote for the *Post* on the psychology of liars. That article has helped me with more than one case."

"Glad to be of service," Py said. "You know, I was reminded that liars come in all flavors the other day when I played golf with my tax accountant. It was the first time we'd played together, and before the round, I asked Rob if he was any good. He told me he played bogey golf. I didn't realize that what he meant was he never wrote down any score higher than a bogey. I saw him take nine strokes on a long par five. Afterward, he loudly announced 'bogey,' and presto, his legitimate score miraculously became a six. That's inventive math."

"He must be good at finding deductions on your tax returns," Archie said.

"He's also as adept as a magician at the old sleight of hand. Once when he hit his ball deep into the woods, he searched along the edge of the trees for a bit then slyly dropped a ball from his pocket. He called out 'here it is,' even though I knew his first ball was hopelessly lost."

"Sounds like one of my suspects making a clumsy attempt to plant evidence."

"He pulled a neater trick whenever he had a short putt. He would place his marker in front of the ball instead of in back of it as the rules call for. Then when his turn came to putt, he'd put the ball back down in front of his marker, thereby moving the ball an inch or two closer to the hole. When I commented on the maneuver, he flew off the handle. 'I never cheat,' he told me. 'I go to church every Sunday.'

"That's when I realized poor old Rob is a narcissist. He may hardly be aware of what he does, since self-delusion is a basic trait of narcissism. Those folks are the center of their own world, and they have such a lofty opinion of themselves that they think they can do no wrong. If someone challenges them about any bad behavior they immediately try to shift the blame to their accuser. That's why it's so dangerous to have a narcissist in a position of power, whether it's running a company or running a country. It's like giving whiskey to an alcoholic. Look at Hitler. He thought he was an Übermensch, a superman."

"Great," Archie moaned. "Now I'll have to be on the lookout for liars who don't know they're lying. There's a complication I could live without."

"A narcissist wouldn't make a reliable trial witness. Chances are he'd put a spin on his testimony to make himself out as the man of the hour."

"How can you stand to play golf with a guy like Rob?"

"He's called a couple of times since we played, but I've managed to avoid another round. No use wasting thirty bucks in greens fees to hear a fellow fabricate his accomplishments. I can do that for free by going down to the Capitol and listening to politicians."

Py took a sip of wine. "One of the most puzzling things about Rob was that he never once complimented me when I hit a good shot, which is simple golf etiquette, but he always patted himself on the back when he hit one down the middle. Everything was about him. I think I might write an article on the influence of narcissism on sports."

"That I'd like to read."

"Here's a fact you can take to the bank. Nothing beats playing golf with someone to discover their true character."

"Okay. Next time I need to size up a suspect, I'll take him golfing."

The Casino Royal was impossible to ignore. The downtown nightclub on 14th Street had a rooftop display of giant horseshoes that blazed with six thousand lightbulbs, like a mini Las Vegas. Washington's upper crust flocked to the Casino to enjoy dinner and dancing between acts headlined by the likes of Johnny Mathis, Tony Bennett, Ella Fitzgerald, and Peggy Lee. When Mae West performed at the Casino, the legendary blond chanteuse brought an entourage of oiled-up bodybuilders onstage, an unexpected sight in the nation's capital.

Tonight, the Casino's six hundred seats were filled with fans of crooner Nat King Cole, all of them waiting to hear him sing his standards and recent hits. The patrons of the upscale nightspot were gussied up in their best suits and cocktail dresses. Next door in the Casino's sister club, the Speakeasy, things were different.

A reproduction of an old-fashioned saloon, the Speakeasy featured young waitresses who paraded around in skimpy outfits, each of them wearing a frilly garter on her black fishnet stockings. While Nat King Cole was warbling "Ramblin' Rose" in the Casino, a ragtime piano and banjo barreled through Scott Joplin's "Maple Leaf Rag" in the Speakeasy. Inexplicably, a cutie on a red velvet swing swayed back and forth while another bit of eye candy indulged in a leisurely bubble bath. The girl on the swing and her friend in the bathtub made no more sense than the empty peanut shells purposely strewn on the floor, but the young clientele seemed to like it.

Xander Riley sat at the saloon's bar nursing a thirty-cent mug of beer while he read the late edition of the *Washington Star*, the once great afternoon newspaper that now played second fiddle to the *Washington Post*. Riley was reading an article about President Lyndon Johnson, who'd just authorized the bombing of North Vietnam and the Ho Chi Minh Trail. Christened Operation Rolling Thunder, the aerial campaign accompanied the landing of the first American combat troops in South Vietnam.

Riley hoped he wouldn't get caught up in that conflict. He had better things to do than slog through a rice paddy toting a rifle. If things went well, he'd soon be on his way to Iraq. He'd read in his encyclopedia that Iraqis weren't religious fanatics like the inhabitants of some of the other Middle Eastern countries. Baghdad had plenty of hangouts where a fellow could have a good time. Maybe he'd meet a nice belly dancer.

Riley was about to lay the newspaper aside when he noticed a short item headlined "Murder at National Geographic." He hurriedly read the piece.

"Earlier this afternoon, the Metropolitan Police were called to the headquarters of the National Geographic Society to investigate a reported homicide. The victim's name has not yet been released, but the *Star* has learned that it was a senior member of the famous organization's research staff. Further details will be available in tomorrow's edition."

Riley folded the paper and took a sip of beer, his thoughts no longer on foreign lands. He didn't even notice when the piano man and banjo player began the toe-tapping "St. Louis Rag."

Located an hour northeast of Washington, Baltimore's wealthy Guilford neighborhood resembled a storybook English village. It was one the choicest places to live in Maryland's largest city. Guilford's streets were shaded by towering trees and lit by old-timey streetlights. Artful flower gardens graced its manicured lawns. The neighborhood's residents shared a sense of well-deserved ascendancy. Even their dogs were aloof.

In his stately brick mansion, William Price settled back in a leather recliner and switched the TV channel to ABC to watch the basketball game between the Baltimore Bullets and the Los Angeles Lakers. Price had the house to himself, since his supple young trophy wife was still enjoying the warmth of Palm Springs.

On this peaceful Sunday evening, Price was a contented man. Everything had gone as planned in Falls Church and Washington. The scales were finally balanced with all of his classmates who'd angered him long ago. He was even happier by the end of tonight's game, which Baltimore won 117-106. Price knew that there was a chance the Bullets might make the playoffs for the first time since the franchise moved from Chicago to Baltimore two years ago.

Price had a lot riding on his team making the playoffs. If he won his bet, it would help him recoup the hit he'd taken in last year's Preakness Stakes, when that nag the Scoundrel lost to Northern Dancer by more than two lengths. Price had backed the Scoundrel simply because he liked the name, but he wasn't used to losing. Losing was for chumps.

Price turned off the TV after the game. He missed the mention of the murder in Washington on the late-night news.

Chapter 11

Monday

Bib hadn't paid much attention to the décor of the Smolletts' home when he and Sergeant Dowden visited earlier. They'd had more important business to attend to. Now that he looked around, he was struck by the apartment's lack of personality. There were no mementoes collecting dust on shelves, and only a few photos hung on the walls. Bib stared at what was unmistakably Joan and Jeffrey Smollett's wedding portrait.

"That was taken in 1945," Jeffrey said. "We met at the University of Virginia but didn't get married until after the war. This summer we'd have celebrated our twentieth anniversary." He said this like a schoolchild reciting a history lesson.

Bib found it hard to believe that the two young people in the photograph were Joan and Jeffrey. They were clinging to each other in their wedding finery, their faces lit with joy. How long had the happiness lasted? Five years? Ten? According to his brother's observations, the Smolletts appeared emotionally distant. But even after their love cooled, they at least had companionship, Bib thought. He was unaware that whenever Joan had been with Jeffrey, her mind was often far away. Now, even the veneer of friendship was gone, and Jeffrey Smollett was alone.

Jeffrey slouched across the room like a man in a daze. Bib was beginning to think he might be mentally disturbed.

"Are you feeling all right today?" Bib asked. "We could come back later if you're not up to an interview."

Jeffrey sat down, slumping in his chair. "No, I'm fine. Ask me whatever you want."

Bib peered at his notebook. "Let's start with the most fundamental question, Mr. Smollett. Do you know of anyone who might have had a reason to harm your wife?"

Jeffrey frowned. "I've been racking my brain ever since you came by with the news. It's hard to imagine somebody having it in for her, although there was that fellow who spilled a drink on her at the dinner party the other night. But that was surely an accident."

"Probably. Did Joan ever talk about any animosity between herself and other employees at National Geographic?"

"Sometimes she criticized people she worked with, but that was only because she was a perfectionist. She couldn't stand to see others being sloppy."

"Anyone in particular?"

"I'm sorry, but I don't remember. I didn't know any of the people she mentioned, so their names meant nothing to me."

Bib realized that Jeffrey must have tuned his wife out completely. It didn't take much effort to picture him nodding and agreeing whenever Joan lambasted one of her coworkers, when he wasn't listening to a word she said.

"Can you tell me why she went into the office on Sunday? Did she say anything about a specific project that she was working on?"

"I wish I could be of more help, but she just said she needed to get ready for work on Monday."

Bib wondered if that included Joan's meeting with his brother. He glanced at Sergeant Dowden, who glowered at the insipid answers they were getting. It seemed that Jeffrey Smollett might need to have labels sewn in his clothes to remember his own name.

Bib reached into his coat pocket and produced a photocopy of the page from the dictionary they'd found in the victim's mouth. He held it out to Jeffrey. "Does this suggest anything to you? We found it on your wife's body. Notice that the word 'library' has been circled."

Jeffrey examined the copy. "I have no idea what it means."

"I have to ask one final question," Bib said. "Can you tell us where you were and what you were doing yesterday between noon and two o'clock?"

"I certainly can." Jeffrey suddenly became more animated. "I'd gone back down to the Tidal Basin to sketch the cherry trees. I do watercolors, you see, and I wanted to capture the trees while they were in full bloom and the light was good. I can show you. I have the sketch in my room."

Jeffrey disappeared into one of the two bedrooms and came back with an open sketchbook. "Here's what I've been working on. It's only a beginning, but I think the composition is quite nice."

Bib was startled by the professional quality of Jeffrey's rendering of the trees and their delicate blossoms. "Where did you learn to draw like this?"

Jeffrey smiled. "From Jon Gnagy."

"Who?"

"The man on television. I got interested in art by watching his program *Learn to Draw.*"

"Do you have any finished work?"

"I'll say. Come look in my room."

Bib and Dowden followed Jeffrey into his bedroom, where one wall was covered with watercolors, all of them scenes from nature—sunsets, spring flowers, fall color, winter scenes—and all of them so artistically rendered that Bib had difficulty believing they could have been created by this mousy, uncommunicative individual. It was a side of Jeffrey Smollett he would never have anticipated. It made him wonder what other secrets the man had.

"These are very impressive," Bib said in earnest. "You've got real talent."

"Oh, I'm only an amateur. That's what Joan always told me when I got to thinking I was getting any good."

You poor, poor man, Bib said to himself. "We've taken enough of your time, Mr. Smollett. Thanks for seeing us. We'll keep you apprised of our progress on the case."

Jeffrey showed them to the door. Once they were out in the hallway, Sergeant Dowden delivered his opinion of the interview. "That was a waste of time."

"Not entirely," Bib said. "We know that his alibi for the time of the murder is—I've got to say this—sketchy."

"We learned something else," Dowden said. "He and his wife slept in separate bedrooms."

Jeffrey Smollett's employer, the National Bank of Washington, had been around since 1809. It was founded as the Bank of Washington, the first local bank in the capital. Three years after being chartered, the bank loaned most of its reserves to the U.S. government to fund the War of 1812, and it later bankrolled much of the early construction in Washington. The list of depositors included some historical names. Statesmen James Monroe, Daniel Webster, and Henry Clay stashed their money there, as did lawyer and poet Francis Scott Key, inventor Eli Whitney, and Supreme Court Justices John Marshall, Roger B. Taney, and Bushrod Washington—George Washington's nephew. Even Davy Crockett, the King of the Wild Frontier, trusted the bank with his savings.

The bank moved its offices a couple of times before settling near the National Mall at 301 7th Street NW. In 1889, a sturdy Romanesque Revival structure was erected there to house the bank. The three-story fortress of marble and granite seemed to symbolize the bank's solidity, and indeed, everything went well for the National Bank of Washington for 140 years. Then in 1949, the United Mine Workers acquired a 76 percent interest in the bank. Some observers might have wondered what mineworkers knew about banking. It was a fair question, one that the directors of the National Bank of Washington had been coping with ever since.

Jeffrey Smollett's responsibilities were far less consequential than guiding the fate of the bank. He was a teller, a financial traffic cop charged with regulating the endless flow of deposits and withdrawals and dealing with the occasional fender bender involving customers who were overdrawn. Few people could match Jeffrey Smollett's ability to muster a breezy "May I help you?" several dozen times a day. He'd been at it for the past fifteen years, and he never appeared flustered or fatigued. If a customer exceeded his level of tolerance, he simply said, "You'd better take that up with Mr. Mayhew," his immediate supervisor.

Sergeant Dowden had called ahead and arranged interviews with Jeffrey's supervisor and two other tellers. Bib and Dowden began with Howard Davis, a teller who'd been with the bank nearly as long as Jeffrey had. Davis was a handsome specimen, with broad shoulders and a strong chin. That's where his physical blessings ended. Whenever Davis made the mistake of smiling, he revealed a set of teeth that resembled weathered tombstones. Bib felt like giving him the name of his dentist and informing him that they could do marvels with cosmetic dentistry these days. Bib found himself looking at Davis's tie whenever the teller spoke.

"Thanks for agreeing to meet with us, Mr. Davis," Bib said.

Davis unveiled his disturbing grin. "I sure hope I can help out old Jeff. It was terrible hearing about his wife, but Jeff had been put upon by that woman for years."

"Is that so?" Bib said. "In what way exactly?"

"For one thing, she corrected him every time he opened his mouth. My wife and I had dinner with them a couple of times, and I tell you, that woman was a piece of work. If I'd have been her husband, I'd have reached across the breakfast table and smashed a grapefruit in her face, like Jimmy Cagney did to his girlfriend in that old movie. I don't know if Jeff ever felt like doing something like that, but if he did he was able to resist the urge. He was always polite and deferential around her. I think he finally stopped talking to her any more than he had to."

"What is Mr. Smollett like here at the bank?" Bib asked. "Is he ever angry or sullen?"

"He isn't the same man that he is at home. He likes to kid around, and you should see him at our office get-togethers. He's always the life of the party."

It seemed obvious to Bib that Jeffrey Smollett had a split personality.

"Yeah, that old harpy turned him inside out and upside down," Davis said. "The real Jeffrey Smollett died the day he married that woman. I'm surprised that he didn't strangle her years ago."

Davis realized what he'd said. "But don't get me wrong. Jeff wouldn't harm anyone. He's too much of a pussycat."

Bib knew that even pussycats could be dangerous if you stepped on their tail.

Teller Clarissa O'Neill was a tall, attractive redhead, no longer young but still on the safe side of middle age. Her lively green eyes reflected an intense sincerity. She spoke softly, enunciating her words with a clarity that indicated a good education. Bib had the feeling that whatever she said could be trusted implicitly.

"I think Jeffrey's something of an underachiever," she replied to Bib's first question. "He should have advanced far beyond his present job." She shook her head as if mystified. "He can crunch numbers like a machine, but somewhere along the line he must have lost his drive."

"How long have you two worked together?" Bib asked.

"I'm a relative newcomer here. I've only been with the bank for three years."

"That's long enough to form an opinion of someone."

The woman smiled. "As I'm sure you know, Inspector, you can usually size up a person you work with in a few days, and often in minutes."

Bib pushed his glasses back in place. "Have you ever socialized with Mr. Smollett?"

The woman hesitated. "We've gone to lunch together a few times. To be honest, Inspector Bib, Jeffrey has always struck me as a lonely man. There's nothing untoward in our friendship, you understand. We usually end up talking about art."

"Did you ever meet his wife?"

"I met her once or twice. I'm embarrassed to admit that I didn't care for her."

"Any reason?"

The woman bit her lower lip as she considered how to frame her response. "She almost acted like she was the only one in the room, if you know what I mean."

"I think I do."

"This is a delicate question, Miss O'Neill, but do you think there's the slightest chance that Jeffrey Smollett might have harmed his wife?"

"You must be joking."

"Then you think it's out of the question?"

"I would be rendered speechless if Jeffrey harmed his wife in any way."

Bib rapped on the doorjamb outside the office of Jeffrey Smollett's supervisor. "Mr. Mayhew, I'm Inspector Bib. I believe you spoke with Sergeant Dowden here on the telephone."

"Come in, come in," Mayhew called, waving the two men inside. Mayhew was an oily fellow, with the plastic smile of a pickpocket. His hair was a shade too black and his face was as pasty as chalk. He looked like he was made up for a role in *The Mikado*, the Gilbert and Sullivan comic opera. *The Mikado* had been a favorite of Bib's wife, and each time they saw the musical together, Bib took as much pleasure in listening to Phyllis's laughter as in the farcical songs themselves. Mayhew seemed ideally suited to play the part of the Lord High Executioner, a character who totes an enormous axe to lop off heads and who blithely draws up a list of villagers who wouldn't be missed. Bib didn't think he'd enjoy working for George Mayhew.

"Caught me at a busy time," Mayhew blustered. He shifted some papers from one pile to another then settled back in his leather executive chair, striking a pose of a man of importance. "What can I do for you? Understand there's some question about our teller Jeffrey Smollett. Murder or some such."

Bib didn't have a chance to reply before the man barreled ahead. "Wouldn't be surprised if he was mixed up in some sordid affair," Mayhew sneered. "Never liked him. Shifty beggar.

Wanted to sack him more than once but I couldn't prove that he'd done anything wrong. Just something about him I don't cotton to."

Bib was momentarily left speechless by Mayhew's venomous outburst. "Has he ever been hostile or aggressive toward you?"

"Downright impudent is the way I'd put it. Always trying to confuse me with some technical rigmarole. Tommyrot, I call it. Rubbish. When I ask a straightforward question I expect a straightforward answer."

"Mr. Davis and Miss O'Neill both speak highly of him."

"Oh, sure, they'd stick together. Tellers are always like that, trying to pull a fast one on management."

Bib knew he definitely wouldn't enjoy working for George Mayhew. He appeared to be a man who'd been promoted beyond his abilities and who took out his resentment over his deficiencies on his subordinates. Bib had worked for a department head like that when he started with the Metropolitan Police. The captain had caused incalculable damage to the morale and efficiency of everyone under him. The staff held an unofficial celebration when the man retired.

Bib couldn't think of a thing to ask Mayhew about Jeffrey Smollett that wouldn't generate more acrimony from the ill-mannered prat. He seized on the one subject that was certain to shift Mayhew's focus—himself.

"Perhaps you could tell me a little about your role here."

Mayhew leaned farther back in his big chair. Bib was worried he might tip over.

"Started out in the mailroom and worked my way up," Mayhew crowed. "Nobody greased my path either. Made it with nothing but the sweat of my brow. Now I've got nine people who report to me."

Bib pitied those unlucky souls. He glanced at his watch. "I can see you've got a lot on your plate, so we'd better let you get back to work."

"No problem," Mayhew said expansively. "Always willing to do my part."

Bib and Dowden conferred in the hallway outside Mayhew's office to decide whether they should interview anyone else, since Mayhew had been such a fiasco. As they talked, a well-dressed middle-aged executive approached. The man had basset hound eyes and the strawberry nose of a devoted tippler. "May I help you?" he asked, clearly wondering why two strangers were lurking about in the hallway.

"No thank you," Bib replied over his shoulder while studying his interview notes.

The executive appeared to resent being given the brush-off on his home ground. "Do you know who I am?" he asked in a peremptory tone.

Bib turned and gave the man a once-over. He wore a full brown beard, the sort that could hide a multitude of sins. In the case of this rotund chap, that likely meant a multitude of chins. A dark brown toupee perched atop the man's bulbous head with the unconvincing lifelessness of a beaver pelt. Why do such fellows try so hard, Bib asked himself.

"No sir, I don't know who you are," Bib replied. He held up his badge. "Do you?"

Bib's response let some of the air out of the puffed-up executive. He recoiled and stared at Bib with his mouth open, then he turned on his heel and scuttled away. Bib didn't know whether the man was someone important or just thought he was, but the Inspector had never had time for posturing. He'd had the privilege of meeting General Eisenhower overseas, so he knew how to recognize the real deal.

"That was Simon Clark," Sergeant Dowden murmured. "He's the president of the bank."

"That's okay. All of my money is resting comfortably back at our credit union."

Sergeant Dowden started the car and pointed it in the direction of police headquarters. "I'm telling you," he said, "after today, I don't know whether to think that Jeffrey Smollett is a harmless schlemiel or a clever murderer."

"I'm with you," Bib said. "If we could only separate personal opinions from objective facts our job would be easy. Unfortunately, every investigation seems like a rerun of *Rashomon.*"

"What the heck is that?"

"It's a movie about a murder and the four witnesses who give accounts of the crime. They each tell a different story, trying to put themselves in the best light."

"Must have been written by a cop," Dowden said.

By the end of the day, every television news addict and newspaper reader in Washington was aware of the murder at National Geographic, an event that shocked and titillated in equal degrees. Monday's *Washington Post* and *Washington Star* splashed their stories across page one, including as many details of the crime as they could obtain from the Metropolitan Police and the Society's own public affairs office.

The stories included brief quotes from Inspector Bib and Pamela Johnson. They both had little to say beyond identifying Joan Smollett as the victim, describing her role at the Society, and stating that investigators were pursuing every possible lead.

Xander Riley had purchased copies of the *Post* and the *Star*. He poured over every word, speculating on how Smollett's death might affect him. William Price read the story in the *Baltimore Evening Sun* while he ate dinner. When he finished the article, he clipped it out and filed it away like some grim souvenir. Afterward, he broke out a bottle of champagne.

Chapter 12

Tuesday

Pamela Johnson looked up from her desk to see a large police-man and a Rumpelstiltskin-like figure in a shabby suit stand-ing outside her door. "Inspector Bib," the pretty blond woman said. "You're as quiet as a mouse. How long have you been standing there?"

"Not long," Bib replied. "You looked so intent on what you were doing that I didn't want to disturb you."

"Please, come in."

"Thank you. You remember Sergeant Dowden."

Johnson gave the sergeant her most radiant Southern belle smile. "Of course I remember him. How are you this morning, Sergeant?"

Dowden gave her the same level gaze that he'd give a drug pusher or an old lady pulling a shopping cart. It was his Mar-shal Dillon look. "Fine, ma'am. Thanks for asking."

"Have a seat, gentlemen," Johnson cooed. "I hope you have some good news."

"We're still in the information gathering stage," Bib said. "That's where we could use your help, since you kindly agreed to be our contact here at National Geographic."

"Just tell me what you need."

"As I mentioned earlier, I'd like your suggestions of who we should speak with to get a better sense of Mrs. Smollett."

Johnson reached for a booklet on her desk. She held it up. "Staff directory. Let me give you the names and phone num-bers of a few people you should meet." Sergeant Dowden had his notebook out to take down the details.

Johnson looked into the middle distance. "Let's see. You'll want to speak with other people in the research department.

Rebecca Wimberly was Mrs. Smollett's number two. She'll no doubt be promoted after the tragedy. I think you'll find her very perceptive." Johnson flipped through the staff directory and gave Dowden the phone number.

"It might also be wise to speak with one of the junior researchers," she said, "to get another viewpoint. I'd recommend Ann Parker. She's young, but she's as smart as they come. You may find her…unconventional in her dress, but don't let that put you off."

Like every good cop, Bib seldom allowed appearances to sway him one way or the other. He'd dealt with too many well-dressed killers—and scraggly bums who turned out to be millionaires.

"I'd also recommend that you speak with our head librarian, since she regularly assists our researchers in verifying articles. Her name is Emily Milhouse.

"You might also want to speak with one of our editors and one of the staff writers. They interact with researchers at different stages in the production of an article. I think you'll find associate editor Vernon Hall helpful. As for which staff writer you should speak with, you might try Doug Smith. He's one of our most talented young writers."

Bib glanced at Sergeant Dowden, who indicated he had everything written down. "It sounds like a good cross section of your staff," Bib said to Miss Johnson. "You could render one further service. Is there an office or meeting room where we could conduct our interviews? We've found it better to question people on neutral ground."

"I think the conference room on the seventh floor is often free. I can call the secretary who schedules the room and have her block out some time for you."

"Thanks. If we could have the room for a couple of hours today and again tomorrow morning we should be able to finish our interviews."

Johnson made the call and arranged everything. "All set," she said as she hung up the phone. "Anything else I can do for you, Inspector?"

113

"Despite what I said about interviewing people on neutral ground, it would save time if I could ask you some questions about Joan Smollett while we're here."

"Sure. Fire away."

"If you don't mind, I'd like to begin by having you tell us a little about your background, where you're from, your job experience, and so forth. It always helps to know something about the history of whoever you're speaking with."

What Bib really wanted was to get a better sense of Johnson's judgment, since experience had taught him that what people said about themselves helped him gauge the validity of what they said of others. It was like reading tea leaves, but every speck of insight helped.

"Well," Johnson began slowly, "I was born and raised in Savannah, Georgia."

"I knew it must have been somewhere south of the Mason-Dixon line," Bib said.

"Is it that obvious? I've done my best to get rid of my y'alls."

"Did you go to college in Georgia?"

"I did. I studied journalism at the University of Georgia. When I was a senior, I was fortunate to receive an internship with a public relations firm here in Washington. That hooked me on working in the capital, and I was even luckier to land a job with National Geographic five years ago. Oh yes, I'm single, I weigh 110 pounds, and my favorite color is blue."

Sergeant Dowden laughed despite himself. He quickly resumed his Marshal Dillon look.

"Thank you, Miss Johnson," Bib said. "Now, I'd like to ask you about Mrs. Smollett. First, what was your opinion of her as a person?"

"I thought she was unique, almost larger than life. She could be direct, but I've never cared for people who beat about the bush. That wastes everyone's time."

"And what did you think of her work?"

"Oh my goodness, she was the best. She was worthy of her role as the head of her department."

"Did you work with her?"

"Only on occasion. Editorial matters and public affairs are rather like church and state, you know."

"My next question is the most important under the circumstances," Bib said. "Do you know if there was anyone Mrs. Smollett didn't get along with here at National Geographic? I hesitate to use the word enemy, but we all know hostility can arise in the workplace."

"That may be true in other organizations, Inspector Bib, but not here."

Bib scrutinized the young woman carefully. He didn't think he'd ever heard a less believable statement. "No tiffs, no arguments? Everything is just sunshine, lollipops, and rainbows?"

"Of course people have animated discussions about editorial issues, but they're never personal, I can assure you. There's no Machiavellian scheming if that's what you're expecting."

"That would make this an atypical establishment," Bib said.

"That's precisely what it is."

"Last question. Do you have any theory as to why the murderer stuffed the page from a dictionary in Mrs. Smollett's mouth, or why the word 'library' would have been circled?"

"None. It's the most bizarre thing about this tragedy. The killer must have been insane."

The seventh-floor conference room turned out to be the perfect place for Bib and Dowden to meet with the staff members suggested by Pamela Johnson. Aside from the conference table, chairs, and telephone, the room was bare, with nothing on the walls to distract the mind. It was superficially similar to the interrogation room at police headquarters. All that was missing were cigarette burns on the table, a dented wastebasket full of used paper coffee cups, and a general air of mistrust.

They began their interviews with Rebecca Wimberly, the assistant head of research and probable successor to Joan Smollett. Sergeant Dowden phoned her and informed her that Inspector Bib would like to speak with her about the case. A few minutes later, she appeared in the conference room doorway. She paused before she made her entrance, waiting until Bib and Dowden turned her way. Bib took note of her pale gray suit, which must have cost more than he earned in a month. Even the designer scarf around her neck would have left a large hole in his paycheck. The woman's long brown hair lay softly on her shoulders, glistening as if a handmaid had given it a hundred brushstrokes.

Bib immediately recognized Wimberly as one of those women bewitched by their own beauty. He saw it in her placid expression of self-satisfaction. The woman swanned into the room and took a seat like she was settling onto a throne. When she looked at Bib, he could sense her expectation of his obeisance and adoration. He didn't know whether to feel pity or revulsion. He pictured her getting up each morning, gazing into her looking glass, and uttering the Wicked Queen's incantation, "Mirror, mirror on the wall, who's the fairest one of all?"

"Good morning, Miss Wimberly," Bib began.

"Ms. Wimberly," the woman loftily pronounced.

"Ah, pardon me." Bib glanced at the diamond ring on the woman's left hand. The stone was the size of a chickpea. It was the sort of ring that women enjoyed waving under their friends' noses to make them envious. Such a large stone must be bothersome, Bib thought, always catching on your clothing when you reached into your pocket. He'd always felt that an enormous diamond wasn't necessarily proof of the depth of a couple's love. Often, it was merely an ostentatious display of wealth. The ring he'd bought Phyllis was much more practical. Oh, who was he kidding? The flyspeck diamond was all he could afford, but the love it represented was as big as any star in the heavens.

Bib pointed to Matthew Dowden. "As Sergeant Dowden here explained to you, we'd like to ask you a few questions about the murder of Mrs. Smollett."

"I'm sure I know nothing that could be of any help."

"Bear with us, Ms. Wimberly. This won't take long."

The woman made a show of consulting her watch.

"Perhaps you could tell us a little about yourself."

"My father is Peter Wimberly," were the first words out of her mouth, as though that fact alone was sufficient to forestall any further questions.

"Interesting," Bib replied. "My father was Joseph Bib. Maybe they met."

Wimberly's dark eyes flared with disdain. "I doubt that."

"You're probably right." Despite his instant visceral dislike of the woman, Bib tried to remain cordial. "Where are you from originally?"

"Boston."

"Ah, a New Englander. Did you attend college in Massachusetts?"

"Wellesley."

Bib didn't need to know anything more about the woman's background. She'd clearly been brought up amid substantial wealth, which in her case had produced the type of disposition he hated having to deal with. He felt like turning the knife. "Not a bad school, I hear."

Wimberly's face nearly imploded.

"Anyway, we only have a few questions to ask you. Could you tell us how you regarded Mrs. Smollett as a person?"

"I'm sorry, detective, but I was brought up not to engage in idle gossip about other people."

Bib wanted to swat the woman. "It's Inspector. Inspector Bib. My sergeant is a detective. And we aren't here to engage in idle gossip, Ms. Wimberly. This is a murder investigation, so please answer the question."

"I thought the world of Joan Smollett," Wimberly said grudgingly. "I admired and respected her."

"And how did you feel about her work?"

"She was the most meticulous researcher at National Geographic, a woman held in awe by other researchers."

"And do you know of anyone she worked with who showed any animosity toward her?"

"Animosity?"

"Yes, someone she might have crossed swords with."

"Researchers have occasional disagreements with writers and editors, but we're all far too civilized to engage in anything as coarse as an outright argument."

Pamela Johnson had said the same thing, but Wimberly's haughty way of couching her opinions was maddening. Bib had nearly reached the end of his tether with her. He was thinking of that grapefruit Jimmy Cagney smashed in his girl-friend's face.

"One last question. We discovered a page torn from a dictionary on Mrs. Smollett's body. For some reason, the word 'library' was circled. Does that suggest anything to you?"

"It suggests that the person who committed this outrageous act hoped to confuse the police. And evidently it's working."

"That will be all, Ms. Wimberly. Thank you for your time."

The woman eased herself out of her chair and slithered out the door.

"She's a beaut," Sergeant Dowden said. "I wonder how she treats her slaves."

"That's not hard to predict," Bib replied. "I could see her plunging an ice pick into someone's neck without the slightest hesitation."

Junior researcher Ann Parker bounced into the room with an expectant look. "I've never been interrogated by the police before," she said. "Where's the lie detector?" The young woman was wearing what appeared to be a Catholic schoolgirl's uniform, complete with white knee socks. She'd added her own touch with a pair of cowboy boots.

"This isn't an interrogation, Miss Parker," Bib said. "That's what we do with suspects. We just want to ask you a few questions to see if you can shed any light on why Mrs. Smollett was killed."

"Oops, got my terminology wrong," she said. "Don't tell that to anyone around here. It might go in my permanent record."

What a contrast this young woman was to the plaster beauty they'd just dealt with, Bib thought. Ann Parker was no beauty herself, more of a petite, spunky leprechaun, with short brown hair, dimpled cheeks, and eyes that sparkled with suppressed mischief.

"We've already spoken with Rebecca Wimberly…"

"Did she mention her father?" Parker asked before Bib could finish his sentence.

"She did. Who is he, by the way?"

"Apparently some whoop-de-do wanker up in Boston. She trots out his name every chance she gets, like it was 'open sesame' or something. She kept her maiden name even though she's married, although I can't fault her for that. Her husband's last name is Butz. Not much cachet there. She probably wouldn't have married the guy if he hadn't been a rich real estate developer. Can you imagine going through life with that albatross for a name?"

"My first name is Archimedes."

"Really? That's so cool. I always wished my first name was Cleopatra. But no, I'm just plain old Ann. As in Raggedy."

Bib found himself taking a liking to this irreverent young woman. She reminded him of his daughter, back when Sylvia was in her rebellious phase.

"Ms. Wimberly wasn't a great deal of help…"

"She wouldn't be."

"…so we're hoping you'll be able to provide some useful information."

"I'll do my best," the young woman said, suddenly serious.

"Let's start with your background. You look young to be working at this prestigious organization."

"Why thank you, Inspector. I'm actually a hoary twenty-five. That's h-o-a-r-y, in case you're wondering."

Bib smiled and Sergeant Dowden looked mystified.

"Where are you from?" Bib inquired.

"Omaha, Nebraska."

"And how did you find your way to National Geographic?"

"I applied for a job right out of college, and they sent me a manuscript to check over as a test. I must have aced it, because I got a telephone call from Mrs. Smollett offering me an entry-level position. And the rest, as they say, is history."

"Did you like working for Mrs. Smollett?"

"Will what I tell you ever get back to Rebecca? To Ms. Wimberly, I mean."

"No, this information is strictly for our own use."

"Okay then. I found working with Mrs. Smollett to be… highly educational."

"Meaning?"

"On one level, she taught me so many things about the role of a researcher that I could never have thanked her enough."

"I sense there's an 'on the other hand' coming," Bib said.

"There is." Parker took a deep breath. "All right, here goes. The other thing I learned from Mrs. Smollett was how not to treat people. She had a total lack of manners. She would walk into my office when I was talking with someone and interrupt us without apology. You wouldn't believe how rude she could be."

"What about her work? Others have said that she was remarkable."

"Oh, she was. Nothing ever got past her, but she could be caustic in dealing with writers. Most of them were terrified of her. Anyone with a pulse can make a mistake, but Mrs. Smollett seemed to glory in pointing them out. Even the senior staff members quailed at the thought of having Joan Smollett pour over their copy. One unlucky fellow inadvertently referred to President Lincoln's 'funeral corsage' in an article he wrote. Mrs. Smollett attached a note to his manuscript suggesting that perhaps the writer's daughter might like to wear a nice 'cortège' to her senior prom."

"That's not very collegial. Do you think that type of comment could have angered someone so much that they might have considered getting back at her?"

"You mean by killing her?"

Bib nodded.

"It's unlikely that any of our staff writers or editors would feel that way. I can't speak to how freelancers might react, since we don't get to know them as well as we do our staffers."

"It sounds to me like Mrs. Smollett's one flaw was an abrasive personality."

"Totally. She may not have been lovable, but she was incredible at her job."

The young woman frowned. "There's another thing you should probably know, Inspector, something that goes beyond the ability to spot writers' mistakes, which is a talent to be admired."

"And what is that?"

"Mrs. Smollett was equally vigilant when it came to the spoken word. She seemed to feel it was up to her to prevent the world from descending into verbal chaos, with no one able to communicate intelligently. What I'm trying to say is that she had an infuriating habit of correcting other people's speech, which she usually prefaced with a condescending chuckle followed by the words, 'I think you meant...'

"Even worse, she sometimes repeated what the other person said under her breath, as if it was so wrongheaded it was comical, and if anyone misused 'who' or 'whom' in her presence, she would roll her eyes and shake her head. More than one National Geographic staffer turned and fled whenever they saw Joan Smollett headed their way.

"The sad part is, the woman had no idea how irritating her comments could be. They were the main reason she was seldom invited to lunch by any of her coworkers. No one wanted to put up with her correcting every little remark they made. She'd have had far more friends if she'd have overlooked the careless slips everyone makes occasionally in casual conversation. But that wasn't Mrs. Smollett's way."

"That's an astute observation," Bib said. He glanced at his notebook. "We have one final item to bring up. When we found Mrs. Smollett's body in her office, we discovered that her killer had stuffed a page from a dictionary in her mouth, with the word 'library' circled. Frankly, that has us stumped. Any thoughts on why a person would do something so odd?"

Parker scrunched up her face, making her look even more like a leprechaun. "That's strange all right. Maybe the word 'library' is the key to the killer's motive, but it would take a PhD in psychology to untangle that."

Parker issued a mischievous laugh. "If I had to guess who'd pull such a stunt, I'd say Rebecca Wimberly."

Bib did a double take. "Are you serious?"

"No, not really."

"Then why make the accusation?"

"Because Rebecca Wimberly hated Joan Smollett with every fiber of her blue-blooded carcass."

"Why?"

"Jealousy, mainly. But also snobbery. She thought Mrs. Smollett was far less deserving to run the research department than a Boston Brahmin with an oversized trust fund and a summer home in the Hamptons."

"You've certainly given us an interesting perspective, Miss Parker," Bib said. "Thanks for your time."

"What do you make of that?" Sergeant Dowden asked after Ann Parker bounced from the room.

"I'm not sure. I wish my wife was here. She was much better than I'll ever be at reading between the lines of what women say about each other."

Chapter 13

Wednesday

Their second day of interviews at National Geographic began in a different setting. Inspector Bib and Sergeant Dowden were in Hubbard Hall, the original headquarters building on 16th Street, which still housed the Society's library. They'd made arrangements that morning to speak with the head librarian, Emily Milhouse.

There was a personal reason why Bib had elected not to ask Milhouse to join them in the conference room over in the new headquarters. He wanted to get a glimpse of the library, which must have figured in so many of the articles he'd read growing up. It had to be one of the world's foremost repositories of cultural, historical, and scientific knowledge, a veritable Fort Knox of information. And Miss Emily Milhouse held the key to the vault.

Hubbard Hall was right out of the Gilded Age, finished with tons of marble and gleaming brass and hung with gold-framed oil portraits of the Society's founders. The National Geographic library was hidden from public view, a secret warren with row upon row of bookshelves, card catalogs, and finely crafted wooden tables where researchers could do their work. A reverential silence lay over the reception area as Bib and Sergeant Dowden approached the main desk.

"Miss Milhouse?" Bib inquired of the slender, thirtyish woman seated at the desk.

The librarian looked up at him over the top of her half-frame reading glasses. "May I help you?" she asked primly. She was wearing a conservative beige sheath dress with a chaste white collar. A small silver cross dangled from a fine chain around her neck.

"I'm Inspector Bib and this is Sergeant Dowden. We're investigating the death of Mrs. Smollett."

The woman took off her glasses, her expression grave. "Yes, I've been expecting you."

Gazing at Emily Milhouse, who wore her long sandy hair in a bun, Bib was struck by how many extraordinarily good-looking women worked at National Geographic. If Miss Milhouse let her hair down, she'd be a dead ringer for Lauren Bacall, although Bib had a hard time picturing her wearing a sexy black satin evening dress while singing a sultry rendition of "How Little We Know" in a Caribbean cabaret, as the young Lauren Bacall did in her screen debut. The seemingly strait-laced librarian appeared to be more the hymn-singing type.

"Is there someplace private where we could talk?" Bib asked.

"We can use the break room. No one should be in there this early in the day."

Miss Milhouse stood up. She was as tall as Lauren Bacall, too. She led the way to the little room where staff members sipped their coffee or sodas while talking about their jobs or their lives or the latest episode of *The Ed Sullivan Show*, where last Sunday night Petula Clark sang "Downtown" and comedians Nancy Walker and Bert Lahr yucked it up as an unhappy married couple.

"Have a seat," Milhouse said, taking a seat herself and pulling her dress down over her knees, which Sergeant Dowden had been quick to notice.

"Thanks for meeting with us, Miss Milhouse," Bib began. "Pamela Johnson suggested you'd be a good person to speak with regarding Mrs. Smollett."

"I hope I'm able to help in some way. I'm still reeling from the news of her death. I said a prayer for her at church after I heard."

Bib smiled to himself. "Are you from around here?"

"I am. My father is with the FBI."

"Is that right? Then you know something about how investigators go about their work."

"Too well. Dad was away from home far too often when I was growing up."

"Did you go to college here?"

"I studied library science at Catholic University."

"I understand that the Society's librarians play a significant role in the editorial process. Pamela Johnson explained that you assist researchers in finding whatever information they need, and she said you often helped Mrs. Smollett with the articles she worked on."

"I had that privilege. We formed a bond over the years."

"You obviously held her in high esteem."

"Mrs. Smollett represented everything that makes the National Geographic Society such a highly respected educational and scientific institution. She was special, both as a person and as an employee."

"In what way?"

"Her dedication, her perseverance in getting things right. She spared no effort. In fact, I think she spent more time here in the library than in her own office. When Mrs. Smollett signed off on a story, you could be sure there were no errors. That sort of commitment is rare these days. Newspapers produce stories so quickly that it's amazing they ever get their facts straight. At National Geographic, we devote however long it takes to do the best job possible. If it's important to the story to know how high an elephant's eye is, then we find out. We don't deal in guesstimates or generalities. If a writer and photographer need six months or a year to complete their work on a major story, then that's how much time they spend. There are no shortcuts to greatness."

"That's a fascinating outlook. Almost Old World."

"Some of us who've been here awhile liken National Geographic to Camelot," Milhouse said. "It does seem like a magical place when you compare it to cutthroat business practices. I hope things never change, but even Camelot didn't last."

"I was told that Mrs. Smollett was employed here for nearly twenty years," Bib observed. "That's a long time."

"Twenty years isn't all that long," Milhouse said. "I've been here for ten years already, and it seems like I just started. The work is so exciting and rewarding that the years fly by. If you don't mind my asking, how long have you been at your job, Inspector Bib?"

"Since 1945."

"Then you know how satisfying it is to commit yourself to what you do. My fiancé prides himself on the fact that he's never worked at any job for more than five years. That kind of job hopping isn't conducive to loyalty, and loyalty is one characteristic that unites everyone who works at National Geographic.

"The Society appreciates that loyalty, too. Employees who reach their twenty-fifth anniversary are given a party, which the entire staff attends. Mr. Grosvenor thanks the person being honored for his or her service, no matter whether they work in the mailroom or the boardroom. That's why you'll find employees who spend forty years or more with National Geographic before they retire, including the top editors."

"Getting back to Mrs. Smollett's death, I need to ask if you have any reason to suspect that another employee might have been involved."

"I'd like to think not, but evil can corrupt the best of us if we're weak."

"Anyone in particular come to mind?"

"Oh no, definitely not."

"Did Mrs. Smollett ever seem stressed or preoccupied, as if something was bothering her?"

"Well, she recently finished working on a challenging article about headhunters in Ecuador. She was over here every day."

"That's interesting. Make a note of it, Sergeant."

Bib hesitated before asking his final question. "I hope this won't upset you, but I'd like your reaction to a disturbing aspect of the scene in Mrs. Smollett's office. We discovered that the killer left behind a page torn from a dictionary, with the word 'library' circled on it. Does that call anything to mind?"

"The Bible itself is considered a library since it's made up of books," Milhouse said, "although there'd be no logical connection in this case. Maybe the madman was making some obscure reference to a mythological library. I could look into it if you'd like."

"I don't think that's necessary. I have a feeling the explanation is far more mundane."

"Then is there anything else you'd like to know?"

"I believe that's all. You've been very helpful."

Bib seemed reluctant to leave. "Would you mind if I walked through the stacks of books? Only for a few minutes."

Milhouse gave Bib a maidenly smile. "I take it you're a faithful reader of *National Geographic*."

"All my life."

"Go ahead. Spend as long as you like."

While Bib drifted up and down the aisles gazing at book titles, Sergeant Dowden amused himself by watching the traffic out on 16th Street. Bib saw one book he'd read not long after he got back from the war, *Man-Eaters of Kumaon*. It was written by British naturalist Jim Corbett, who was responsible for hunting man-eating tigers and leopards in India's Kumaon region in the early 1900s. One rogue tiger Corbett wrote about killed more than four hundred people. Bib recalled how he'd yearned to visit exotic India after reading that book, but with a new job, a young wife, a baby daughter, and bills to pay, that had remained an unfulfilled dream.

Twenty minutes later, Inspector Bib collected his car-gazing sergeant and they returned to the conference room where they'd held their previous interviews. Next on their list of staff members to speak with was writer Doug Smith. A telephone call by Sergeant Dowden brought the young man hustling down the hall from his office, which was on the same floor.

The bearded, dark-haired writer stepped through the doorway and assumed a rigid pose. "Smith, Douglas. Petty Officer 2nd Class. B635441. Reporting for duty."

Bib responded in kind to the young writer's offbeat military introduction of name, rank, and serial number. "At ease, Petty Officer Smith," the Inspector said with a smile.

The lanky young writer grinned at the two men and came on into the room. "I'm glad you recognize a veteran," he said, "although I wasn't exactly a conquering hero. About all I did was float around the Mediterranean enjoying shore leave in some of the most compelling locations on earth. Like the recruitment posters say, join the Navy and see the world."

"Have a seat," Bib said, "and tell us a little more about your background. It sounds intriguing."

"Aye aye, sir." Smith made himself comfortable and launched into a brief account of his 32 years. "My adventures began in an obscure little town in a pastoral realm that natives refer to as 'Muhzuruh.' After my stint in the Navy, I attended the University of Missouri School of Journalism. My degree opened doors for me, first on a boating magazine, then on a medical journal, and finally here with National Geographic. I'm married to my high school sweetheart, we have no children yet so we're free to entertain ourselves however we please, and I'm as happy as a clam with my job."

"You're a lucky guy," Bib said.

"I can't tell you how much I love this place," Smith continued. "I subscribed to *National Geographic* when I was 15, with money I earned mowing lawns. It was always my dream to work here. When I was hired, I felt like I was taking holy orders. It's wonderful being on a publication where the top decision makers are real journalists, and all of them dedicated to this organization. There aren't any mercenary interlopers mucking things up. If that crowd ever takes over, they'll have us doing endless sensationalized stories on Nazis, sharks, and ancient Egypt."

Smith didn't mention that he was cursed with the itch to be a novelist, a pursuit that crushed the souls of most of those foolish enough to try it. Despite being aware that there were far too many mystery novels being published, Smith had written a couple himself, books that had sparked a tremendous outpouring of apathy. One reason few people paid attention to Smith's novels was that he wrote almost exclusively for himself. His personal interests colored his fiction to such a degree that many readers were left cold.

A friend of Smith's suggested that if he spent more time creating a brisk, coherent plot—without any long-winded digressions on the layout of Barcelona or the history of the dulcimer—he might reach a wider audience. Curiously, the dismal sales of his novels didn't faze Smith. His attitude was "readers be damned." Half the fun of writing was pursuing subjects that fascinated him. Sometimes, however, he fantasized that an influential critic might come across his forgotten work after he was dead and proclaim him a literary genius. That would be a hoot, he told himself—becoming the Vincent Van Gogh of remaindered paperbacks.

"Pamela Johnson praised your work here," Bib said. "She thought that you might have valuable insight on the subject of our investigation."

"Pam's a sweetheart through and through, but I'm not sure if I'm an unbiased judge of Mrs. Smollett."

"Why's that?" Bib asked.

"I didn't care for her or the comments she made on my copy."

"I understand she was thorough in her fact checking."

"I'll give her credit for that. All the staff writers appreciated her backing us up, but that's a researcher's job. What galled us was that she looked upon herself as the arbiter of good writing, even though she'd never written anything of merit herself. Criticizing someone else's writing is the cheapest commodity on the market. I once told a friend that when Mrs. Smollett turned out a flawless ten thousand–word piece, then I'd start taking her extraneous comments to heart."

"Was she disliked by all the staff writers?" Bib asked.

"Most of us. One chap claimed he'd rather have amoebic dysentery than deal with her, and another fellow described her as an aggravating little mouse scrabbling over his stories and chewing holes in the paper. We sometimes speculated on which of us would end up throttling the persnickety woman. That was all in jest, you understand, but she irritated the hell out of a lot of people."

"Might one of the staff writers have taken his irritation a step further?"

"I doubt that, but I do have to say that there are some seriously big egos around this place. As a Midwesterner, it took me awhile to get used to certain people ignoring me when I said good morning on the elevator. What you've got to understand is that National Geographic is like an exclusive club. When I landed a job here, the head of the personnel office told me they receive ten thousand applications for every editorial staff position they fill. Some folks seem to have let that fact go to their heads.

"Also, there's a band of Ivy Leaguers about, and between you and me, I think some of them were hired because of their family connections, which gives them an elevated sense of their own importance. Of course, that suspicion is probably the product of my mile-wide streak of jealousy. You see, no matter how smart I may be or how competent I am as a writer, I'm still just a bumbling small-town kid socially. I ain't got none of that there savoir faire."

"There's one facet of Mrs. Smollett's murder that seems incomprehensible," Bib said. "The killer stuffed a page torn from a dictionary in her mouth, with the word 'library' circled."

"Whew, that's a real Edgar Allan Poe move. Right up there with sealing someone behind a brick wall. I can't picture anyone I know committing murder, let alone leaving that kind of cryptic, oddball message."

"Thank you very much, Mr. Smith. You've been quite candid with us."

"I hope I didn't overdo it. Mrs. Smollett may have been a pain in the rear, but she didn't deserve to die like that. I hope you catch whoever did it."

"We will, Mr. Smith. We will."

Associate editor Vernon Hall reminded Bib of Wally Cox, the star of the old TV comedy *Mister Peepers*. Like the character Mr. Peepers, who was a junior high science teacher, Hall had dark, slicked-back hair and the unathletic appearance of an academic. Hall's round eyeglasses gave him an owlish look, and his bow tie topped off the image. He'd never be mistaken for a member of the Washington Redskins, other than a water boy perhaps.

Hall's job was a step above that of staff writer, just as his office was one floor higher. The moment Hall opened his mouth, though, Bib saw that the man's senior editorial position hadn't given him the sense of self-importance that Doug Smith described.

"Howdy," Hall said as he strolled into the conference room. "So you're looking into Mrs. Smollett's untimely demise. I've got to say, I don't envy you gents."

Bib and Dowden exchanged looks of mystification. "Good morning, Mr. Hall," Bib said. "Please, have a seat and tell us why you don't envy us."

"Actually, it's Dr. Hall, but 'Mr.' is okay. I earned a doctorate in biology down in Austin and taught high school science for a couple of years—until I came to my senses and realized how much I dislike teenagers."

Yep, the fellow's Mr. Peepers all right, Bib said to himself—on steroids.

"After my foray into teaching," Hall continued, "I edited a technical journal for a few years, and after that I washed up on the shores of the Potomac River. I've been with National Geographic for fifteen years now, so between my science background and my experience as an editor I can recognize a tough assignment when I see one."

"Such as?"

"Consider how a scientist works. He may devote years of research to a single project. Eventually, he comes up with a hypothesis and then tries to prove its validity to his skeptical peers. You, on the other hand, have to research a new set of facts and prove your findings with every case you undertake—and I'm sure you handle far more projects than the average scientist does. People can't wait ten years for justice to be served. That's why I don't envy you."

"I don't know whether I should feel flattered or depressed," Bib said.

"I'd vote for flattered, since that was my intention. I think the police have a thankless task, and they do it very well."

"If we weren't on duty, I'd take you out and buy you a drink for that," Bib said. "Unfortunately, Sergeant Dowden and I need to stick to our investigation."

"Of course. Tell me how I can help."

"We've been asking staff members to give us their opinion of Mrs. Smollett, first what she was like as a person and then how they assessed her job performance."

"Boy oh boy," Hall muttered. "The answers to those two questions are diametrically opposed."

"I think I know where you're headed," Bib said, "based on what others have told us."

"Okay, I'll be frank. Did I like Joan Smollett? No. Was she good at her job? She was more than good. She was fanatical. I tended to think of her as a necessary evil."

"I understand you worked with her both as a writer and an editor."

"That's correct, and both roles presented their difficulties. To give you an example of what it was like to work with Mrs. Smollett as a writer, I slipped up once in a piece I wrote about President Lincoln's funeral. You wouldn't believe what that woman wrote in a note she sent me."

"You mean the corsage/cortège business?"

"Good gracious, is that common knowledge?"

"No, nothing like that. We heard about it from one of the researchers we spoke with concerning Mrs. Smollett's work habits. The researcher told us in confidence, and she didn't mention your name."

"Thank God for that. Once a silly mistake like that gets around the building, you're the butt of endless jokes. Doesn't do much for the reputation. Anyway, the point is she could be hard on a writer's ego, and there's nothing as fragile as a writer's ego.

"As far as working with her as an editor, I had to weigh her research comments and decide which fixes in a writer's copy were warranted. Being an occasional writer myself, I feel an obligation to preserve the voices of other writers. I don't want our stories to be reduced to some generic geo-speak. Mrs. Smollett made my job more complicated by the volume of her comments, many of which strayed from the area she was responsible for—the factual accuracy of the copy."

"Everyone we've spoken with has indicated that the frustrations of working with Mrs. Smollett wouldn't be enough to cause anyone on the staff to harm her. Do you agree with that assumption?"

"One hundred percent. Shoot, we all have to work with people we may not like, but only a person who's a bit off would contemplate murdering someone over a petty grievance. I'd be astounded if you found your killer among the staff of National Geographic."

"One final item. We discovered a page torn from a dictionary stuffed in Mrs. Smollett's mouth. The word 'library' was circled. Does that suggest anything to you?"

"It simply reinforces what I said earlier. I don't envy you for having to decipher such riddles."

Chapter 14

Thursday

On Thursday morning, Bib got a telephone call from Carl Hoskins, the chief medical examiner. The autopsy on Mrs. Smollett's body was complete and the lab results were in. "Stop by when you can and I'll go over everything with you," Dr. Hoskins said. "And I should warn you. Be prepared for a surprise."

Visiting the autopsy suite was Bib's least favorite duty. The smell of disinfectant made him shudder. It brought back memories of visiting his wife in the hospital when she was dying. Bib had read that odors can trigger some of our strongest memories. He could vouch for that. One whiff of the nauseating stench of disinfectant left him wandering down the long, dark road he knew too well.

Bib steeled himself for the off-putting task ahead and pushed through the swinging double doors of the autopsy suite. As always, he'd donned a surgical mask to spare himself some of the unpleasantness.

Dr. Hoskins looked up from the stainless-steel table where the body of Joan Smollett lay. Hoskins was a crew-cut ex-Marine with a vise-like grip and a fondness for wisecracks. Luckily for Bib—particularly for his right hand—the M.E.'s own hands were in no condition to be clasped in greeting when he was in the midst of his gruesome work. Bib, however, could never escape the witticisms.

Dr. Hoskins pointed to the wound on Smollett's neck. "It wasn't an ice pick," he announced. "The wound's too shallow. More like a knitting needle or some such. Whatever it was, it was tipped with poison. Curare to be precise. That's what killed the woman."

"Curare? That's a new one."

"Never run into it in thirty years in the business," Hoskins said. "About as rare as your average conservative supporting a new welfare program."

"So the poison was introduced through the wound?"

"Yep, just like some of those Indian tribes do with their blow-gun darts. The poison works on the nervous system. Paralyzes the target and they drop dead in no time. Our victim here wouldn't have had long before she lost control of her muscles. That's why she was found pitched forward on her desk."

"Could that explain the hideous look on her face as well?" Bib asked.

"I don't think that she was ever a very attractive woman," Hoskins quipped, "but yes, it's possible that shock was responsible for her death grimace. She'd have had time to stare at her killer in disbelief before she died, even though she couldn't move. A horrible way to go. If her killer was especially warped, he or she could have stood there and watched her die."

"Where would anyone obtain curare?" Bib asked.

"I'd say your best bet would be somewhere in the Amazon rainforest," Hoskins replied.

Bib suddenly recalled a comment Emily Milhouse had made. She'd told them that Mrs. Smollett was working on an article about headhunters in Ecuador.

Back in his office, Bib called Sergeant Dowden and gave him the news. "Telephone National Geographic and find out who wrote the article on headhunters that Mrs. Smollett was working on. If it's someone on the staff, get down there right away and haul him in for questioning. If it's not a staff member, get his contact information."

Ten minutes later, Dowden appeared in the doorway of Bib's office. "It's a freelance writer named Xander Riley. The guy's been showing off in lectures with some of the toys he brought back from Ecuador." The sergeant waved his note-book. "I found out where he's staying."

"Let's go," Bib said.

The opulent, history-steeped Mayflower Hotel backed up to 17th Street, catty-cornered from National Geographic headquarters, with its main entrance on Connecticut Avenue. Since 1925, the hotel had been a fine place to sip a cold drink and watch assorted swells going about their business. Harry Truman called the hotel "Washington's second-best address."

In 1927, Charles Lindbergh received National Geographic's prestigious Hubbard Medal in the Mayflower following his solo flight from New York to Paris. In 1933, while staying in Room 776, newly elected President Franklin D. Roosevelt wrote his inaugural address, a speech that contained the most famous line about the Great Depression: "The only thing we have to fear is fear itself." And in 1945, Prime Minister Winston Churchill told an off-color joke to the person seated next to him at a state dinner held in the Mayflower. To Churchill's embarrassment, the acoustics of the room carried his voice to other startled guests, including the president.

When Bib and Dowden parked their unmarked car in front of the grand hotel's elegant marquee on Connecticut Avenue, the uniformed doorman marched over to tell them it was a no-parking zone. Bib held up his badge and the two officers proceeded inside. The glittering, block-long first floor was like a scene out of a Fred Astaire and Ginger Rogers movie. It was the sort of setting where Fred and Ginger often danced, Fred in white tie and tails and Ginger in a wispy ball gown. After Bib made an inquiry at the reception desk, a hotel official took him and Dowden up to Xander Riley's room, which they discovered was unoccupied.

Dowden whistled as he gaped at the unbelievable luxury of Riley's suite. "This fellow must be rich," he said.

The Inspector picked up a book lying on the end table beside the king-size bed. It was a copy of *The Arabian Nights*, the collection of Middle Eastern and Asian tales about Aladdin, Ali Baba, Sinbad the Sailor, and other folk heroes. He held the book up for Dowden to see. "He must also be into fantasy."

The two officers turned toward the doorway when they heard someone enter the suite. "Excuse me," the startled adventure writer said. "What are you doing in my room?"

Bib walked over to the tall, handsome young man. "Are you Xander Riley?"

"Yes I am, but you haven't answered my question. What are you doing here?"

Bib showed him his badge. "Come with us, please."

The interrogation room at police headquarters was like an old friend to Bib. He felt at home there. It was where he'd cracked so many of his cases that he'd lost count. The suspects he dealt with ranged from high-powered businessmen who mistakenly thought they could outsmart their poorly dressed interrogator to tough guttersnipes who expressed contempt for the scrawny cop sitting across the table.

There were two things every suspect questioned by Archimedes Bib soon learned. One was that he was in charge and the other was that they were as helpless as newborn kittens in his hands. Riley was no different from everyone else who'd sat in his chair before him.

"We understand that you recently worked with Joan Smollett," Bib said. "As you must know, she was murdered in her office last Sunday afternoon. We've learned that she was poisoned with curare."

Riley seemed to shrink. "Curare?" he mumbled. He leaned forward with a look of outrage. "And of course you automatically think that I had something to do with it."

"It's a logical assumption. I don't imagine Mrs. Smollett could have been working with anyone else who had an opportunity to procure curare."

"But what reason would I have for killing her?"

"That's what we intend to find out."

"Look, she was just a researcher. She corrected a few misspelled words in my stories, that's all. I certainly wouldn't kill her over such a trifling matter."

"The head librarian said Mrs. Smollett had to spend an inordinate amount of time on your current article. How do you explain that?"

"It's set in an inaccessible part of the world, in the wildest region of Ecuador. I'm sure she had to spend extra time trying to find information on the subject."

Bib regarded him in silence. Riley looked back uncomfortably. He felt like he was gazing into the hypnotic eyes of a cobra.

"I'm told your lectures for National Geographic included a discussion of curare—along with a demonstration of how to use a blowgun and poison darts. That very much puts you in the frame."

"Okay, so I talked about curare," Riley said, "and I brought back some poison darts from my trip. But that doesn't mean I was the only one with access to them. I had a couple of blowguns and two quivers of darts, along with a bunch of other artifacts. Several weeks ago, I turned over everything I didn't need for my lectures to the folks in Explorers Hall, including one of the blowguns and a quiver of darts. They've been holding my stuff in storage until they set up the exhibit that's supposed to accompany my article in the May issue of the magazine. That means any number of people could have taken a dart— if that's actually what was used to kill Mrs. Smollett, which I doubt you can prove."

Bib continued to stare at Riley. "One final question. Where were you last Sunday between noon and two o'clock?"

"Sunday between noon and two o'clock? I can't remember where I was at exactly that time. Could you?"

"Please try."

"Well...oh yeah, I went jogging down on the Mall after lunch."

"By yourself?"

"Sure."

"Then no one can vouch for your whereabouts?"

"No they can't, but I was out jogging. I wasn't busy killing Mrs. Smollett."

Bib closed his notebook. "Sergeant Dowden, please take Mr. Riley back to his hotel."

"Then you're not arresting me?" Riley said with relief.

"Not today, but please don't leave the Washington area."

"I wouldn't think of it," Riley replied. "I've still got work to do here."

"So do I, Mr. Riley," Bib said.

That afternoon, Inspector Bib and Sergeant Dowden arranged to meet with the curator of Explorers Hall. They found him in his second-floor office going over plans for an exhibit of Navajo pottery and weaving.

Peter Nance was a suntanned gentleman with an abundant shock of white hair. Nance got his ruddy glow by spending his weekends in search of peace and quiet at his cottage in Rappahannock County, Virginia. Nance had been attracted to the setting because of its rural beauty, along with the fact that the entire county didn't possess a single stoplight. From his back deck, Nance could see the Blue Ridge Mountains of Shenandoah National Park. On Monday mornings, it was difficult for the man to tear himself away and make the seventy-mile drive back to Washington.

"What can I do for you?" Nance asked after the introductions were made.

"We're investigating the murder of Mrs. Joan Smollett," Bib replied, "and this morning we learned that she was killed with the poison curare. We understand that you hold several artifacts brought back from Ecuador by freelance writer Xander Riley, including poison darts used by the indigenous headhunters that figure in his upcoming article and exhibit."

"That's true," Nance said. "The obvious implication that you're making is that Mr. Riley's darts were used to commit the crime."

"That does suggest itself," Bib said. "If you would, please tell us how those artifacts have been stored."

"I'll show you."

Nance led the way to a line of storerooms down the corridor from his office. He took a key from his pocket and unlocked one of the doors. "In here, gentlemen."

Bib and Dowden followed the curator into a large room with metal shelving. Nance led them over to the shelves where Riley's South American paraphernalia was neatly arranged. Bib was intrigued by the array of blowguns, bows and arrows, bead necklaces, feathered headdresses, and other handcrafted items.

"Holy moly," Sergeant Dowden said when he noticed the frightful little faces of the three shrunken heads Riley had acquired. "Would you look at those poor suckers."

"Grim, aren't they," Nance said. "I'm sure they'll be the star attraction of our exhibit. People do love gruesomeness—as long as it doesn't touch them personally."

Bib's eye was drawn to the bamboo quivers full of footlong needlelike darts. The light brown fletching of the darts appeared to be made from animal fur or some sort of feathery material. "What's the name of the Indian tribe that makes these things?" Bib asked.

"The Jivaros. They live in the Amazon rainforest of southeastern Ecuador and northern Peru."

"Who has access to this room?" the Inspector asked.

"Only the curatorial staff."

"How many people is that?"

"Myself, my secretary, and four workmen. However, everything you see here is listed on the Explorers Hall inventory sheet, so a few other people could have known those darts were in storage, although they wouldn't have had access to them. We keep the storage rooms locked when they're not in use. Naturally, the rooms have to be unlocked whenever our workmen are going in and out to set up displays or to bring in items to be stored."

"Does anyone keep an eye on the rooms while they're unlocked?"

"We don't have a guard standing watch, if that's what you mean, but it would take a Japanese ninja to be able to slip in here undetected and steal something. They'd have to get by my secretary for one thing. Her desk commands a view of the doors to the storerooms."

"And all of this material has been here the whole time?" Bib asked.

"Everything except the few artifacts Mr. Riley used in his two lectures at Constitution Hall. Pamela Johnson was in charge of those. She dropped them off this morning, after the final lecture. That took place last night I believe."

Bib didn't know what to make of the situation. Even though a number of people might have known that the poison darts were in storage, he couldn't see why anyone associated with Explorers Hall would have a reason to murder Mrs. Smollett. Their worlds were so far apart as to make such a connection remote. Still, he needed to interview them to be certain. "We'd better speak with your staff," he said to Nance.

The curator extended an arm to usher the policemen out. "You can use our conference room."

Bib spoke to Mr. Nance's secretary first. Jane Messi was exactly that—messy in appearance and thought. She must have dressed in the dark from the look of her mismatched skirt and blouse, and her hair whirled around her head as if she'd just emerged from a cyclone. Her mind also appeared to be in a whirl. Before she told Bib whether she knew Joan Smollett, Messi spun off on her own line of thinking.

"You don't look like a sleuth," she said. "At least not the way they're supposed to look. You know, a handsome, well-dressed man like Nick Charles or a tough guy like Joe Friday. You look more like a librarian. Do you carry a gun?"

"I'm sorry to disappoint you, Miss Messi, but could you please answer my question."

"What was it you asked me?"

"Did you know Joan Smollett?"

"Does she work here?"

"Thanks very much. That will be all."

"You never said if you carry a gun."

"No. I rely on my bodyguard to protect me." He pointed to Sergeant Dowden. "Except on weekends, when I'm working at the library. Then I carry a gun."

Bib was convinced that Jane Messi could never murder anyone. If the thought ever entered her head, she'd likely forget to bring the murder weapon with her.

The four workmen assigned to Explorers Hall—a carpenter, an electrician, a painter, and a general helper—were at least more coherent, if not actually more helpful. They all wore the same khaki outfits. Maybe they bowled together after work.

Carpenter Doug Chambers was a small, balding man with a wispy mustache that would have been better left at home. He was acquainted with Mrs. Smollett.

"Sure, I knew her. I worked in our carpenter shop before they transferred me to Explorers Hall. I installed some bookshelves for her once. She called me back three times to make little adjustments. Said the shelves weren't quite straight. A very fussy lady, Mrs. Smollett was."

Bib didn't think Chambers would seek revenge over some misaligned bookshelves.

Bo Harper, the electrician, was a fast-talking young man with a fondness for chewing gum and a talent for making it crack. Bib hurried the interview with him so he wouldn't have to listen to the annoying sound.

"Did you know Mrs. Joan Smollett?"

"Isn't she that tall cashier lady in the gift shop?" *Crack.*

The third workman, painter Harry Gambel, had no conspicuous physical shortcomings or exasperating habits. The tall, gray-haired man must have confused strangers when he told them he was a painter. From his distinguished bearing, they probably thought he painted portraits or landscapes instead of walls. If he ever grew a goatee and sported a beret it would really mislead people.

Gambel was aware that Mrs. Smollett had been murdered. "My wife works in the Society's secretarial pool, so she knew the woman. Not someone she looked forward to working for."

"Have you or any of the other workmen ever encountered any unauthorized person entering the Explorers Hall storage rooms?" Bib asked.

"She wasn't unauthorized, but I saw Jane Messi fooling around in one of the rooms last week. Silly girl was trying on hats from an exhibit on the Victorian era."

Steve Huntley was the crew's general helper—the man assigned to schlep artifacts from the storage rooms to Explorers Hall. A towering black man, he could have lifted Bib with one hand. He spoke in a gentle, melodic voice, the same voice he used when he sang the blues in dark, smoky bars of Southeast D.C. He went by the name Skip Huntley professionally, and he could play his battered steel body resonator guitar with the flair of his idol, Skip James. No one at National Geographic but a few of the black custodians had ever seen him perform.

Huntley had never heard of Joan Smollett.

Bib treated Sergeant Dowden to a cup of coffee following their futile afternoon. They took their coffee with them to a bench in the courtyard of Sumner School, where they could look at National Geographic headquarters across M Street. The rush hour was just beginning. The cars whizzing past on the one-way street were traveling west toward Connecticut Avenue, a block away. At some point, Virginia residents would be turning left to head home and most Marylanders would turn to the right.

"What do you think, Matt?" Bib asked.

"As usual, nobody knows nuthin'."

"Somebody does. National Geographic is filled with smart people, and one of them has outsmarted us so far."

Chapter 15

Friday and Saturday

Riley picked up Pamela Johnson after work in a rented Thunderbird, a low-slung silver coupe that throbbed with the intoxicating power of three hundred horses. The wind whistled past the windows like a banshee's scream as the long, sleek Ford raced east on Highway 50 toward Annapolis, Maryland, where the couple planned to spend the weekend together.

Johnson ran her hand over the car's sumptuous black leather seats. "You certainly go in for the best," she said.

"Nothing's too good for my Pam."

Johnson ruffled Riley's hair. He took her hand and kissed the back of it. "You'll have to show me around Annapolis," he said. "I've never been there before."

"That makes two of us."

Riley flashed his rakish smile. "Then we'll discover it together. And let's not forget an important reason for this little romantic excursion."

"I thought romance *was* the reason."

"It is, but behind that is a spirit of celebration. I've completed my lectures to general acclaim. Mr. Grosvenor hasn't shown me the door. And Wednesday was St. Patrick's Day, which my lecture at Constitution Hall prohibited me from celebrating in the proper fashion. I intend to make up for that this weekend with a pint or two of Guinness, like a good Irishman."

Johnson opened her purse and took out a travel brochure. "Top Attractions in Annapolis," she read out loud, showing Riley the pamphlet. She started flipping through the pages. "Hmm. Did you know that Annapolis was temporarily the capital of the United States after the Revolutionary War?"

"Nope. Did you?"

"Of course. Every educated American knows that."

"Yeah, sure."

"Let's see, what shall we do. The historic district. Check. The Naval Academy Museum. Definitely. The Annapolis Maritime Museum. Probably. The Maryland State House. Maybe. Chesapeake Bay sailing tours. Yes, if we can."

Johnson turned several more pages. "My gosh, there's more to see and do here than we could hope to accomplish in a weekend. And listen to this. The Chesapeake Bay is the largest estuary in the country and the third largest in the world, and it has over 3,600 species of plants and animals. We really do have to take a cruise."

"It all sounds fantastic," Riley said, "but let's take our time and enjoy a few sights rather than try to do everything. We can start with a walk in the historic district and go from there."

Riley pulled into Annapolis at dusk. Negotiating the narrow streets of the downtown area, he parked beside a three-story Victorian-era hotel with a wide, inviting front porch. "Here we are, madam. Our weekend accommodation, the Flag House Inn, built in 1879 by a Welsh shipbuilder and guaranteed to meet your high standards."

"Oh, Xander, it's perfect," Johnson gushed.

Inside, they were shown to their third-floor room. Like the rest of the inn, it's simple period furnishings reflected an understated elegance. As soon as the bellhop left them, Johnson leaped onto the king-size bed. "We can stay right here the whole weekend."

Riley wiggled his eyebrows suggestively like Groucho Marx. "I like your thinking," he said, "but what say we meander about first and get a bite to eat. I'm famished." He stood by a window that overlooked the jumble of shops and restaurants lining the brick streets of the city's historic district. "Looks like everything we need to see is within walking distance."

Just down the street from the inn, they found the historic Middleton Tavern, which had been serving fresh local seafood since 1750. Johnson consulted her travel brochure. "Hey, if this old clam shack was good enough for George Washington, Thomas Jefferson, and Benjamin Franklin, then it ought to be good enough for us."

The smells coming from inside the rustic brick restaurant convinced them they were in the right place. Once they were seated in the antique-filled dining room, Riley ordered a plate of oysters. "I wonder if these actually spark the libido," he said.

Johnson touched his hand. "I don't think you need them."

After the oysters, they stuffed themselves on the largest, most delicious crab cakes either of them had ever eaten. Johnson pushed her empty plate away and leaned back with a sigh. "I can't hold another bite. Let's get outside and start walking before I explode."

Annapolis Harbor was steps away from the restaurant. They strolled about the waterfront, gazing at the sleek sailboats tied up along the City Dock. The lights of the harbor winked on the dark water, and the cool breeze off the Chesapeake Bay was a bracing tonic. "It's lovely," Johnson said. "A real fairy-tale setting."

Riley put his arm around her and pulled her close. "Then let's head back to our room and see if fairytales come true."

The next morning, Johnson sat on their unmade bed, clad only in one of the white terry cloth bathrobes the inn provided. The top of the robe gapped open, and she'd hiked the lower part up to her thighs. A map of Annapolis they'd picked up last night was spread out in front of her. "What shall we do first?" she asked Riley, who was lying back propped up by his pillows.

Riley gave the svelte young woman a wolfish look. "With you sitting there like a *Playboy* bunny, there's only one thing I want to do."

Johnson grabbed one of her own pillows and smacked him with it. "Get serious. We've got one full day to enjoy ourselves before we have to head home on Sunday, so let's decide on our itinerary."

"You're an organized little lady, aren't you?" Riley sat up and scooted over so he could view Johnson's map. He pulled her robe off her shoulder and kissed her bare skin. "Why don't we begin with a tour of the Naval Academy Museum?" He kissed her on the neck. "Then we can proceed to the Annapolis Maritime Museum." He nuzzled her ear. "After that we can…" He slipped his hand inside her robe. She tossed the map on the floor and pushed Riley onto his back, pouncing on him like a wild animal. Sightseeing would have to wait.

An hour later, they emerged from the Flag House Inn to find the sun beaming down on a sublime Annapolis day. The Naval Academy Museum was a short walk from their inn. The museum was filled with displays of uniforms from different eras, arcane nautical equipment, and paintings of old ships and famous mariners. What captured Riley's interest was a gallery crammed with model sailing ships, each one corresponding to a life-size vessel, some of which dated back to the 1600s. The details of the models were incredible, with their tiny canons and intricate masts and lines.

Johnson finally had to tug Riley away. "Nice as these little replicas are," she said, "once you've seen two or three dozen you've seen them all."

Riley gave her a sheepish look. "I tried to build a model of Old Ironsides when I was a kid. I gave up when it was turning out to look more like a Chinese junk."

"If you like boats, then let's go find a real one. This town is supposed to be America's sailing capital, so let's get with the program."

Johnson checked her travel brochure and found a cruise that sounded good—a two-hour tour leaving from the City Dock aboard a Chesapeake Bay skipjack, one of the classic workboats used in oyster dredging.

The 75-foot-long, sloop-rigged sailboat tied up at the City Dock was a reminder of the Bay's dwindling skipjack fleet, which once numbered well over a thousand boats. With its low, racy silhouette and immaculate white hull and white sails, the skipjack could have been built for a millionaire yachtsman instead of a crew of hardworking oystermen.

Riley and Johnson climbed aboard just five minutes before the boat pulled away. The spring wind was brisk, so the sails filled quickly. The boat heeled over as it gathered speed. Johnson huddled in Riley's arms against the wind. The brilliant sunlight reflecting on the choppy water forced her to squint. She looked up into Riley's face with the joyous expression of the young.

"This does beat looking at model boats," he said with boyish enthusiasm.

Gazing out over the broad, slate gray waters of the Chesapeake, Johnson wished the cruise would last far longer than two hours.

Saturday was shopping day for Jeffrey Smollett, only he wasn't out to buy bread and milk. He stood in front of the Lord & Taylor department store on Connecticut Avenue, trying to work up his courage. After studying the smartly attired male mannequins in the window for a while, he entered the store with lingering apprehension and sought out a salesclerk in the men's department.

A young ginger-haired salesman smiled when he saw Jeffrey shambling up the aisle in an ill-fitting 1950s business suit, one of the closetful of grotesqueries Jeffrey wore to his job at the bank. After they were married, Joan had picked out all of Jeffrey's clothes.

The young salesman could have been the fifth Beatle, with his tight-fitting sharkskin suit and pointy shoes. "Morning, sir," he said. "How may I help you?"

Jeffrey examined his own drab, shapeless clothing. "I need a new look," he replied.

"Certainly, sir. What sort of look were you hoping for?"

Jeffrey glanced around the department, seeing all the handsome men in snazzy suits and sport coats. He turned back to the salesman and eyed his clothes. The sixties look of shiny fabric and narrow lapels almost frightened Jeffrey. Did he dare to dress like that?

"I want to look like you," he said with a laugh. "Or at least as close as possible."

The salesman gave Jeffrey's tired suit a quick inspection, tugging on the excess material around the waist of the coat and appraising the large, out-of-date cuffs of the baggy trousers. "I think that's a wise decision. My name's Reg. Let me show you some suits from our new Brooks Brothers collection."

A few minutes later, Jeffrey stood before a full-length mirror. He hardly recognized himself. The light blue silk-blend suit Reg picked out had miraculously turned a colorless doormat into a dashing figure. The coat was narrow at the waist and the shoulders more padded than anything Jeffrey had ever worn. He smiled at his reflection. Joan would never have approved of such stylishness. She'd probably have said he looked like a gigolo or a pimp.

"I like it," he said to Reg. "What else have you got? And by the way, I'll need one suit that's a little more subdued. I have a funeral to attend."

By the time Jeffrey left Lord & Taylor, he was a new man, outwardly at least. He'd chosen five business suits and a pair of sport coats with complementary trousers. Among his purchases was a dark, double-breasted suit he intended to wear to Joan's service. He relished the thought of turning up at his wife's funeral looking like a distinguished London barrister. For a moment, he considered buying a bowler hat and a black umbrella to complete the look. He did buy a few of the skinny ties that were in vogue, and he added one other accessory—a tan English driving cap. He had a special use in mind for it.

Jeffrey took his purchases home, where he put on a white turtleneck sweater along with his new brown plaid trousers and burgundy blazer. Donning his driving cap, he flipped off the lights in the apartment and headed out the door. He was ready for Phase Two of the Jeffrey Smollett Resurrection.

The long taxi ride up 16th Street to Silver Spring, Maryland, was costly, but since it would be a one-way fare, Jeffrey didn't mind. He gave the driver a generous tip and hopped out of the cab in front of the British Motor Cars dealership. Spread out before him was a gleaming trove of imported automobiles, crowned by a glorious selection of Austin-Healey 3000s, the most beautiful sports car ever built. Jeffrey had never voiced his passion for the sleek convertible to his wife for fear of ridicule. Now he stood gazing at them with the enchanted look of a young boy staring in a shop window at the new bicycle he wanted for Christmas.

Jeffrey snapped out of his trance of wishfulness and began walking through the lot, admiring the cars. The Big Healeys, as the 3000s were called, came in a variety of solid colors—red, black, blue, green, silver, gold, and cream, along with several two-tone combinations. Jeffrey's favorite had always been British racing green, with brown leather seats and wire wheels. He'd once thought of building a toy 3000 from a kit he saw in a store, but, again, there was Joan. She'd have told him he was being childish. But Joan was no longer looking over his shoulder, no longer correcting him or telling him what to do. Now he could do whatever he wanted, and more than anything in the world he wanted to own an Austin-Healey 3000—a real Austin-Healey 3000.

A genial older salesman—a Perry Como look-alike in a tan wool cardigan—eased up to the side of the car Jeffrey was hovering over, his dream version in British racing green. "She's a honey, isn't she?" the salesman remarked. "This one's a Mark III, the latest model. She's got more horsepower than the Mark II and comes standard with power-assisted brakes."

"I know," Jeffrey said.

"Care to take her for a spin?"

"That's why I'm here."

While the salesman went inside to get the key, Jeffrey settled into the driver-side bucket seat. He visualized himself roaring along in a European road rally with the wind in his hair. He was guiding the car through an imaginary hairpin turn when the salesman returned and opened the passenger-side door. Jeffrey removed his hands from the wheel in embarrassment.

"Don't worry," the salesman said in a cordial tone as he climbed inside. "Everyone who sits in one of these beauties for the first time does the same thing. Where were you—Monte Carlo?"

"No place special. Just somewhere on a winding road with the wind in my hair."

"That's what it's all about, isn't it? What say we put the top down?"

The salesman handed Jeffrey the key. The throaty purr of the engine was the most erotic sound he'd ever heard. He removed his driving cap, eased the car into first gear, and drove out of the lot. Soon they were whipping along Highway 29— with the wind in their hair.

The salesman didn't have to make a sales pitch. He could tell the car was sold when he saw the smile on Jeffrey's face. Back at the dealership, they completed the paperwork in under an hour, then Jeffrey climbed into his new car, donned his jaunty cap, and drove off in the general direction of home. He was in no hurry. His only other errand for the day was to stop by the Dupont Circle shop where he was having some of his watercolors matted and framed so he could hang them around the apartment.

On Saturday night, Riley took Johnson to an atmospheric waterfront restaurant in Eastport, the maritime district located on the south side of Annapolis Harbor. They could see vessels of every size and description moored beyond the restaurant's windows. Across the harbor, boats were sailing into the Annapolis Yacht Basin and the inlet to the City Dock. The reflections of the boats' red, green, and white running lights sparkled like rubies, emeralds, and diamonds cast upon the water. The setting sun painted the clouds gathering over Annapolis with crimson and gold.

"What do you feel like tonight?" Riley asked as they perused their menus.

"Everything looks good."

The rockfish and crab entrée they decided on turned out to be the culinary high point of their stay, and the pricey French Sauvignon Blanc went down easily. By the time they finished eating, Riley and Johnson had both lapsed into a dreamy state of bliss.

Back in their room, the only light came from the nearby historic buildings. The city lights cast a dim glow, barely enough for the couple to see each other's faces as they cuddled in bed. Johnson traced Riley's chin with the tip of her finger. "Xander, how much longer are you going to be here?" she asked in a wistful tone.

"All night."

She punched him in the chest. "You know what I mean. How much longer before you take off on another of your wild adventures?"

Riley gave the question some thought. He wondered if it would spoil things to tell her about his notion of traveling to Iraq. He fell back on his long-standing conviction that equivocation was always the best policy when it came to relationships with women. "You're not getting rid of me anytime soon. I'll be staying for the opening of the exhibit in May for sure. After that, who knows? I might settle down and write a book."

Johnson sat up. "Seriously? That would be terrific. I'll bet you could write a humdinger of a book about your adventures. The Society might publish it, or one of the big New York publishing houses."

"Whoa, girl. Next thing I know you'll be planning my publicity tour."

Johnson fell back against her pillow with a hurt look. "I just want the best for you."

Riley held her face between his hands. "You are one sweet Georgia peach, Pam." His kiss lasted long enough to stave off Johnson's curiosity for the present, then they were in each other's arms. Afterward, the pretty young blonde nestled against Riley's side.

"Pam, there's something I need to tell you," he said.

Johnson propped herself up on an elbow and studied him. She expected him to say that he loved her, but what Riley said was far from a profession of love.

"I was questioned by the police on Thursday morning," he told her.

Johnson sat up in alarm. "What about?"

"They've got it into their heads that I was involved in Joan Smollett's death."

Johnson leaped out of bed. "Oh no. Why?"

"They've determined that Mrs. Smollett was killed with curare, so naturally they thought of me. Why wouldn't they? I'm the only guy around National Geographic with darts tipped with curare."

Johnson threw on her bathrobe and paced back and forth. "What did you say to them?"

"I pointed out that most of my artifacts, including some of the poison darts, have been in storage at National Geographic for several weeks, and that someone else could have stolen one of the darts and used it to kill Mrs. Smollett."

"How did they react?"

"They obviously realized it was a possibility. Otherwise, they might not have let me go."

Johnson sat on the edge of the bed. "Oh, Xander. This can't be happening."

"Don't take it so hard, hon. Even if I did feel like murdering her at times, I didn't do it. You've got to believe me."

"I know you didn't kill her, but if the police can't come up with any other likely suspect, they're bound to focus on you."

Riley stared out the window. "I suppose you're right. I'll just have to hope that fellow Bib does his job and finds the real killer."

Johnson began crying uncontrollably.

Chapter 16

Sunday

On Sunday morning, Riley and Johnson tried to recapture the magic of the previous day. After breakfast at their inn, they set off on a walking tour of the historic district recommended in Johnson's travel brochure. They made their way to State Circle, a road ringing the Maryland State House. Johnson's brochure informed them that the dignified brick building with the impressive white columns and tiered dome had been built in 1779 and had served as the U.S. Capitol from late 1783 to the summer of 1784.

"Looks interesting," Riley said. "Shall we take a peek inside?"

Johnson shrugged. "I don't think so. It's just an old building."

"Don't you want to walk where Washington and all his pals once walked?"

"We've been doing that ever since we got here."

"Can't argue with that," Riley said, attempting to keep the mood light. "What say we pop over to that old church?" He indicated St. Anne's Episcopal Church, a plain brick structure in the center of Church Circle, another roundabout a block to the west. Riley took the brochure from Johnson and read one of the facts about the church. "Says here they broke ground on that building in 1696. Now that is old."

"Maybe we should head home, Xander," Johnson said. "I'm all toured out."

Annapolis had lost its allure. The happiness Riley and Johnson felt when they arrived in the historic city had vanished like the petals of a night-blooming flower. Even the weather had turned gloomy, with a gray veil of clouds hiding the sun. There was no point in prolonging their weekend escape, so they went back to the inn, packed up, and checked out.

Johnson had hardly said a word all morning. By the time their big silver Thunderbird hit Highway 50, she'd sunk into a state of melancholy silence. All she could think about was the possibility of Riley being charged with murder. It was simply unimaginable.

Riley peered at Johnson out of the corner of his eye. He tried to start a conversation a couple of times before giving up. This is one moody chick, he said to himself. Her reaction the night before when he told her he'd been interviewed by the police had seemed way overdone. He wasn't worried about being hauled in for the crime, so why was she so upset?

Riley began to wonder if he was getting in over his head with Johnson. She was becoming a mite too serious. Maybe he needed to put some space between them for a while. There was always the nubile Rachel Mathers in the payroll office to fall back on. Yeah, that sounded like fun, in more ways than one. Anyway, it wouldn't be much longer before he headed off to Baghdad, where these niggling woman problems could be forgotten. He might find someone there like Ramona, the spirited airline stewardess who'd welcomed him to Quito. He hoped the women of Baghdad would be as hospitable. He was anxious to become acquainted with the sights of that city as well.

Jeffrey Smollett had settled on the Foundry United Methodist Church as the best location to hold his wife's funeral. The church was a couple blocks from his apartment, on the other side of Stead Park on 16th Street. He and Joan had never attended services there. In fact, they'd never been inside a church since the day they were married, and neither professed any strong religious feelings, but a Methodist church seemed like a nice middle-of-the-road place to gather. He definitely didn't want any overly fancy venue, and the other nearby option, St. Thomas Episcopal Church, seemed too austere even to suit Joan's spartan taste. Jeffrey spoke with the minister of the Foundry Church and made the arrangements. It would be a modest service.

Jeffrey thought it was interesting that presidents Abraham Lincoln, Andrew Johnson, and Rutherford B. Hayes had attended services at Foundry, back when the church was smaller. The present Gothic Revival building was dedicated in 1904. On Christmas Day, 1941, President Franklin D. Roosevelt attended a service there with British Prime Minister Winston Churchill following the Japanese attack on Pearl Harbor and the declaration of war against the Axis Powers. Jeffrey felt that Joan would have been pleased to know that so many luminaries had patronized Foundry before her. She always did like to hobnob with big shots.

Jeffrey had decided to forgo the visitation traditionally held before a funeral. Since he was the only family member, and because he didn't know any of Joan's friends or coworkers, there seemed to be no reason to have complete strangers pat him on the arm and tell him how sorry they were for his loss. He'd also opted for a closed casket. He doubted if anyone else wanted to view Joan's body. He said his brief goodbye before the service began and motioned for the attendant to close the casket lid. It was like shutting and locking the door to a house you'd known for years but had no intention of ever returning to. As irrevocable as closing the casket had been, Jeffrey felt no sense of loss. He'd lived with Joan for almost twenty years, and now he no longer would.

At two o'clock on Sunday afternoon, Jeffrey sat by himself in the family pew at the front of the Foundry sanctuary, a large all-white room with an arching ceiling and minimal decorations—stained-glass windows along the sides and a triptych depicting Jesus and his followers behind the altar, surmounted by stained glass. The purity of the church's understated ornamentation illustrated the adage that less is sometimes more.

The organist had been softly playing a somber Bach melody for several minutes, allowing time for those coming to pay their respects to be seated. Jeffrey refrained from turning around to see who'd arrived. He wouldn't know their names if he did, and he was sure the turnout would be small. He was correct.

Seated behind Jeffrey were Joan's fellow researchers Rebecca Wimberly and Ann Parker. Pythagoras Bib was also in attendance, carrying the flag for National Geographic's upper management. Associate editor Vernon Hall sat to one side, representing the senior editorial staff. Librarian Emily Milhouse sat alongside Pamela Johnson, who'd just made it back from Annapolis in time for the service. Clarissa O'Neill, the red-haired teller from the National Bank of Washington, was also present, Jeffrey's one friend in attendance. A few members of Joan's high school class also came—Reverend Tom Clark and his wife Brenda, insurance salesman Tim Wilson and his wife Vicky, and dress saleslady Margery Kendall. It was a paltry turnout, making a sad occasion sadder.

When the organ music faded away, Foundry's young minister took his place behind the pulpit and delivered a generic eulogy. Not knowing the deceased, there was no way he could deliver a more meaningful message. He made the usual observations on the fleeting nature of life, God's undying love, and the promise of a better world that awaited the faithful. He finished with a reading from John 14:27, containing words Jesus spoke to his disciples: "Let not your heart be troubled, neither let it be afraid." It seemed like a nice sentiment.

Following the minister's presentation, two of Joan Smollett's coworkers delivered more personal eulogies. Rebecca Wimberly spoke first. Ann Parker nearly gagged as she listened to Wimberly's effusive praise of Joan Smollett, a woman Wimberly hated. Even though the unvarnished truth was seldom spoken at funerals and the dead usually grew in stature, Wimberly's hypocritical veneration was beyond the pale. Of those present, only Ann Parker knew that Wimberly's words were as empty as a politician's promises. When Wimberly mentioned how much she'd miss Mrs. Smollett, Parker realized what a consummate liar the woman was. It must be a product of good breeding, Parker told herself.

In contrast to Wimberly's insincere comments, the admiration that librarian Emily Milhouse expressed for Joan Smollett appeared to be heartfelt. Evidently, she'd just seen Mrs. Smollett's laudable qualities and none of her faults. Perhaps she'd never been subjected to any of Smollett's withering remarks. More likely, Milhouse's opinion of Mrs. Smollett was an example of how varied people's perceptions of others could be. Beauty truly was in the eye of the beholder.

Following the eulogies, the mourners all stood and sang "Nearer My God to Thee," then the service closed with the minister leading them in the Lord's Prayer. When the organist began playing the recessional, the minister escorted Jeffrey Smollett to the rear of the sanctuary. Jeffrey had decided on a private interment in the plot in Falls Church where Joan's parents were buried, and since he couldn't bear going through the ordeal of a reception, the funeral was over.

Jeffrey shook hands with the guests as they left, thanking them for coming. Rebecca Wimberly made a great show of consoling Jeffrey, the very thing he'd been hoping to avoid. As Wimberly exited the church, she was considering how to redecorate and rearrange the furniture in her new office. When Ann Parker shook Jeffrey's hand, she was struck by what a surprising impression the man made. In his new double-breasted suit, he looked positively handsome. Parker would never have imagined Joan Smollett being married to anyone so urbane.

Vernon Hall told Jeffrey that his wife had been the most dedicated fact-checker he'd ever worked with, and the willowy Emily Milhouse said there would never be another Joan Smollett at National Geographic. Pamela Johnson mumbled a few quick words of condolence and hurried away. She couldn't get the minister's quotation from the Bible out of her head. "Let not your heart be troubled, neither let it be afraid." Probably not one person in a million ever went through life with an untroubled heart and the absence of fear, she thought. She certainly hadn't.

Py Bib and Joan's other classmates made the customary noises, reminiscing about high school days they'd shared with Joan, memories that meant nothing to Jeffrey, although he made a brave effort to seem heartened by what they said to him. Funerals demanded so much pretending.

Jeffrey's coworker Clarissa O'Neill was the only guest who gave him a hug. He caught a hint of jasmine as she leaned close. Clarissa squeezed Jeffrey's hand and passed on, thinking how different her friend looked. He appeared to have shed ten years, and he stood much straighter than she remembered, as if an invisible weight had been lifted from his shoulders. Jeffrey watched her walk away, observing what smashing legs she had. He'd never noticed before.

After the service, Jeffrey climbed into his shiny new Austin-Healey 3000. As he drove away, he turned on the radio. The Beatles were still bemoaning the fact that money couldn't buy them love. Jeffrey thought of Clarissa O'Neill and smiled. Clarissa knew how to laugh, and Jeffrey hadn't had much laughter in his life for years. After a decent interval of mourning had passed, maybe he'd ask her to accompany him on a Caribbean cruise, or they could travel to Europe and spend their days wandering the famous art galleries. There was so much in life to enjoy. They could even send their grumpy supervisor a postcard. For the first time in ages, Jeffrey Smollett was looking forward to the future.

While Joan Smollett's funeral was going on, pharmaceutical king William Price was playing golf at the Elkridge Country Club in Baltimore. He had his best round of the year and won five thousand dollars from another extravagant magnate.

It was Bib's turn to host his brother for Sunday dinner at his Georgetown townhouse. The evening assumed a familiar pattern, since Py usually asked the obliging Amara Brown to cook his favorite Jamaican meal—jerk chicken served with a green salad, rice, fried plantains, and coco bread. Py always brought along a couple of Jamaican Red Stripe beers for himself and a bouquet of a dozen long-stemmed red roses his friend Barbara selected for Amara's bedroom.

Amara had started their dinner the night before by rubbing the chicken with her homemade jerk sauce, made from a recipe handed down in her family for generations. The stars of the recipe were the fiery Scotch bonnet peppers beloved by Jamaicans. When combined with a lengthy list of spices, brown sugar, soy sauce, onion, garlic, and lime juice, the result was a pungent concoction fit to satisfy the taste buds of the most finicky islander—or two Yankee city slickers.

The brothers seated themselves on the patio to watch Amara tend the chicken on the beat-up barbecue grill Archie had bought years ago, back when he'd put on a show of knowing something about outdoor cooking to impress Phyllis and Sylvia. Somehow, Amara always managed to acquire a supply of pimento wood, which Jamaicans used to impart a sweet, smoky tang to their dishes. The aroma of the roasting chicken was enough to transport anyone who'd ever been to Jamaica back to those sunny shores.

"Amara, you're a treasure," Py declared. "That chicken smells fit for a king. When's it going to be ready, for goodness sake?"

Amara responded with a throaty chuckle and the common island saying "Soon come," which essentially meant "Hold your horses, it'll be ready when it's ready."

While Archie nursed his bottle of Canada Dry ginger ale and Py his Red Stripe, the setting sun burnished the limbs of the weeping cherry tree in the corner of the backyard. The tree's delicate blossoms had mostly fallen by now, covering the ground with a circular carpet of petals that were slowly turning brown. Archie's elderly neighbor lady's fluffy white Persian cat sat on the fence between their adjoining yards, drawn by the tantalizing smell of the chicken.

"Sorry, no handouts tonight, General Grant," Archie called to the animal. The cat squinted its eyes at its neighbor with an aggrieved look.

"How did Joan Smollett's funeral go?" Archie asked.

"It was a depressing affair. Despite Joan's towering ego and fierce dedication to her job, the woman isn't leaving behind much of a legacy. Jeffrey looked like a new man, though. Apparently, death becomes him." Py drained the last of his Red Stripe and set the bottle aside. "I heard you gave our staff a good quizzing this week. Learn anything of interest?"

"I learned lots of interesting things, but very little that's conclusive. The people I talked with fall into two camps. They either say Joan Smollett was an admirable woman who represented the best of National Geographic's traditions or she was a termagant that no one enjoyed working with. Take your pick."

"What about Jeffrey and his coworkers at the bank?"

"Nothing conclusive there either. Jeffrey came off as a hazy introvert when we spoke with him, except when he began talking about his hobby."

"Let me guess. Collecting stamps."

"No. He does watercolors, and darned good ones, too. He said he was sketching the cherry trees down at the Tidal Basin when Joan was killed."

"And the people at his bank?"

"That was the biggest surprise. We spoke with two of Jeffrey's fellow tellers, and both of them said he was a clever, engaging person when he was at work. We also talked with his supervisor, but that poor guy was suffering from a terminal case of general disgruntlement. We concluded that Jeffrey took his punishment at home without a whimper, and that he came alive when he was away from his wife."

"Nothing unique there. Humans often display wildly different personalities around different people. I remember being flabbergasted by a man I work with. I'd always regarded him as rather dull until I saw him at a party at another coworker's home. He was playing the classical guitar like an expert. He was ambidextrous and could play left-handed or right-handed. It was amazing. He knew Charlie Byrd and had sat in with Byrd's group at the Showboat Lounge, over on 18th Street."

"It's a miracle I ever solve any of my cases," Archie said, "what with suspects changing their personalities as easily as they change their clothes."

"Chicken about ready," Amara announced. "Give me five minutes to put everything together inside and dinner will be served."

"Thanks, Amara," Archie said. "We'll be in shortly." He turned to his brother. "I haven't mentioned the curare."

Py looked confused. "Curare? What about curare?"

"It's what killed Joan."

"That's one for the books. What have you found out?"

"The curare was administered by stabbing Joan in the neck with a thin sharp object. The only person connected with National Geographic who has a link to the poison is a freelance writer named Xander Riley. He's written a story on the head-hunting Jivaro tribe of Ecuador, and he brought back some Jivaro artifacts, including blowguns and poison darts."

"Did Riley have any connection with Joan?"

"She was fact-checking his article."

"Then it sounds like you've got your man."

"We interviewed him, and he of course denied having any animosity toward Joan. Then he pointed out that the folks who set up the exhibits in Explorers Hall have had some of his poison darts in storage for several weeks, so others could have had access to them."

"I take it you spoke with Peter Nance."

"We interviewed Mr. Nance and everyone who works for him. None of them appear to have any motive to harm Joan, and it would have been difficult for an outsider to slip into the room where the darts were stored and make off with one."

Py looked pensive. "Curare, curare. What was I reading about that recently? Oh yes, I read an article about there being potential new medical uses for curare. It's been used for decades to treat certain diseases, including epilepsy. A fair amount of research is being devoted to developing additional uses."

"You're not suggesting that a medical researcher killed Joan, are you?"

"Yes and no. Bill Price's pharmaceutical company up in Baltimore might be experimenting with curare. I don't want to cast any aspersions, but we know that Bill seemed to have an axe to grind with Joan."

"You're right, and we also know that Bill has anger issues. Remember what I said about him still smashing his hand against walls?"

Amara stuck her head out the patio door. "Dinner," she called in her lilting voice.

Archie and Py got up and gathered their empty bottles.

"Matt Dowden and I may have to take a road trip tomorrow," Archie said.

For a little while, crime was forgotten as Archie, Py, and Amara sat down at the dinner table and gave themselves over to the wondrous sensations of jerk chicken. Amara even provided the music, a bootleg collection by a new Jamaican group calling themselves The Wailers. Archie was partial to their song "One Love."

Chapter 17

Monday and Tuesday

The next morning, Bib realized at once that he'd made a mistake. Matthew Dowden could negotiate the busy streets of Washington with ease, driving with forceful confidence. On the highway to Baltimore, however, he revealed a frightening habit. He was a tailgater.

As the sergeant cruised perilously close to the bumpers of the vehicles ahead of them, Bib very nearly pushed his right foot through the floorboard stomping on an imaginary brake pedal. Finally, he couldn't stand it any longer.

"Sergeant, what's the recommended distance between cars traveling on the highway?"

"A car length for every ten miles per hour of speed."

"And how fast are you going?"

"Sixty-five."

"And how long is a Ford Galaxie sedan?"

"About seventeen feet."

"Let me see, if my calculations are correct, that would mean there should be at least a hundred feet between our car and that tractor-trailer ahead of us. How far ahead would you estimate the truck actually is?"

"Um, maybe twenty feet. Sorry, sir."

Bib sat back with relief as the sergeant slowed down to allow the recommended interval between vehicles.

The drive to Baltimore took a little over an hour due to the heavy Monday morning traffic. Sergeant Dowden located Price Pharmaceuticals with ease. He had the homing instincts of a pigeon. The large two-story building was in an industrial park in the north of the city, with a prominent sign out front. No one could miss the fact that William Price had arrived.

At the imposing first-floor reception counter, Inspector Bib asked to speak with Price.

"Do you have an appointment?" the young woman behind the counter inquired.

Bib showed her his badge.

"Oh, I see." The young woman picked up the phone and dialed Price's office. "Hello, Betty, there are two policemen here who would like to speak with Mr. Price."

The receptionist gave Bib a taut smile while she waited for Price's secretary to check with her boss. "Yes," she said when the secretary came back on. "All right, I'll tell them."

"Mr. Price will be happy to see you. Room 201. Take the elevator to your left."

Bill Price was waiting in the reception area outside his office when Bib and Dowden appeared. "Archie," Price boomed. "You're a little off your usual beat. What brings you up here to my neck of the woods?"

"Hello, Bill. This is Sergeant Dowden. We'd like to ask you a couple of questions relating to the murder of Joan Smollett. You know about her death, I assume."

The welcoming veneer faded from Price's face like the sun going behind a cloud. "Sure, I read all about it. A real tragedy. I don't know what I can tell you, but come on in my office and we can talk."

Price's office was roughly the size of a basketball court. The expansive rear windows looked out over a parklike setting, where the company's workers could take their lunch breaks in good weather. The walls of the office were hung with photos of Price glad-handing well-dressed businessmen. There were also photos of Price playing golf and others where he was standing next to various dead animals with a rifle in hand and a smarmy grin on his face. Bib took it all in with a rising feeling of distaste.

"Have a seat," Price said as he ensconced himself behind his massive desk. "Now what can I do for you?" he asked once his guests were settled.

Bib knew that if he conveyed the slightest impression that Price was under suspicion in a homicide case the man would likely blow up and they'd get nowhere. He decided to take a different tack, one that played on Price's vanity. "We could use your expertise in getting a handle on a technical issue, Bill."

Price appeared to relax. "Be glad to help if I can. What sort of issue are we talking about?"

"Our medical examiner says Joan was killed with curare."

"I'll be damned," Price said. "That stuff can be lethal all right, but it also holds real promise for use in medicine. You might not know it, but we've been doing some research to develop new medical uses for curare. It could be worth a fortune. Hell, the Amazon rainforest probably has hundreds of unidentified plant species that could help with all kinds of medical problems."

"Then we've come to the right person."

"I'm no scientist, Archie. All I can tell you is that curare can kill if introduced into the bloodstream. Beyond that, you'd have to speak with one of my lab boys."

"That would be great. And I hope you wouldn't mind if we had a look around your plant. I've never visited a pharmaceutical company before. It must be interesting."

"Sure, we get school groups all the time." Price buzzed his secretary and asked her to have his public relations man report to his office.

"Dick Phelps will give you a tour and get you to the right person to answer your questions," Price told them.

Bib stood up to leave. "Thanks very much, Bill." He paused in the doorway. "I was sorry to miss some of the reunion events. Did you make it to all of them?"

"Every one," Price said. "Had a lot of fun."

"That must have been tiring. When did you make it home?"

"Left D.C. on Sunday afternoon. It was quiet when I got back. My wife's out in Palm Springs, basking in the sunshine."

Bib waved goodbye. "Good to see you, and thanks again for the help."

Price's PR man was waiting in the outer office. He led Bib and Dowden down the hall. As soon as the two policemen were out of sight, Price buzzed his secretary again. "Give Gus Richards a call and tell him to have my Learjet ready as soon as he can. I've decided to join Marybeth in Palm Springs. I can't let her have all the fun."

Dick Phelps fit Bib's image of a corporate representative. Tall and serious, Phelps spoke with the voice of authority. "I understand you'd like to see a little of our operation. Most of what we do is too technical for the average visitor to fully comprehend, but we do have some displays that give a general idea of how a pharmaceutical company operates."

"Bill told us you're doing research on possible medical uses for curare," Bib said.

"We are, but you should know that Price Pharmaceuticals does a limited amount of original research."

"Isn't research the lifeblood of pharmaceutical companies?"

"That's true for the mega companies, but Mr. Price saw a way to run a viable business without the big costs incurred in research. We wait until the patents have expired on marketable drugs, and then we produce generic versions. Since the companies that created those drugs spent millions in research, they have to charge hefty prices to recoup their investment, but with our generic versions we can undercut their prices substantially. That simple strategy has made Bill Price a millionaire many times over."

"He seems a clever man."

"Extremely clever."

The tour that Bib and Dowden were given was superficial. They were shown a few exhibits that might have entertained schoolchildren and a model lab that wasn't much more than what Bib remembered from his college science classes. He didn't ask to interview any scientists about curare. What he wanted was a chance to question one of Price's employees in private to gain insight on the boss.

That opportunity came after Phelps concluded his tour and escorted Bib and Dowden back to the first-floor reception area. "I hope you gentlemen have a safe trip home," Phelps said with the practiced solicitousness of a PR specialist.

"Thanks for showing us around," Bib said. He hesitated. "Would you mind if we used the men's room before we headed back to Washington. It's a long drive."

"Of course," Phelps said. "Down the hallway on your right."

Once Phelps disappeared, Bib and Dowden meandered down the hall. Bib stopped in front of the first open door they came to. A studious-looking young man sitting behind a desk looked up from a thick ledger. "May I help you?" he asked.

Bib showed the man his badge. "I wonder if you could spare a moment to chat with us. My sergeant and I are curious about what it's like to work for a successful businessman like William Price."

An impish smile lit the young man's face. "C'mon in," he said. "And shut the door."

Bib and Dowden did as the fellow asked. "Thank you very much," Bib said, "and I promise you that anything you tell us will be off the record."

"Very well then. So you want to know what it's like to work for Bill Price. I imagine if you asked almost anyone here for their candid opinion, they'd say that Price is a royal pain in the keister. They'd most likely tell you that he's an arrogant man who's jealous of anyone who makes him feel inferior and who takes pleasure in subjugating his employees."

"In other words," Bib said, "he's not as good at personal relationships as he is at business."

"If you want the definitive story on Bill Price's personal relationships, you should speak with his trophy wives."

"Wives? How many does he have?"

"He's on his fourth. He treats them all like merchandise, and once they show a bit of age, or if he gets tired of them, he trades them in for a newer model, just like he does with his expensive foreign cars."

The man winked. "Of course, I'd never say any of this about Mr. Price myself. I think he's a saint, the most brilliant, humble, generous human being I've ever met. I would mention that one trait most successful businessmen share is that they know how to take advantage of others, and William Price is an excellent businessman."

Bib pushed his glasses back in place. "Thank you for your honesty."

Out in the parking lot, Bib slipped into the driver's seat for the trip back to Washington. He wasn't feeling up to having his sergeant behind the wheel. "That was helpful," he said to Dowden. "It sounds like Bill Price wouldn't win any Boss of the Year awards."

Dowden was looking over a company brochure he'd picked up. On the back was a photo of William Price, CEO and grand pooh-bah of the whole shebang. "I know he's your high school classmate, sir, but I wouldn't trust this guy with my lunch money. He strikes me as the type of rich old boy who thinks he can get away with anything."

Dowden held out the photo of Price for Bib to see. "Maybe we should show this to the National Geographic guard who was on duty the day of the murder. See if he happened to notice if this mug was prowling around Explorers Hall."

"That, my esteemed colleague, is an excellent idea."

By late afternoon, William Price was sprawled asleep on a poolside chaise lounge at the exclusive La Quinta Resort in Palm Springs, California. The brawny, hairy-chested mogul could have passed for a bear in hibernation. Lying next to him was his young wife, the former Marybeth Sanders. Marybeth still possessed the charms that had won her the Miss Maryland title in 1960, charms that had caught the eye of William Price as he watched the pageant on television with his soon to be jettisoned third wife.

The talent that Marybeth demonstrated at the beauty pageant was singing and playing the acoustic guitar. Her rollicking rendition of the Hank Williams country classic "Jambalaya" had the audience bouncing in their seats. Marybeth's short fringed skirt and white cowboy hat set at a flirtatious angle had the male judges thinking shameful thoughts, and the way she wiggled about to the lively tune added several points to their scorecards.

The audience had no idea that Marybeth couldn't play any other song on the guitar. With only two chords, G7 and C, "Jambalaya" was one of the easiest songs in the universe to master, especially since all Marybeth did was strum. As to her singing, her infectious enthusiasm went a long way in overcoming her deficiencies, and when she shouted, "C'mon, everybody, sing along," she had the crown within her reach.

Marybeth's musical performance scored well, but what put her over the top was her true talent—parading around the stage wearing a winsome smile and the few square inches of cloth of a bright red bikini. She'd perfected the art of displaying her assets to best advantage through hours of practice, posing in front of her bedroom mirror in her underwear night after night. Although her stage routine was simple, it merited praise. As Marybeth later declared, she put as much effort into her dipping and swirling as that perky little bitch from Takoma Park put into her fancy-schmancy Chopin prelude.

Marybeth had also put a good deal of effort into negotiating the terms of the prenuptial agreement she signed with William Price. Even though she considered her husband a loathsome brute, she found it hard to resist the high six-figure sum she would receive should their marriage come to sad and unforeseen termination, an event she prayed for every night.

Marybeth regarded Price as he slept. Why did he have to show up and spoil the fun she was having with Troy, the resort tennis pro? Ah well, it wouldn't be long now before the lout grew tired of her and she could get on with her life, in a significantly better financial condition.

Just then Bill Price emerged from hibernation with a stupefied look. "Hey, babe," he said, rubbing his eyes with his meaty fists. "Why don't you slip over to the bar and grab me another mai tai. And get one for yourself."

"Sure, hon."

Price ogled his young wife's prizewinning backside as she dipped and swirled toward the poolside bar. When Marybeth returned with their drinks, Price touched his glass to hers and took a sip. "You know, babe," he said. "I've been thinking. Why don't we hang around for a few more days? I'm in no hurry to get back to Baltimore, and I wouldn't mind playing a little golf out here."

Yippee, Marybeth said to herself. She wouldn't have to say goodbye yet to her boy toy, Troy. "Sounds swell, hon. I was going to suggest that. You don't get to play nearly enough golf back home, and out here you've got lots of courses and all the partners you could want. I'll bet you could beat the pants off most of them, too."

Marybeth gave him her Cheshire cat smile of faux marital bliss. "And while you're enjoying your golf, I can take a few more tennis lessons. You wouldn't believe how much better I've gotten in the short time since I've been here." Marybeth checked her wristwatch. "As a matter of fact, I have another lesson scheduled in half an hour, so I'd better scoot on back to our room and change."

While Marybeth was scooting, Price cast an appreciative glance at the curvaceous, top-heavy cabana girl, whose name, he'd learned, was Wendy Gibbs. Wendy was an ambitious young lady. She was hoping her new silicone breast implants would help her land a fat cat sugar daddy. She didn't know how much longer she could continue supplying aging, leering tycoons with liquor solely for tips. She wanted the whole cookie jar, not the crumbs.

As Wendy bobbled past in her short shorts and halter top, Price raised his mai tai in salute. "Nice afternoon, Wendy."

"It sure is, Mr. Price."

"Please, call me Bill."

Wendy giggled and gave him a dramatic profile view.

171

The next morning at 10 a.m., Bill Price took a few warm-up swings on the first tee at La Quinta Country Club, a desert course popular with movie stars, champion golfers, and dedicated duffers such as former President Eisenhower, whose political opponents complained that while he was in office he spent more time on the Palm Springs golf courses than in the White House.

Price's playing partner was a rotund shoe manufacturer named Roscoe Fortescue. Price had met Fortescue in the hotel bar, and he disliked the man from the get-go, not only for his corny jokes—Fortescue said that making shoes had left him well heeled—but also for his ridiculous names. To Price, Roscoe sounded like a name you'd give a mule, and Fortescue reminded him of a mincing British dandy.

"What say we make it interesting?" Price said before his first shot. "A thousand a hole?"

"All right by me," said Fortescue. He'd sized up Price as an easy mark, a lumbering oaf who thought sheer power was the key to golf. Fortescue may have resembled the Pillsbury Doughboy, but he had a swing as sweet as Slammin' Sammy Snead's. By the fourth hole he was four thousand to the good. That's when Bill Price got resourceful. However, despite Price's foot wedges to improve his lie in the rough and his creative scorekeeping, Roscoe Fortescue walked away with a check for a tidy eighteen grand at the end of their game.

That was chicken feed to Price, but the indignity of losing— especially to a tubby nincompoop like Fortescue—rankled. The only way to repair his damaged ego that Price could think of was to make a conquest in some other sphere. His mind naturally turned to Wendy Gibbs. That afternoon, after Marybeth scooted off for another tennis lesson, Price smothered the cabana girl with attention. It was a pairing that promised mutual benefits. As far as Miss Gibbs was concerned, Price gave every indication of fitting nicely into the financial category she was hoping for. She, on the other hand, fulfilled Price's emerging fancy for a buxom new bimbo.

Before long, the avaricious Miss Gibbs was wrestling with a trained bear named Bill in her staff quarters. Little did they know that in another room not far down the hallway, Marybeth had gone love-all with tennis pro Troy No Last Name, a blond Adonis whose forehand was a thing of beauty. He was a master of his racket.

That evening at dinner, Price told Marybeth how much he'd enjoyed his day.

"Good round, hon?" Marybeth inquired.

"You could say that."

The couple agreed they would stay on at La Quinta for the rest of the week.

Chapter 18

Tuesday

Washington's Tabard Inn had been welcoming diners and overnight guests since 1922. Named for the English hostelry in Geoffrey Chaucer's *Canterbury Tales,* the Tabard Inn occupied a prime location on N Street off Dupont Circle, a few blocks from National Geographic headquarters. Out front, the inn featured the whimsically wild landscaping of an English garden, which echoed the artsy, unconventional décor inside. In the Tabard Inn's early days, local society ladies sipped their tea and exchanged gossip in cozy comfort. During World War II, the inn served as a boarding house for women in the Navy.

Tonight, the Tabard Inn welcomed the brothers Bib. After Archie's trip to visit Bill Price in Baltimore, Py was anxious to learn if his brother was any closer to identifying Joan Smollett's curare-wielding killer. They found a quiet corner in the inn's spacious old lounge, a wood-paneled sanctuary with vintage furniture, heavy beams on the ceiling, quaint old prints on the walls, and a stone fireplace that could have warmed Chaucer's motley collection of pilgrims while they spun their tales of life in 14th-century England.

Py Bib was friends with the manager of the Tabard Inn, who made sure the brothers were comfortable before sending a waitress by to take their order. They decided on a light meal of gazpacho and Caesar salad, even though the menu included some inviting Southern favorites. Archie ordered a tonic and lime and Py a glass of Chardonnay.

Their young waitress was dressed all in black, with a distinctive tattoo on her left forearm, a fearsome red dragon. "Celtic?" Py inquired, pointing at the tattoo. That brought a polite smile to the girl's pretty face. "And if I'm not mistaken," he continued, "that's the red Welsh dragon that defeated the white dragon of the Saxons, which was supposedly a harbinger of the eventual defeat of the English."

"You know your mythology," the girl said.

Py gave his brother a crafty look after the girl left. "I can't resist trying to impress young ladies. And the dragon was easy to identify. It's on the national flag of Wales."

"Shall I call her back and tell her you're not quite as clever as you appear to be?"

"Heavens, no. That little ploy will guarantee the girl keeps an eye on our table."

"You're really slick with your inducements. Amara goes on and on about you after your visits. I guess a dozen red roses is all it takes to make someone a knight in shining armor."

"It's not just the roses," Py said. "It's how you present them to a lady that counts. Sir Lancelot didn't win Guinevere's love by tossing a bouquet of flowers at her. You've got to make the lady feel special. That's easy to do with Amara, since she is special."

Archie looked into the middle distance. Py didn't realize how close to the mark he'd come. Without Amara, Archie knew he couldn't go on living in a home with so many memories.

"All right, let's have it," Py said. "What did you learn about our questionable classmate William Price?"

"I learned that he runs his empire up there in Baltimore with the Midas touch. His public relations man said his company undercuts the competition by producing mostly generic drugs. And they are doing research on curare, so Price could nab some if he wanted to.

"One unexpected thing I learned is that Bill is a big game hunter. His office is full of photographs of himself with his trophies. I've always been leery of big game hunters. Maybe it's an unfair assumption, but they strike me as trying a little too hard to emphasize their manliness—especially dilettantes like Bill, who have no reason to hunt other than for thrills. The idea of killing animals for sport makes me cringe."

175

"The psychology of men who hunt is fascinating," Py said. "For some of them, it stems from deep-seated primal instincts, the old caveman with a club routine. Interestingly, hunters often proclaim their love of the animals they kill, which seems a tad contradictory, although Native Americans revered the animals they depended on, like the buffalo."

"My bet is that Bill Price hunts to prove something to himself," Archie said. "You have to wonder if he might want to test himself against 'the most dangerous game'—another human, like that crazy Russian did in the old Joel McCrea movie."

"That premise made for an exciting tale," Py said, "but in real life, it would be a stretch." He sat back as their waitress set their chilled soup and crisp romaine salads in front of them. He tasted the gazpacho. "Mm, just like mother used to make."

Archie cocked an eyebrow. Their mother had been better at math than cooking. "Matt Dowden and I had a revealing conversation with a young man who works for Price," he said. "We asked him what Price is like as a boss, and the young fellow said that he's arrogant, jealous of others, and runs roughshod over his employees as well as his wives, of which there have been four so far. Bill sounds a lot like your golfing buddy Rob—always putting himself first."

"He could be exhibiting Rob's narcissism," Py said. "That might explain his taunting of Joan Smollett with the copy of *Don Quixote*. He may have been trying to say 'I'm better than you,' which would be consistent with narcissistic behavior."

"Are narcissists prone to violence?" Archie asked.

"They can be. There are actually different types of narcissists. One includes people who think they're infallible and all powerful. They feel they deserve special treatment, and they display little empathy or compassion. Another type includes people who feel aggrieved due to envy or resentment of others. Their unhappiness makes them crave attention. Both types can explode in rage if they feel slighted, and neither can tolerate criticism. No one likes to admit being wrong, but narcissists just can't do it."

"Amiable folks," Archie said.

"One factor to be aware of is that narcissists tend to be bullies and cowards. They often try to mask their own fears and inadequacies by picking on the weak or defenseless, and that doesn't always mean physical violence. A bully can get his kicks just by intimidating, embarrassing, or making fun of someone. Given those considerations, it's possible that Bill Price could be nothing more than a run-of-the-mill head case."

"Maybe so, but I'm keeping him on my list of suspects for now. In the long history of crime, there are sure to have been plenty of bullies who committed murder."

"Of course. All psychology can do is suggest probabilities. There are few certainties where humans are concerned. I would point out that a man with Bill Price's personality would more likely commit murder in a fit of anger. The use of curare to kill Joan indicates forethought."

"You do like complicating things, don't you?"

"What's a brother for?"

Archie took a sip of his drink. "We discovered one other important piece of information when we spoke with Bill. He has no confirmable alibi for the time of the murder. He told us he drove home Sunday afternoon and that his wife was out of town, so there's no way for him to prove that he didn't make a quick stop at National Geographic to repay some old debt. And despite probabilities and personalities, we can't dismiss the fact that he's one of only two people we know of who had access to curare."

"Where does this leave your investigation?"

"Matt and I discussed all the suspects on the drive home from Baltimore. We kept coming back to Xander Riley as the leading candidate. First, there's the fact that he doesn't have a confirmable alibi either. He said he was jogging on the Mall at the time of the murder."

"Yeah, him and dozens of other guys."

"Even more incriminating is the fact that he was working with Joan on his story about headhunters, and that she was having to put in quite a lot of extra time in checking over his manuscript. There could have been disagreements that might have set him off."

"Have you found out why it took Joan longer than usual to check his story?"

"Riley claimed it was because the article is set in a remote part of Ecuador."

"Maybe he's one of those writers who are defensive about their copy, not wanting anyone to change a word. That can lead to confrontations. The opposite of those touchy fellows are the writers who don't care if an editor's red pencil leaves their manuscript looking like it's bleeding, as long as they get paid. If I were an editor, I'd prefer to work with the ones who fight to preserve their writing, since to me that would indicate a greater commitment to their story. Someone who doesn't care one way or the other what an editor does to their copy would make me wonder how much time they actually devoted to the piece."

"Which kind of writer are you?"

"I'm an exceptionally careful writer who never makes mistakes and is a delight to work with."

"Modesty always was your strong point."

"To be honest, with the popular psychology stories I write, I'm happy to have a researcher or editor back me up. I spend so much time trying to make complicated concepts understandable for general readers that it's easy to bollix up the minutiae. Believe me, I'd rather undergo a severe edit than see my name on a story that's full of howlers. You can never live those down."

"Let me ask you a question that we asked the people we interviewed at National Geographic. Do you think it's possible for a writer to get so worked up over a story that he'd resort to murder?"

"The circumstances would have to be far from normal. Offhand, I can't think of a thing that might lead a National Geographic writer to kill someone."

"That's what everyone else said. Unfortunately, in my line of work, the circumstances usually are far from normal."

Just then their server stopped by to check on them. "Can I get you anything else?"

"We'll have another round of drinks," Py said.

"I'm not halfway done with my first drink," Archie said as the girl walked away.

"I know, but I wanted to make her feel useful. She seems really nice."

"You mean cute."

"Is she cute? I hadn't noticed."

"Getting back to reality," Archie said, "there are three other people I can't rule out. First there's Jeffrey Smollett, a man who was browbeaten by his wife to an extraordinary degree for years. Most men would have left a woman like that, but Jeffrey stuck by her side."

"Do you have any idea how many men and women remain with spouses they no longer care for?" Py asked. "I'm talking about people who can barely stand to be in the same room together."

"I'm guessing you're going to say a lot."

"From what I've read, the number is extraordinarily high, and mainly for one reason. Most people are afraid of change. They're hesitant to alter the routine of their lives. They worry about where they'd go if they left, how they'd handle their finances, that sort of thing. Hard as it is to believe, some men stick with a wife they can no longer tolerate simply because they don't want to have to do their own laundry."

"You make a splendid advocate for marriage."

Py held up his left hand and wiggled his fingers. "Do you happen to see a ring?"

Archie glanced at the wedding ring on his own left hand, which he'd never taken off since Phyllis passed away. Py saw his brother's reaction and immediately felt ashamed of his remark. "You were one of the lucky ones," he said quietly. Archie forced a smile.

"Any convincing argument for suspecting mild-mannered Jeffrey Smollett?" Py asked. "He didn't appear to be gloating at Joan's funeral."

"Three. The insurance money, his flimsy alibi, and his split personality. The records are filled with examples of mild-mannered men who murdered their wives. And they often do it with poison, although I've never read about a case in which the husband used curare. That's why Jeffrey is far down on my list of suspects. There doesn't seem to be any way he could get a supply of curare. However, that's not true of your assistant head of research, Rebecca Wimberly. It's a long shot, but she might have obtained one of those poison darts that were in storage. Maybe she bribed one of the Explorers Hall workmen. She'd have plenty of money for that."

"Sounds to me like you're clutching at straws," Py commented. "I'd say she's an even more unlikely killer than Jeffrey Smollett."

"Do you know her?"

"Only to say hello."

"I'm ashamed to admit it, but I took an instant dislike of the woman. She struck me as a real Lucrezia Borgia type—vain, haughty, privileged. I wouldn't want to share a glass of wine with her for fear she might add a pinch of arsenic. It wouldn't take much imagination to see her eliminating anyone who stood in the way of her getting what she wanted. And from what I've learned, she very much wanted Joan Smollett's job."

"Is that right? I miss out on all the juicy office intrigues stuck in my ninth-floor aerie."

"One of the junior researchers claims Wimberly hated Joan. We haven't gone any further in looking into Wimberly, but if all the other candidates wash out, we may have to do that." Archie sighed. "Maybe we'll catch a break soon."

"You said you had three other subjects you couldn't rule out. Who's the third one?"

"The other possibility is someone I call Suspect X."

"And who might that be?"

"An individual that we haven't yet identified who was clever enough to lay their hands on one of the poison darts. It seems improbable that an unauthorized person could have slipped into the Explorers Hall storage room, but I've been surprised before by the ingenuity of murderers. We once arrested a marathon runner who learned to scale the side of a building just to be able to gain access to the apartment where his ex-girlfriend lived. He might have gotten away with her murder if he hadn't fallen three stories and broken both of his legs while he was making his getaway. The perp didn't run any more marathons after that."

"What does Sergeant Dowden think about the case?"

"Matt's usually closemouthed, but I could tell he thought I was crazy for releasing Xander Riley. He may have a point. We're having a devil of a time finding out anything about the man's background. According to public records, he seems to have materialized out of nowhere a couple of years ago. We need to pull him in again and press him for details on who he is and where he came from. All we know is that he says he grew up in an orphanage and knocked around a bit before taking up writing."

"That's nebulous, although it makes for a romantic resume. You know, poor orphan boy makes good."

"Romantic or not, I don't like loose ends." Archie chuckled. "I forgot to mention something else we saw in Bill Price's office. There were photos of him playing golf. Maybe the two of you should get together."

"No thanks. I already have a wacko partner I can play with."

"Matt had an inspired idea about Price. He picked up a company brochure with Bill's photograph on it and suggested showing it to the guard who was on duty in Explorers Hall on the fatal day."

"And?"

"The guard told us that he'd never seen the man. We also showed him a photo of Xander Riley. He said he recognized Riley but didn't recall seeing him the day of the murder."

The girl with the tattoo reappeared, but Archie and Py had finished their dinners and were ready to leave. "You can bring our check, please," Py said with a wink.

When the girl returned with the bill, Py paid in cash, leaving a hefty tip. He then thanked the girl in Welsh to see how she'd react. *"Diolch,"* he said.

"Croeso," she responded.

The girl took a Tabard Inn business card from her apron and wrote on the back of it. She laid the card on the table in front of Py, gave him a sweet look, and walked away.

On the back of the card was a telephone number.

Archie dropped off Py at his apartment and drove on home. He could smell coffee when he walked in the door. Amara had made a fresh pot before retiring to her bedroom, where she always watched television before going to sleep. Her favorite shows were comedies. Bib could hear her laughter all the way in the kitchen while he was pouring a cup of coffee.

He took his coffee into his study, where he put on the new Glenn Miller LP he'd bought recently. *The Best of Glenn Miller* had many of his wife's favorite songs on it, including "In the Mood," which came out the year they were married. Every time Bib listened to the song, he thought of dancing the swing with Phyllis, something he'd never done with any other woman. He was a reluctant dancer, but Phyllis got so much joy from whirling about to the music that he led her onto the floor whenever she grabbed his hand and said "Let's dance," always with a joyous smile.

Bib settled into his easy chair and listened to the music with a smile on his own face. He looked around the room, which was filled with mementoes from the happiest years of his life. Across the room was the enormous rolltop desk he and Phyllis had discovered in an antique shop in Clarendon, Virginia. The desk had been in bad shape, but Phyllis spent an entire summer refinishing it, which was why he would never get rid of it, even though it took up half the room.

Bib picked up his copy of the highly praised novel *To Kill a Mockingbird,* which he'd been trying to get into for a week or more. It was an amazing story, but every time he started reading it, the character of Atticus Finch's daughter Scout led him to think of his own daughter, and the next thing he knew he was reminiscing about Sylvia's childhood years, a golden stage that seemed like a fleeting dream.

Bib laid the book aside and concentrated on the music. "Don't Sit Under the Apple Tree with Anyone Else But Me" was playing now. The song had been a hit during World War II. Its lyrics told the story of a young couple pledging to remain true to one another while the man was away during the war. Bib had served with many men who'd given in to temptation during their years in Europe, but the very notion of being unfaithful to Phyllis had repelled him to the point of physical illness. The only thing that had kept him sane during those terrifying years was the thought of Phyllis and their baby girl waiting for him back home.

He turned off the phonograph and went to bed before he disappeared down the rabbit hole of longing for the past.

Chapter 19

Riley displayed his Hollywood-perfect teeth in a captivating smile, turning up his lady-killer persona to maximum voltage. At his best, he could charm a princess out of her tiara. Rebecca Wimberly seemed receptive to the man's charisma. She sat across the table from him on the shady brick patio of the Iron Gate, a popular N Street restaurant in the same block as the Tabard Inn. Lush banks of wisteria enclosed the patio, creating the feeling of sitting in a private garden in Greece or southern Italy. Riley made certain that Wimberly would notice the absurdly expensive Breitling wristwatch he was wearing by touching his chin. He knew that he had her within his grasp when he saw her appraising it.

"I can't tell you how much I appreciate your agreeing to have lunch with me, Ms. Wimberly," Riley oozed.

"It's my pleasure. And please, call me Rebecca." Wimberly was confident she was dealing with someone from her own social set. Class will tell, she said to herself.

"All right, Rebecca. And I hope I'm not being too forward if I ask you to call me Xander."

"I'd love to. I've never known anyone before with such an unusual name. Is it short for Alexander?"

"I don't know. One of the nuns in the orphanage where I grew up chose it. She said it's from the Bible, and that it means 'defender of man,' although I can't think why she'd have given me such a grandiose name."

"Perhaps that part of your life is yet to come."

Riley doubted it. The only man he intended to defend was Numero Uno. "By the way, I want to congratulate you on your promotion. I heard you've been made the new head of the editorial research department." A liberal application of butter always helped.

"Thank you, Xander. Actually, I've been named the interim department head."

"I'm sure that's just a formality. You're the natural successor. The powers that be probably feel they should wait a bit after Mrs. Smollett's funeral before they name her permanent replacement. Decorum and all that."

"It would be an honor should it come to pass, and I'll have some big shoes to fill. Joan Smollett was such a towering figure."

"She was, although she could be tough on writers. Or maybe it was just me."

"No, I think Mrs. Smollett was uncompromising with all the writers she worked with. She was excellent at her job, but her occasional severity did strike some of us as excessive. I think you'll find a different atmosphere in the research department from now on."

"That's great to hear, Rebecca. Do you know that Mrs. Smollett had the gall to accuse me of manufacturing some of the incidents I described in my story about Ecuador? I was never so angry in my life. A writer's reputation is everything, and I've worked hard to make a good name for myself."

"I wouldn't worry about that. Whatever Mrs. Smollett did is all in the past, including any unwarranted criticisms."

Riley breathed easy for the first time since that old bat Smollett had begun to home in on his sham adventuring.

When the waiter came to take their order, Wimberly laid her menu aside. "Why don't you order for us, Xander. I'm sure I can rely on your judgment."

Ann Parker wasn't very happy with her latest assignment. As a junior researcher, she was often given less desirable stories to work on. But this job stunk. After Rebecca Wimberly boarded her golden chariot and ascended to her new role as interim head of editorial research, she'd given Parker the lowly task of clearing out Joan Smollett's office. Wimberly told her to box up all of Smollett's personal items for her husband. Parker was then supposed to make an inventory of Smollett's work files so that Wimberly could reassign the stories.

Parker was muttering to herself as she went through Smollett's desk. Stirring around in someone else's private junk made her feel unclean. Fortunately, she didn't find much that could be classified as private. There were no photos of Smollett's family, so the only things Parker found to add to the box to send home were a manila folder conveniently labeled "Personal" and a few strange knickknacks—a fortune-telling Magic 8 Ball, a ceramic rooster, a pencil holder with the University of Virginia logo, and, for some odd reason, a toy mousetrap. The most surprising thing she found was a copy of Dale Carnegie's *How to Win Friends and Influence People.* Now there's a book Smollett never bothered to read, Parker told herself.

Setting the box aside, Parker began going through the file organizer on Smollett's desk. Mrs. Smollett had been working on several stories, most recently an article on African wild dogs and Xander Riley's story about the headhunting Jivaros of Ecuador. Wild dogs didn't appeal to Parker all that much, but she decided to take a look inside the Riley folder. She'd always wondered how someone could shrink a human head. When she opened the folder, she found a brief typed note on top. Parker drew in her breath as she scanned the note. Mrs. Smollett had outlined her doubts about Riley having visited some of the places in Ecuador he wrote about. She cited a number of instances that seemed to prove Riley was a fraud.

The most shocking part of the note was the handwritten addendum at the bottom. "When I confronted Mr. Riley with these examples of his dubious claims, he said I would face serious consequences if I ever mentioned my suspicions to anyone." Smollett's signature appeared below the addendum.

Ann Parker sat staring at the note, then she took the folder next door to Rebecca Wimberly's office. When Parker tapped on the door, Wimberly looked up with an expression of annoyance. "Finished already?" she asked sourly.

"Not yet," Parker replied, "but I found something interesting." Parker laid the open folder on Wimberly's desk and pointed to Smollett's note. "I think we should show this to the police," she said.

Wimberly quickly read the note. She looked at Parker, then she closed the folder and gave it back to her. The snobbish researcher pictured the handsome, cultivated writer she'd just had lunch with. He was a paragon compared with the vulgar woman whose position she'd rightfully be assuming.

"This is delusional nonsense," Wimberly said. "Mr. Riley would never do what she claims. Take this folder back where you found it. And get rid of the note."

Parker didn't know how to respond. This was important evidence in a murder case, and her superior was telling her to destroy it. She returned to Smollett's office and put the folder away. She slipped the note into her purse.

Parker spoke softly into the telephone. "Inspector Bib, this is Ann Parker, one of the staff members you interviewed at National Geographic."

Bib grinned as he recalled the feisty young researcher. "What can I do for you, Miss Parker?"

"I have a document you need to see, but we can't meet here at headquarters. Do you know the coffee shop on M Street near our building?"

"Yes, but why the mystery?"

"I can't talk about it right now. How soon could you meet me there?"

"Twenty minutes. Do you mind if I bring along Sergeant Dowden?"

"It might be better if a uniformed policeman didn't show up. People would be curious."

When Bib walked into the coffee shop, he spotted Ann Parker sitting at a table in a far corner. She was hard to miss. She wore a bright orange skirt with a vivid pink sweater, like two different flavors of sorbet. She had her back to the door, but

Bib recognized the petite researcher's short brown hair. "I hope I haven't kept you waiting," he said as he took a seat. Bib noticed that Parker's spunky attitude was missing. "Now, what about this document you spoke of?"

Parker looked around to make sure no one from her office was in the coffee shop. "What I'm going to show you may relate to Mrs. Smollett's murder," she said. "But you have to know that giving you this could get me in big trouble with my boss." She took Smollett's note from her purse and slid it across the table. "Rebecca Wimberly told me to destroy this, so if she ever finds out that I gave it to you, my career at National Geographic could be over."

Bib picked up the note and read it twice. He laid the note on the table and looked at the brave young woman who was putting her job on the line to bring this to his attention. "You say Rebecca Wimberly told you to destroy this?"

"Yes," Parker whispered.

"Suppression of evidence in a murder investigation carries a stiff penalty," Bib said.

"Oh boy. I'm gonna be sacked for this."

"No, young lady, you're not. You're going to be credited for your courage. Rebecca Wimberly won't be going to jail because of what she did, and she won't be retaliating against you either. I promise you that."

Inspector Bib tapped on the open door of associate editor Vernon Hall's eighth-floor office. "Good afternoon, Dr. Hall," Bib said. "Do you have a couple of minutes?"

"Sure. C'mon in and have a seat. I could use a break. I've been going over the travel expenses of one of our most profligate staff writers. One charge he's turned in on his recent trip to Libya is for 'camel rental.' Can you beat that? I wonder if Avis runs the camel concession."

Bib laughed and took a seat. "I need to acquaint you with a new development and ask for your advice. Your young researcher Ann Parker gave me an important document this afternoon. It's a note from Mrs. Smollett that could prove crucial in solving her murder."

"What sort of note?"

Bib handed Hall the message. When Hall finished reading it, he whistled. "This is damning all right. It could be that you've caught your killer."

"We'll see how that pans out," Bib said as he took back the note. "The main reason I'm here is to ask you how to handle a ticklish situation. Miss Parker told me that she showed the note to Rebecca Wimberly, and that Ms. Wimberly told her to destroy it."

"You've got to be kidding. What could have possessed the woman to do that?"

"Who knows, but Miss Parker is concerned that she'll be punished by Wimberly when this comes out. I'm hoping you can tell me how we can make sure that doesn't happen."

"You're darn tootin' I can tell you. I'm going to get that woman up here pronto and put the fear of God in her. If she so much as frowns at Ann Parker, I'll come down on her so hard she'll need help dressing herself in those fancy designer outfits she wears."

"Thanks, Dr. Hall. And if you aren't aware of it, Ann Parker is as smart as a whip. She gave me some incredible insight into Joan Smollett's personality. I think Miss Parker deserves some kind of reward for having the strength of character to come forward about this note despite being told by her superior to keep her mouth shut."

"Don't you worry about that, Inspector. I've got a feeling Ann Parker is due for a promotion, and a significant raise."

Bib drove back to his office and phoned Sergeant Dowden. "Things are finally breaking our way," Bib said. "Stop by and I'll show you something that will make your day."

When Dowden walked in, Bib handed him Joan Smollett's note. A smile spread across the big man's face as he read what the woman had written. "Gotcha, you bastard," he said.

189

Bib stood. "Let's go pick him up, Sergeant."

That turned out to be easier said than done. Riley wasn't anywhere to be found around National Geographic headquarters, and he wasn't in his room at the Mayflower Hotel. Bib and Dowden checked at the hotel's front desk to see if he might have mentioned anything about where he was going when he dropped off his room key.

"Mr. Riley did make a comment about having to arrange his future travels," the desk clerk told them. Bib handed the man his card and asked him to telephone police headquarters when Riley returned.

"Our Mr. Riley has no idea where he'll soon be traveling," Sergeant Dowden said to his boss as they walked away.

With his safety assured thanks to his masterful schmoozing of Rebecca Wimberly, Riley had decided to move ahead with his next adventure. The wonders of Baghdad were beckoning. He just needed to work out the details on how to set up his trip. Once he had a handle on that, he'd bring that peabrain Plummer on board with his plans.

Riley felt his old self-confidence returning as he neared the Iraqi embassy, a beige brick building on the corner of P and 18th Streets NW. A third-story balcony out front looked like a fine place for an Iraqi vocalist to sing his country's national anthem, Riley noted, if they had one. He sashayed into the building and asked the gorgeous raven-haired young woman at the reception desk if he could speak with someone about traveling to Iraq.

The woman's name badge said she was a Miss Hussein. From the little reading he'd done about Iraq, Riley remembered that Hussein meant "good-looking." If Iraqi women are all like this doll, he thought, I may have to extend my stay.

"Of course, sir," the receptionist replied. "I'll see if our cultural attaché has a moment to help you." When she spoke, cute little dimples crinkled her cheeks. She picked up the phone and made a brief call. "Mr. Hussein will be right with you," she said.

"Is everyone in Iraq named Hussein?" Riley asked jokingly.

"It's a very common surname," the woman said. "Like Smith here in your country."

Seconds later, a lean, sinister-looking man with oily black hair and a thin Errol Flynn mustache appeared, like a genie popping out of a bottle. From the look of his five o'clock shadow, it was a good bet that Mr. Hussein had to shave twice a day. He beckoned to Riley, who followed him down a long hallway to an office looking out on P Street, where people were scurrying past on their way toward Dupont Circle.

The man hadn't spoken a word of greeting. He sat behind his desk and pointed to the chair in front of it. Riley took a seat, turning on his debonair smile in an effort to thaw this frosty fellow. For an instant, Riley pictured the man pushing a button on his desk and sending him tumbling through an opening in the floor to a secret inquisition chamber below. He'd read stories about the rampant political treachery in the Middle East.

The man took a pad from a desk drawer and reached for a pen. "Name?" he commanded in a deep, reverberating voice that was startling. Riley gave the man his name with as much jauntiness as he could muster.

"Have you ever been to Iraq before?"

"No, never. But I've heard your people are very…"

"The purpose of your visit?" the commandant demanded.

"Tourism."

The man hesitated in his note-taking and gave Riley a steely look. "Tourism," he repeated, as though he didn't believe him, then he wrote something down.

What does this guy think I am, Riley said to himself—a subversive out to start a revolution, or some wild-eyed evangelist wanting to convert his people?

"Destination?" the man continued.

"Baghdad. I've heard it's…"

"The length of your stay?"

"A week or two," Riley said meekly.

"That will be all." The man kept scribbling furiously, as if completing an important dossier. When he finished, he laid down his pen and reached into his desk. He took out a large brown envelope and held it out to Riley. "Here is everything you need to know about traveling to Iraq, along with your visa application form."

Suddenly, Mr. Hussein beamed, revealing a mouthful of pearly teeth. "Have a wonderful trip, sir," he said like a jolly Dutch uncle.

Riley grabbed the envelope and got the hell out of there before the man changed his mind and pushed that button on his desk. He took a cab back to the Mayflower, where he settled on a barstool in the lounge and ordered an Irish whiskey. After that grilling, he needed a drink.

Fetching his key from the registration desk, he returned to his room. He flopped down on the king-size bed and began conjuring up images of dimpled, dark-haired Iraqi women. Fifteen minutes later, someone knocked on his door. Riley was surprised to find Sergeant Dowden standing outside.

Riley stared at Inspector Bib across the battered table in the interrogation room at police headquarters. Riley tried on a smile but it didn't fit.

"Mr. Riley," Bib began in a tired voice, "it's my duty to inform you that we're arresting you for the murder of Mrs. Joan Smollett."

"You can't be serious," Riley blurted. "I told you that I'm not the only one who had access to those poison darts."

"But you're the only person with a strong motive for putting Mrs. Smollett out of the way."

"What are you talking about? I had no cause to harm her."

Bib took Mrs. Smollett's note from a folder and pushed it across the table. "This note says otherwise. You said she'd face significant consequences if she told anyone about her belief that you falsified parts of your story on the headhunters of Ecuador."

Riley gulped and looked down at the note. It seemed to take him forever to read through it. "I…I don't know what to say." He sat up straighter. "This is a lie, I tell you. Joan Smollett never liked me. She'd have done whatever she could to harm my career."

"It looks like it was her career that was harmed," Bib said. "And we have every reason to believe that you're the one who did it." Bib turned to Matthew Dowden. "Sergeant, please escort Mr. Riley to a holding cell."

Riley sat on the narrow, rock-hard bunk in his cell and looked around him in a daze. It seemed inconceivable, but he was actually in jail, arrested for murder. The overpowering stench of disinfectant that assaulted his nostrils wasn't nearly as bad as the sight of the thick steel bars that shut him off from the world, enclosing him in a claustrophobic six-by-eight-foot space. It was his worst nightmare come true. He had a hard time catching his breath, as if the confines of the tiny chamber were suffocating him.

How did people survive under these conditions, he wondered. It was inhumane. His thoughts started racing. He visualized himself in various idyllic settings—strolling on a pristine beach in California, walking down a busy boulevard in Rome, driving through the colorful, sun-splashed Sonoran Desert. All of the images represented something he'd always taken for granted, the freedom to go wherever he wanted. That freedom now felt like the most precious thing in the world. Would he ever enjoy it again? How could this be happening? He'd been arrested. *Arrested.*

Chapter 20

Wednesday

Pamela Johnson decided it was time to start drafting the press release announcing the upcoming "Headhunters of the Amazon" exhibit in Explorers Hall. She cranked a piece of paper into her IBM Selectric and began typing.

The National Geographic Society is proud to announce an exciting new exhibit coming to its Explorers Hall museum. Opening to the public on May 1, "Headhunters of the Amazon" will accompany an article appearing in the May issue of *National Geographic,* written by adventurer Xander Riley. Mr. Riley is the author of the popular article "Treasures of the Orinoco" that ran in the journal two years ago.

The new exhibit will showcase an amazing array of artifacts that Mr. Riley gathered during his expedition into the Amazon rainforest of southeastern Ecuador, a region inhabited by the fiercely independent Jivaro people, whose traditional culture features the unsettling custom of headhunting. Among the artifacts are the Jivaro blowguns and poison darts used in hunting and intertribal warfare.

Other artifacts in the exhibit will include a collection of beautiful feathered headdresses and bead necklaces, along with various utilitarian objects representing the daily lives of the Jivaros. The most fascinating items to be displayed will be the shrunken heads that Mr. Riley acquired from the Jivaros, at no small personal risk. Tickets for the "Headhunters of the Amazon" exhibit can be purchased in Explorers Hall or at 202-555-7588.

Johnson removed the draft and read it over. Penciling in a couple of minor corrections, she added the release to the file folder she'd started on the exhibit. A few days before it was time to distribute the release, she'd run it past Peter Nance in Explorers Hall.

Johnson put the folder away and turned to the next matter on her calendar, contacting the photo department to arrange for coverage of MBG's participation in a meeting of the White House Historical Association. Before she could make the call, her telephone started ringing. Johnson was surprised to discover who was on the line.

"Good afternoon, Miss Johnson," Inspector Bib said. "I hope I'm not interrupting, but I have some important news."

"Hello, Inspector. Has there been a break in the case?"

"There has. We've arrested Xander Riley for Mrs. Smollett's murder." Bib waited for Johnson's response, but there was only silence. "Miss Johnson?" Bib said.

"I…I'm sorry, Inspector, but this is quite a shock. I'd heard that you interviewed Mr. Riley, but I had no idea he was a serious suspect."

"We obtained some new evidence today. Mr. Riley has incriminated himself with some injudicious comments he made to Mrs. Smollett, which she documented in writing."

"I see." Johnson fell silent again. "Would it be all right if I visited Mr. Riley? This is devastating news for the Society, and I'd like to hear his side so I can let others here know how things stand."

"Of course. Stop by whenever you want."

"Thank you for informing me about this, Inspector."

"I know it's not the best news, but those are the facts. If I find out anything else you should know, I'll give you a call."

Word of Riley's arrest was too much for Johnson to bear. She closed her office door and sat at her desk in a stupor. Soon she was blubbering like a child. When she heard a knock on her door, she did her best to gain control of her emotions. Blowing her nose and wiping her eyes, she croaked, "Come in."

Johnson's secretary, kindly, gray-haired Deborah Kaplan, opened the door just far enough to reveal her face, which was etched with concern. "Are you all right, Miss? I could hear you crying all the way outside."

Johnson sniffed. "Thank you, Deb. I'm..." Before she could finish her sentence, she was sobbing again.

Mrs. Kaplan didn't know whether to advance into the room and try to comfort her boss or leave her to her misery. "Oh my, Miss Johnson, did someone close to you die?"

The question sparked an even greater flood of anguish. Johnson gestured for Mrs. Kaplan to shut the door.

"I'll leave you alone then, Miss, but if you need anything at all, you buzz me."

Few people would describe the exterior of St. Matthew the Apostle Catholic Church as breathtaking. Seen from Rhode Island Avenue, the flat redbrick and sandstone facade of Washington's downtown cathedral was as plain as a country barn. The effect was misleading, for the church's unpretentious entrance didn't prepare visitors for what was inside. Opening the door and stepping into St. Matthew's was like opening an oyster shell and finding a magnificent pearl.

Anyone entering the church for the first time was staggered by the opulence. It left them turning in circles to take it all in. All around were richly detailed paintings, glorious stained glass, and splendid marble and wood inlays. Mighty rose-hued marble columns lined the sides of the nave under a vaulted ceiling, with a soaring blue-tinted dome floating like a celestial crown above the giant mosaic of the famed apostle behind the main altar.

Built between 1893 and 1913, St. Matthew's was originally a parish church. In 1939, it was designated a cathedral. The funeral of President Kennedy was held there in 1963, and services for other dignitaries had also taken place there. For Catholics who worked nearby, St. Matthew's was convenient for attending midday Mass or for meditating in soothing silence at any time, and anyone needing to unburden themselves could go to confession Monday through Saturday.

Pamela Johnson made the short walk from headquarters to St. Matthew's. After lighting a candle and praying for Xander Riley to be exonerated, she sat in a pew and contemplated the portraits of saints in the niches along the sides of the nave. If only those holy figures would step down from the wall and share their wisdom. A sprinkling of other visitors sat in the church's vast interior, most of them staring at their hands.

Eventually, Johnson worked up the courage to approach the confessional, a cubicle with one entrance for the troubled and one for the man of the cloth who could supposedly deliver comfort and absolution. But could he? Johnson's step was tentative. She was unsure of what she would say to the priest, but she was driven to speak with someone. Since learning of Riley's arrest, she felt like she was the one trapped in a lonely cell.

Others were ahead of her in the queue to enter the confessional. What might their burdens be, she wondered. Infidelity? Envy? Greed? Deceit? She knew something about that last sin. More than once, she'd been dishonest with herself. How hard it was to lead an upright life.

When her turn came to step into the confessional, Johnson made the sign of the cross and spoke the usual words of contrition. "Bless me, Father, for I have sinned." She panicked when the priest asked her to enumerate her transgressions. After a period of silent turmoil, she uttered a few banalities, prayed for forgiveness, and hurried away with the priest's words ringing in her ears. She felt no sense of absolution, and the customary act of penance the priest prescribed seemed hollow and sadly inadequate.

"You've got yourself a visitor, Mr. Riley," Sergeant Dowden announced in his Marshal Dillon growl.

Riley looked up with a forlorn expression. "Who?"

"It's Miss Johnson from National Geographic. C'mon. I'll take you to her."

Riley sprang off his bunk as Dowden swung back the heavy steel door. Riley followed the strapping sergeant to a large room where a few other prisoners were talking with friends or family members. An armed guard stood near the door, surveying everything that went on.

Pamela Johnson rose from her seat when Riley entered the room. She assumed a businesslike manner, not wanting to parade her feelings in front of Sergeant Dowden. Her relationship with Riley was no business of his or Inspector Bib's. Once Dowden left, she wrapped Riley in a fierce hug. As happy as she was to see him, she started crying again.

Riley wiped away her tears. "None of that, Pam. You don't need to carry on. I'll be out of here in no time." He guided her to a quiet corner, taking her hands in his as they sat down. "It's great to see you. You wouldn't believe what it's like being cooped up in one of those tiny cells. It's like being locked in that trunk Houdini used in his famous escape trick, except in this case there's no secret maneuver for getting out. And the smell. Ugh."

"Sounds awful. Do they at least give you something to read?"

"The only thing to read is a sign on the wall listing the regulations. I don't even want to tell you about those."

Johnson took a paperback book from her purse. "Here's a copy of Hemingway's *The Old Man and the Sea*. I hope that you haven't read it."

"Thanks, Pam. And no, I haven't read this one, but Hemingway is one of my favorite authors. His book *Green Hills of Africa* influenced my decision to try my hand as an adventure writer."

Riley's unyielding bunk had made a rumpled mess of his normally spiffy cargo pants and safari jacket. "Do they allow you to change your clothes?" Johnson asked, attempting to laugh. "You're beginning to look like a vagrant."

"A nice man gave me a pair of dungarees and a blue work shirt, but I haven't tried them on. I hope they're the right size. I want to look my best while I'm pounding rocks on the chain gang. The nice man told me I could take a shower in the morning with the other prisoners. I'm looking forward to that. The fellow in the cell across from mine keeps staring at me as if he'd like to get to know me better."

Johnson's face took on a solemn look. "Is there any chance they'll let you out of here?"

"There's supposed to be an attorney assigned to my case, so I can ask him about bail, although I'm not sure how that works. Never been in the hoosegow before."

Johnson started sniffling again. She blew her nose and got hold of herself. "Why did the police decide to arrest you? I thought there was a possibility that someone else could have gotten one of those poison darts."

Riley took a deep breath. "They found a note from Mrs. Smollett saying that I'd threatened her."

"Did you really do that?"

"I guess I sort of did. You see, the woman accused me of making up things in my article on Ecuador, and I warned her not to spread that around. I wasn't threatening to harm her physically, but I'd have raised a rumpus if her meddling hurt my career with National Geographic. I might have even taken her to court for defamation."

"Then you can use that in your defense."

"I'll run it by the dime-store lawyer they assign me and see what he thinks."

In a remarkably short time, Sergeant Dowden appeared in the doorway. "Time's up," he announced.

Riley and Johnson stood. Johnson badly wanted to kiss Riley, but she restrained herself and shook his hand. As Dowden led him away, Johnson pictured Riley sitting alone in his cell, wearing his dreadful jail clothing. She thought of him laboring at some useless prison job and growing old and gray after years behind bars. She imagined guards beating him with their nightsticks and other prisoners abusing him in ways too horrible to contemplate. It was worse than the tortures of the Nine Circles of Hell in Dante's Inferno.

Johnson's taxi stopped at National Geographic headquarters, but she couldn't bring herself to return to her office. She was afraid of meeting someone and having to put up a false front of composure while knowing she might burst into tears at any moment. She resolved to take a walk to settle herself before she went back to work. The Renwick Gallery was a few blocks down 17th Street, on Pennsylvania Avenue. She'd often visited the Renwick to see its displays of American arts and crafts, which filled her with admiration for the artisans who kept alive the time-honored traditions of weaving, glassblowing, furniture making, and other handicrafts.

Built to resemble the Louvre, the fanciful mid-19th-century redbrick structure was America's first dedicated art museum, originally housing the Corcoran art collection. Inside, Johnson found her way to the area featuring the work of contemporary quilt makers. Her grandmother had made quilts, and Johnson had always marveled at how the woman laboriously pieced together intricate patterns from scraps of cloth. Her grandmother's work had seemed skillfully made, but as Johnson looked at the quilts in the exhibit, she realized that quilting could be raised to the level of art.

Taking her time, she strolled past dozens of quilts with different themes, thinking of the extensive planning and execution each had required, like assembling an enormous jigsaw puzzle. When she glanced at her watch, she was startled to see that she'd been there for half an hour already. She needed to get back to her office, although her visit was time well spent. The lovingly crafted treasures had worked their magic on her, and she felt ready to face her job again.

By the time she got back to headquarters, however, her mind had lapsed into the cycle of worry she'd hoped to shake. Her secretary greeted her cheerfully and didn't ask why she'd been gone for so long. Johnson looked through the phone messages Mrs. Kaplan had left on her desk, then set them aside. Instead of making calls, she went to the window and stared at nothing. She turned around when she heard a light knock on her door. Mrs. Kaplan came in carrying a cup and saucer.

"I thought you might enjoy a hot cup of chamomile tea," she said. "They say it calms the nerves," she added, looking inquiringly at her boss.

"Thank you so much, Deb. You're very considerate." Johnson took a sip of the steaming brew. "Mm, that's just what I needed."

Mrs. Kaplan smiled and went back to her desk. Johnson shuffled through her phone messages again and began returning the calls. Getting back into the swing of things gradually shifted her mind away from Xander Riley. She looked up when Mrs. Kaplan appeared at her door.

"Sorry to bother you Miss, but I just got a call from Mabel Mayweather. Mr. Grosvenor would like you to stop by as soon as possible."

Johnson felt like she'd been punched in the stomach. "Did Mrs. Mayweather say what it was about?"

"No, only that it was urgent."

On the tenth floor, Johnson nervously approached MBG's secretary. "Good afternoon, Mrs. Mayweather. I got your message that Mr. Grosvenor wants to see me."

"Hello, Miss Johnson," the president's dour watchdog said. "I'll see if Mr. Grosvenor's free." After a brief call, she waved Johnson ahead. "Go right in."

Johnson put on the best smile she could manage and walked into the chamber of inquiry. "You wanted to speak with me, Mr. Grosvenor," she said brightly.

"Yes, I do," Grosvenor replied. "Please have a seat."

Johnson had always thought of MBG as a kindly old gentleman. With his gray hair and craggy features, he reminded her of an erudite Benedictine monk. Now he looked more like a hawk eyeing a mouse—and she was the mouse.

"I was saddened to learn that one of our freelance writers has been arrested," Grosvenor said. "As I understand it, the police have charged Mr. Xander Riley with the murder of Joan Smollett. Is that correct?"

"Yes sir, it's true."

"We've had some trouble with Mr. Riley before. In particular, the issue of his rash action in shooting a blowgun dart over the audience during his lecture at Constitution Hall. I dismissed that error in judgment after he convinced me that he understood the foolhardiness of what he'd done and promised to desist from such theatrics."

"I heard about your meeting with Mr. Riley, sir, and I can assure you that he was thoroughly repentant over his actions."

"Yes, well, be that as it may, being repentant won't do him much good if he's convicted of murder."

"Sir, if I may, I'd like to personally vouch for Mr. Riley's character in this matter. I've worked with him on several occasions, and he strikes me as an honest, sensible individual. While I'm not privy to everything the police have found in their investigation of Mrs. Smollett's death, I expect Mr. Riley to be exonerated."

"Unfortunately, Miss Johnson, personal opinions regarding someone's guilt or innocence carry little weight. What I'm concerned about is how this reflects on the Society. How will it look when the newspapers report that one of our writers is in jail on a murder charge? I'm inclined to cut our losses. I lean toward cancelling Mr. Riley's article and the accompanying Explorers Hall exhibit immediately."

"I admit that his arrest might persuade some people to criticize the Society, but no one with any sense of fairness should react that way. After all, isn't anyone accused of a crime supposed to be considered innocent until proven guilty?"

Grosvenor stroked his chin and studied the young woman in front of him. "Indeed, the presumption of innocence is the bedrock of our legal system."

"Furthermore, a person's guilt has to be proved beyond a reasonable doubt before they can be convicted of a crime. Some may jump to conclusions about Mr. Riley's guilt, but the

National Geographic Society shouldn't be among them. We should stand by him as long as possible."

"You make a strong case, Miss Johnson, and I've always trusted your judgment." Grosvenor fiddled with a glass paperweight engraved with his initials, a gift from Jacqueline Kennedy. "All right. We'll not do anything to punish Mr. Riley unless we know he actually deserves it."

"Thank you, Mr. Grosvenor. I think that's the right way to handle this situation." Johnson returned to her office, feeling relieved that she'd averted at least one disaster.

Mrs. Kaplan left at five o'clock as usual, but Johnson stayed late that night. At 7:30, she removed a cardboard mailing tube from her desk and dropped it into her briefcase. She then took a taxi to Pier 4, a commercial wharf on Water Street in Southwest D.C., on the Washington Channel across from East Potomac Park and the Jefferson Memorial. There she boarded the M.V. *George Washington,* a Potomac River cruise boat accommodating over three hundred passengers. At eight o'clock, the boat departed on its "Moonlight Cruise" to Mount Vernon, an hour to the south.

Despite the billing, there was little moonlight on this starry night. The river was a dark void, except for where the lights of the boat illuminated the water ahead. Johnson found a place to stand on the open upper deck, where she watched the lights of the city flicker like fireflies in the night. She imagined herself on a cruise through Paris on the Seine, floating past the Eiffel Tower, Notre Dame Cathedral, and other storied sights. She'd never been to Paris but had always wanted to go. All she'd ever lacked was a lover to share the experience with. Traveling by herself to the City of Light held no appeal at all. Maybe someday, if things worked out, she and Riley might make the trip together. If things worked out.

As the M.V. *George Washington* passed the lights of Alexandria, Johnson thought of the nights she and Riley had shared in her apartment. There was something about Xander Riley that she couldn't put her finger on. At times, he seemed like the proverbial boy next door, familiar and always there when you needed him. At other times, when he had a faraway look in his eye, he seemed like a stranger. He might have been a time traveler from another age for all she knew. The one thing she was certain of was that he fascinated her.

She took the mailing tube from her briefcase and stared at it, trying to decide what to do.

Chapter 21

Thursday

After one night in his revolting cell, Xander Riley understood the full meaning of the term stir-crazy. Unless he got out of his cramped cubicle soon he was going to start banging his head against the wall. At the first opportunity, he asked to speak with Inspector Bib about the prospect of bail. He was sitting on his bunk and gazing at the floor when the Inspector found time to speak with him. Bib knew the look Riley wore very well. It was the forlorn aspect of a criminal bummed out by the fact that he'd been caught.

"You wanted to see me?" Bib said.

Riley managed a feeble grin. "Hello, Inspector. Any word on when Perry Mason will be stopping by? If he's busy fooling around with Della Street, I may have to ask my buddy Mick to represent me, assuming I can lure him away from his favorite barstool."

Bib gave Riley a smile for keeping up a pretense of bravery. "Your court-appointed attorney will be seeing you later today. For your sake, I hope that he's as good as Perry Mason. I think you'll need it."

"You really believe I murdered Mrs. Smollett, don't you?" Riley said.

"There doesn't seem to be much doubt, although there's one thing I don't understand. Why did you take her wallet? There couldn't have been much cash in it."

Riley looked up with a startled expression. "You say her wallet was stolen?"

"As if you didn't know."

Riley suddenly laughed. His handsome young face was transformed from utter despair to jubilation. "That's wonderful."

Bib did a doubletake. "Come again?"

"It proves I had nothing to do with her murder."

"And how do you figure that?"

"Listen, Inspector, I may not be an angel, but I'm no killer, and I'm certainly not a thief. Why would I need to steal the wretched woman's wallet? I'm from one of the wealthiest families in New Jersey."

"What? I thought you were supposed to be a poor kid who pulled himself up by his bootstraps."

Riley smiled apologetically. "Yeah, I invented that business about growing up in an orphanage in New York." The prisoner hung his head. He decided to make a clean breast of things. "That was a nice little story, but I'm actually from the other side of the Hudson. Newark, to be exact."

"Newark?" Bib said in astonishment. "I didn't think anyone was from Newark."

"Hey, Newark's got a lot going for it. It's the largest city in New Jersey, and as the local wags are fond of saying, the bright lights of Hoboken are just twelve miles away."

"Any other surprises?" Bib asked.

"Yep. My name isn't Xander Riley. It's Jacob Stein. My father was Solomon Stein, the owner of a prosperous chain of new car dealerships in Newark. When he died, I inherited the whole kit and caboodle, which for the past few years has enabled me to live out my fantasies. Without having to worry about money, I've been able to try my hand at whatever strikes my fancy, even if I have to fabricate a new identity and tell a few whoppers along the way, such as inventing tales about going off on exciting wilderness expeditions."

Bib seemed thunderstruck. "So you're saying that everything we believed we knew about you—the plucky orphan boy, the daring adventurer—is all so much hooey."

"I'm afraid so."

"Then that's why we couldn't find any documentation about you in the public records."

"There wouldn't be, would there?"

"You'd better tell me the whole story."

The newly unmasked Jacob Stein gathered his thoughts. "After I graduated from college, the logical path for me would have been to return home and help run our Chevrolet dealerships. Being the son of the owner, I could have done anything I wanted, from helping to manage the business end to being a huckster in our television ads. But I couldn't see myself living as an office drudge or a simpering salesman on TV. That all sounded so boringly dreary. I'd majored in English literature in college, and I wanted to lead an exciting life like I'd read about in books.

"After leaving the family business in the care of my uncle, I tried my hand at being a chef, which had always struck me as an interesting job. Later, I bummed around the world on my own for a while. You should see all the stamps in my passport. Among other things, I've led ghost tours in London and dealt blackjack in a Sydney casino. Then one day I got the idea of writing about my travels, only what I'd been doing up to that point was pretty tame. That's when I thought of becoming an adventure writer. However, there was a tiny flaw in that plan. You see, I have particular aversions to danger and deprivation. That's why I faked my two stories for *National Geographic* about trekking into the wilderness."

"How could you have hoped to get away with that? It was inevitable that someone like Mrs. Smollett would eventually catch on to you."

"Clearly it's hubris, but I've always felt that I have a talent for pulling the wool over people's eyes. In the case of the article on Ecuador, I purchased all the Jivaro artifacts in a curio shop in Quito, then Jake Plummer took a few photos of me in a safe, accessible area of the Amazon rainforest not far from the city. After that, Jake traveled into the remote territory where the headhunters live in order to flesh out the visual end of the story. We did the same thing with our article on the Orinoco. I bought the "treasures" I wrote about in a shop in Caracas, and Jake headed off down the river with some guides."

Stein felt the need to justify himself. "It was like any other assignment for *National Geographic,* except I didn't have to give up the comfort of a first-class hotel."

"How did you get your photographer to go along with your subterfuge?"

"I discovered a little something about his past that would be embarrassing if it became generally known. Nothing against the law, mind you. Just a bit of ill-considered behavior."

"You mean you blackmailed him into working for you?"

"Blackmail is an unsavory term. I simply persuaded him with irrefutable reasoning. And I didn't take advantage of him financially if that's what you're thinking. I paid him more than he'd ever made on any of his previous assignments. The only downside was that he had to work under trying conditions, with the possibility of risk. Jake shouldered that part of our work together while I spun the tales that evoked the romance of adventure travel. Those stories were good, too, if I do say so myself. I thought of my role as being similar to that of a writer-director on a movie, like John Huston. Others might be involved in the production, but I supplied the script and orchestrated the performances."

"You're a very imaginative fellow, Mr. Riley...I mean, Mr. Stein." Bib wrinkled his brow. "But how do I know that what you're telling me now isn't another load of bunkum?"

"I'll give you the contact information for my Uncle Noah in Newark."

Pamela Johnson decided she had to get out of Washington. She needed someplace quiet where she could think. She settled on a short trip to visit her parents in Savannah. After calling her office and telling her secretary she was taking a couple of days off, she took a taxi to Union Station, where she boarded the *Champion,* the daily Atlantic Coast Line train linking New York and Miami. She didn't feel up to the ten-hour drive home, and a train ride was more conducive to uninterrupted thought. She'd packed for a long weekend, making sure to throw in a book and a couple of magazines. Even as she shoved the reading material into her bag, she knew she'd probably spend most of the time staring out the window of the train.

From Washington, the *Champion*'s southbound route ran through Richmond, Virginia, with stops in a few smaller towns before reaching Charleston, South Carolina, and Savannah, Georgia. The train's streamlined pink and silver locomotive was a familiar sight as it raced through sleepy burgs where kids waved wildly in hopes of coaxing a blast from the *Champion*'s ear-splitting air horn. Johnson knew every mile of the bucolic route. She'd been up and down this line twenty or thirty times over the years.

Once the train left Richmond, Johnson settled back in her comfortable coach seat and gazed at the verdant Virginia countryside rushing by. She took out the latest issue of *LIFE* magazine, which featured Julie Andrews on the cover exhibiting her wholesome smile. Johnson opened the magazine to the story about the actress's latest movie, *The Sound of Music,* but before she'd read a word her mind drifted off on a storm cloud of misgivings. The clacking of the train's wheels on the rails seemed to keep repeating *Xander Riley, Xander Riley.*

Coming into Savannah created feelings unlike any Pamela Johnson ever experienced in other cities. Two hours earlier, the train had passed through Charleston, which had all the charm and grace of a genteel Southern town, but for a native of Georgia, Charleston was only an appetizer. Savannah would always be the entrée.

Johnson's pulse quickened the moment the train crossed the Savannah River. By the time the *Champion* steamed into the Savannah train station, she was thinking of summer days spent strolling through Forsyth Park beneath a bower of giant live oak trees hung with swags of Spanish moss. She could almost hear the sound of water splashing in the park's iconic white stone fountain, which little kids danced around with youthful exuberance and couples posed in front of for photographs.

As a former longtime resident of the historic port, Johnson had done both of those things.

A few blocks north of Forsyth Park was St. John's Cathedral, where the young Pamela Johnson had been accepted into the Catholic faith through baptism, confirmation, and communion. She'd attended her parish elementary and high schools, being steeped in religious studies and taught the secular subjects that prepared her for college up in Athens. Hers had been a quiet, regulated upbringing—until the raging hormones of her teenage years took hold.

Johnson smiled as she recalled the country lane on the edge of town where she and high school beau Philip Dunn had engaged in a little hanky-panky after their senior prom. Trying to climb into the backseat of his parents' '55 Buick while wearing an elegant evening dress with a full petticoat had required considerable effort, like trying to cram a Christmas tree into a closet. They'd both wrestled with that uncooperative dress until Philip located the zipper in back and they were able to leave the cumbersome thing in the front seat. Putting the gown back on afterward while inside the car was no easy trick either.

One thing every person who grew up in Savannah learned was the history of their city. If you stopped anyone on the street above the age of twelve, there was a good chance they could rattle off the fact that Savannah had been founded on the Savannah River in 1733 by James Oglethorpe and his fellow passengers on the good ship *Anne*. Oglethorpe named America's thirteenth colony after England's King George II. The first capital of the state of Georgia, the port city played important roles in both the American Revolution and the Civil War, and it grew rich on the cotton trade in its early years.

The original city was dotted with over twenty squares, which had been preserved as public parks bursting with semitropical lushness. Dozens of restored homes and buildings in the historic district gave the city the feel of a Deep South time capsule. Johnson had grown up in an antebellum brick townhouse off Lafayette Square, near St. John's Cathedral. Her father,

Dr. Harold Johnson, a courtly gentleman that Pamela had never heard raise his voice, ran his general practice from their home, so Pamela had grown used to seeing patients of all ages entering his office.

Pamela's mother, Priscilla, the Johnson family wit, worked as a docent on the Savannah historic homes tour. She knew more about the city's famous and infamous residents than anyone other than the local history teachers. Priscilla could spin humorous tales about every elite Savannah family, every eccentric patriarch, every legendary beauty, and every society scandal that was worth knowing. At the age of fifty, she could still fit into the *Gone with the Wind* gowns she'd been wearing on the homes tour for the past twenty years, and there wasn't a trace of gray in the lustrous blond hair she'd passed on to her daughter.

It was Priscilla who picked up Pamela at the train station. After the obligatory hugs and kisses, they drove through town toward Lafayette Square. "You sounded stressed when you called to tell us you were coming," Priscilla said with a sideways glance. "Anything we need to talk about?"

Pamela looked out at the green serenity of Madison Square on East Harris Street. "Maybe we could talk tonight after Dad finishes work." She gave her mother a tight smile. "I'd rather not have to go through everything twice. Let's you and I enjoy ourselves this afternoon and then we can have a family pow-wow after dinner."

"All right, if you're sure it can wait."

"It can. I'm not dying or anything. It's just a bit of a personal dilemma."

"Your father specializes in those. He read a book once."

For the first time since receiving yesterday's traumatic news, Pamela laughed a genuine laugh. "What do you say we drive down to the waterfront? I've missed the smell of the river and the sound of the boats."

"River Street it is then," her mother said, turning left on Abercorn and heading north. As they approached the historic

Colonial Park Cemetery, a burial ground established in 1750, Pamela broke down and started crying. She remembered the walks she and her friends used to take in the shade-dappled old cemetery, where they marveled at the ancient, lichen-covered tombstones and crypts, speculating about the lives of the people who'd lived in Savannah two centuries earlier. Now, the thought of tombstones and death brought her back to the terrifying quandary she'd been struggling with.

Her mother pulled over and stopped the car. "Now listen to me, missy," Priscilla said. "I want you to tell me what's bothering you here and now. Your father can wait. He'll probably trot out some medical mumbo jumbo anyway."

Pamela leaned over and embraced her mother. "Oh, Mom, I don't know what to do. A man that I care for very much is in terrible trouble."

"What kind of trouble?"

Pamela had difficulty getting the words out. "He's…accused of murdering a woman who worked at National Geographic."

"Goodness. Do you think he might have done it?"

"I know he didn't, but I can't think what I should do."

"What can you do, honey? It will be up to a court now. If you're certain he didn't do it, then stand by him and let him know how much you care."

Pamela looked into her mother's eyes and hugged her again. "I'll try," she said.

"Do you want to share this with your father tonight?"

"Let's not. You've given me the only advice that makes sense. No use burdening him as well."

"All right. Do you still want to go down to the river?"

Pamela sniffed and nodded.

They held hands as they walked down the old stone steps that led to River Street, a narrow brown cobblestone lane constructed two hundred years ago from the ballast stones carried by ships entering Savannah's harbor. In those days, steamboats docked along River Street to be loaded with the bales of cotton that brought wealth to Savannah. Today, huge container ships plied the river, sailing past the golden-domed City Hall that had presided over the waterfront since 1904, when it replaced a century-old predecessor. Steamboats still docked along River Street, but now they hauled tourists and dinner guests instead of trade goods.

As Pamela and her mother walked along, the broad river caught the afternoon sunlight, turning the water into a sheet of hammered bronze. A ship headed toward the Atlantic, its decked stacked several stories high with colorful containers, like towering stacks of Lego blocks. The young couples strolling along River Street reminded Pamela of the carefree walk she'd enjoyed with Riley in Annapolis before he told her he was a murder suspect.

"Where do you and Dad want to eat tonight?" she asked her mother, trying to chase thoughts of murder from her head.

"As soon as your father heard you were coming, he made reservations up there." Priscilla pointed toward the Boar's Head Grill and Tavern, a restaurant perched above them overlooking the river. Occupying part of a restored cotton warehouse dating to 1780, Boar's Head specialized in steaks and local seafood. With its antique brick interior and simple furnishings, the restaurant gave diners the feeling of stepping back in time.

"The restaurant's only been there a few years," Priscilla said, "but we love it. Your father decided to take you there because they serve one of your favorite dishes."

"Shrimp and grits?" Pamela asked.

"Some of the best in town."

At eight o'clock, Dr. Harold Johnson opened the door to the restaurant and bowed to his wife and daughter. "After you, ladies," he said with his soothing drawl.

The sound of Dr. Johnson's mellow voice could lower a worried patient's blood pressure several points, and when he laid a reassuring hand on someone's arm, it seemed to convey a sense that all would be well. Faith healers put great stock in the laying on of hands, and while Dr. Johnson was a man of science, he knew there was a magical quality in the touch of a fellow human being.

Dr. Johnson immediately sensed that something had upset his daughter, but he didn't want to spoil their evening by delving into it right away. There'd be plenty time in the next few days to coax her into talking about her problem. He was used to dealing with people who came to see him but were reluctant to discuss what was on their mind. He suspected that Pamela's issue had to be a serious matter if it had driven her to suddenly come home on a weekday.

"Do I have to ask for your preferences," Dr. Johnson said after they were seated, "or shall I go ahead and order the usual for everyone? Shrimp and grits for you, Pam, and lamb chops for your mother."

Priscilla made a face at her husband. "Smarty pants. Just for that I'm ordering a different dish. I'll have the bouillabaisse."

"And you, daughter?" Dr. Johnson asked.

Pamela ran her eye over the menu. "I think I'll have…um, the shrimp and grits."

Dr. Johnson smiled. "And I'll have my usual ribeye steak."

Pamela began to relax by slow degrees during the course of the evening. Savannah was weaving its spell. After dinner, they sat in their family room at home and sipped their coffee. When they all turned in for the night, Pamela lay in bed in her old room and listened to the ticking of the grandfather clock in the front hallway. *Tick-tock, tick-tock,* the venerable timepiece measured out the hours with mechanical precision. Pamela listened until the mesmerizing sound lulled her to sleep.

Chapter 22

Friday

The two hundred-mile train trip from Washington's Union Station to Newark's Penn Station would take a little over three hours. It was an outing Bib would rather have missed, but he had to corroborate Jacob Stein's story. Years ago, Bib had passed through Newark on the way to New York, where he'd treated Phyllis and Sylvia to a weekend in the city over the Christmas holidays. They'd done all the usual tourist things— skating at Rockefeller Center, attending the Rockettes' show at Radio City Music Hall, shopping at Macy's on 34th Street. That was the last time Bib had been to New York. The memories of that happy trip were blotted out when Phyllis was diagnosed with breast cancer not long afterward.

Bib gazed out the window at the fertile Maryland countryside. Fields were starting to green up again after the bleak months of winter. Bib was alone on this excursion. He'd told Sergeant Dowden there was no use for both of them to spend an entire day on the train. Dowden could hardly contain his glee. Bib had telephoned Stein's uncle, Noah Stein, and arranged a meeting. Mr. Stein said he'd be happy to tell Bib anything he wanted to know about his nephew. He even invited Bib to lunch.

The train followed the Northeast Corridor, the route linking Washington and Boston, one of the busiest daily commuter lines in the country. The coaches swayed and shuddered like a carnival ride, but instead of five minutes duration, this ride went on for hours. Passengers staggered up and down the aisle as if they were drunk. Only the conductor had his sea legs under him, although Bib supposed they should properly be called rail legs.

Bib was reminded that rail travel offered an opportunity to see the areas of cities that never made it into publicity photos. The tracks of the older eastern rail lines often passed through the worst parts of town, the slums and warehouse districts that had been left behind as the cities grew. Bib found those blighted neighborhoods fascinating for the history they revealed, yet most passengers averted their eyes, preferring not to be reminded of the daily struggles of the people who lived and worked in such places. Bib's job routinely took him into the worst parts of Washington, so he'd come to realize that life went on in a tenement much the same as in a penthouse. The furnishings and weaponry were simply different.

By the time Bib's train reached the outskirts of Newark, he'd gone through every scenario he could think of involving someone other than Jacob Stein having murdered Mrs. Smollett. If anyone managed to gain access to the Explorers Hall storage room, it had to one of the workers they'd interviewed—or a thief on the order of Adam Worth, the 19th-century "Napoleon of Crime" that Sir Arthur Conan Doyle used as a model for the archvillain Professor Moriarty in the Sherlock Holmes stories. The one hitch in that idea was the preposterous notion that a person with the skills of a master criminal would be working for National Geographic.

Bib thought of janitor Bill Foster. He was Johnny-on-the-spot in finding Smollett's body. Could he have had a run-in with the researcher? Bib scoffed at his own supposition. What would he come up with next? The president of National Geographic sneaking down from his tenth-floor office to murder Mrs. Smollett? Bib needed to give it a rest.

Emerging from Newark's Penn Station, Bib hailed a taxi and gave the driver the address for the largest of the half-dozen dealerships owned by the Stein family. The Solomon Chevrolet dealership on Broadway was a sea of shiny new vehicles. Bib barely made it halfway across the lot before being accosted by a rangy salesman wearing a bolo tie and a cowboy hat. The man bore an uncanny resemblance to actor Slim Pickens. Bib pictured the salesman sitting astride a plummeting atom bomb and waving his hat like a bronco rider, as Pickens did in the movie *Dr. Strangelove.*

"Lookin' for anything special?" the fellow asked with a wide, toothy grin. "We just got in a shipment of new Impalas that'll knock your socks off."

Bib had once owned a used 1952 Bel Air that had cost him a fortune in repairs. "Actually, I'm here to see Noah Stein."

"Mr. Stein's a busy man. You sure I can't help you?" The salesman wasn't going to let a commission slip through his fingers that easily.

"I'm not looking for a car. I have a meeting with Mr. Stein."

The salesman's grin evaporated. "Oh. Head on into the showroom and ask the young lady at the front desk to speak with Mr. Stein." As he said this, he was scanning the lot for other potential customers.

Bib did as the salesman suggested. The giddy blonde behind the desk phoned Stein's secretary and told her that an "Inspector Fib" from Washington, D.C., was here to see Mr. Stein.

Minutes later, a short, gray-haired gentleman in a dark pinstripe suite approached Bib with his hand outstretched. "Noah Stein," the man said in a pleasant voice. Bib thought Stein looked like a kindly uncle, and he must have been for him to consent to run the business while his nephew hopscotched between careers as if playing musical chairs.

"Thanks for agreeing to see me, Mr. Stein," Bib said.

"My pleasure, and before we get down to business, let's go have a bite to eat. There's a deli nearby that serves the best corned beef sandwiches you ever tasted."

Bib checked his watch and saw that it was already the lunch hour. "Sounds great."

The sandwiches turned out to be as good as Stein had promised. After the two men finished eating, Stein looked across the table with a serious expression. "Now, how can I help you, Inspector? Or perhaps I should say, how can I help my dear nephew Jacob?"

"First, let's make sure that we're talking about the same person." Bib showed Stein the mug shot they'd taken. "Is this your nephew?"

Stein admired the photograph. "Yes, that Jacob. He takes a good photo, doesn't he? Even in a mug shot he looks distinguished."

Bib put the photograph away. "As I told you over the phone, we arrested your nephew in connection with a murder that took place at National Geographic headquarters. Yesterday, your nephew revealed to me that he isn't who he's been passing himself off as. He's been posing as a freelance writer named Xander Riley."

Stein burst out laughing. "At least he could have made up a good Jewish name."

Bib suppressed a smile. "All along, he's insisted that he had no reason to murder the victim, and when I happened to mention that the woman's wallet had been stolen, he said he definitely wouldn't have robbed her, since he was from one of the wealthiest families in New Jersey. I need you to corroborate that information and also to give me your honest opinion of your nephew. In other words, do you think there's any possibility that he might harm someone?"

"I understand," Stein said. "First, let me assure you that Jacob is a good boy. He's just a victim of his own flamboyant imagination. He likes to playact, to dress up and pretend to be someone else—something more romantic than the pampered son of a rich car salesman. He performed as a mime in college, for Pete's sake. After he graduated from Dartmouth, he attended the Culinary Institute of America. He used to tell people he'd been recruited by the CIA.

"After a few months as a fry chef, though, he'd had his fill of working in a steamy, grease-filled kitchen. When he came up with the idea of becoming an adventure writer, I shook my head. He couldn't have been any more ill-suited for that. Shoot, he dropped out of Boy Scouts because he couldn't stand the discomfort of camping. Adventure writer…ha! The closest

Jacob ever came to adventure was walking through a shopping mall on his own for the first time."

Stein stared at his hands. "When Jacob told you he was from a wealthy family, he wasn't exaggerating. My brother Solomon and I were in a Nazi concentration camp, Inspector. After the war, we came to this country with little more than the clothes on our backs. In five years, Solomon owned his first new car dealership. In ten, he owned a string of dealerships all over Newark. He provided jobs for every member of his family, including me. Every year, Solomon donated a hundred thousand dollars to B'nai B'rith. So yes, Jacob is from a wealthy family.

"As to your question about whether he would harm anyone, let me tell you a story about Jacob when he was a boy. For his tenth birthday, Jacob begged his father to buy him a BB gun. Solomon was always a soft touch, and he gave his son what he wanted. After his birthday party, Jacob took his new BB gun outside. A few minutes later, he came back in the house, bawling his head off. He'd shot a robin, and when he picked it up he was horrified by what he'd done. Part of the little bird's brain was hanging out. Jacob buried that bird, and the next day he gave away his new BB gun to a friend. So when you ask me if Jacob could harm another human being, I have to say that would be the most farfetched thing I've ever heard of."

When Inspector Bib arrived back at Metropolitan Police headquarters, he freed Jacob Stein. His search for the killer of Joan Smollett wasn't over.

The smell of frying bacon wafted through the Johnson house shortly before sunrise. The enticing aroma took Pamela back to her childhood, when she used to snuggle deeper under her covers and wait for her mother to call out "breakfast" from the foot of the stairs. The way her mother pronounced the irresistible summons made it sound like two words—*brek...fust.* As she'd done when she was growing up, Pamela crawled from bed and stretched like a waking cat. Then she washed her face, brushed her teeth, combed her hair, donned her bathrobe, and went stumping down the stairs on the way to the kitchen.

"There you are, sleepyhead," her fathered drawled. "We thought you were going to stay in bed all day." As usual, Dr. Johnson was seated at the breakfast table with the *Savannah Morning News* in his hands. He peered over the top of the paper. Except for his gray hair and wrinkles, the scene was the same as it had been a dozen years ago.

Priscilla Johnson busied herself at the stove, tending the bacon, eggs, biscuits, and gravy. She waved her spatula at her daughter like a magic wand. "Sit yourself down, dear, and prepare yourself for a real Southern breakfast."

"I'm always glad when you visit," Dr. Johnson said. "Usually all I get for breakfast is toast and marmalade."

"Oh hush," his wife said. "You know I always fix you a nice breakfast on the weekend."

"I concede the point, but what about the rest of the week?"

"Did you ever consider that you might fix me a nice breakfast once in a while?"

"I see in the paper we might get some rain," Dr. Johnson said.

Priscilla winked at her daughter as she set the platters of steaming food on the table. "That ended his complaining, didn't it?"

Dr. Johnson laid his newspaper aside and filled his plate. "Got any big plans for today?" he asked Pamela.

She glanced at the clock on the stove. "I was thinking I might go to early Mass."

Dr. Johnson looked at his wife, who imperceptibly shook her head, forestalling any comment from her husband. Last night, he'd asked if she knew what was troubling their daughter. Priscilla had hinted that her dilemma was romantic in nature, leaving out the part about her friend's arrest. Pamela would have to be the one to bring that up.

"That sounds like a good idea," Dr. Johnson said. "If I didn't have patients scheduled I'd go with you. But then maybe you'd rather go by yourself."

"Oh no. You and Mom would be welcome," Pamela said.

They could tell she didn't mean it. "I think we'll let you go on your own," Priscilla said. "We get over to St. John's every Sunday, and Father Samuel might think something was wrong if we started showing up on weekdays. Nothing much ever gets by him."

The early morning sunshine tinted the streets with an orange glow as Pamela strolled through her old neighborhood to the Cathedral of St. John the Baptist. The cathedral's regal white and gold exterior and soaring twin spires gave it the look of a medieval castle. At least that's how it had always struck Pamela when she was a child. She used to think how lucky she was to be able to attend a church fit for royalty. Her best friend went to the local Lutheran church, a simple brick building with what seemed to Pamela like a poor excuse for a steeple. Though she'd never mentioned it to her friend, Pamela often wondered how anyone could get in the proper mood for prayer in such humdrum surroundings.

The inside of St. John's was as lavish as the outside. Every surface of the interior was decorated with elaborate religious symbols—a throng of saints, angels, and biblical characters. It might have seemed gaudy and overdone to some, but for a faithful Catholic, it was as close to heaven on earth as it was possible to be. Anyone who couldn't get in the mood for prayer while enfolded in the splendor of St. John's probably couldn't get in the mood anywhere.

Pamela Johnson was in the mood for prayer. She found a seat and listened to the cathedral's pipe organ swell with the sacred music that accompanied the introductory rites preceding the liturgy. Pamela bowed her head and prayed fervently for the release of Xander Riley. God recognized the blameless, she reassured herself, and the blameless should never be punished for the sins of others. Pamela knew in her heart that Xander was innocent. Surely if she prayed long enough and hard enough, God would hear her.

"What's on the agenda for the rest of the day?" Priscilla asked her daughter when she returned from Mass.

"I've been thinking about a long walk on the beach."

"It might be a little cool if a sea breeze is blowing over on Tybee Island."

"That's all right. I'll take a sweater, and I don't plan to go in the water. I just want to hear the sound of the waves and the cries of the seagulls. There's nothing more relaxing."

"The gulls always sound lonely to me," Priscilla said.

"I've always thought they sound like they're laughing."

"Maybe that's what they are doing." Priscilla fussed with straightening the pillows on the sofa. "I'd tag along, but I need to do some shopping for dinner tonight. You can take one of the cars. Do you want me to pack you a lunch?"

"You don't need to. After that hearty breakfast I doubt if I'll get hungry, and if I do, I can get a snack over there."

While Pamela was at Mass, Dr. Johnson had suggested that Priscilla should stick by her daughter's side today, but Priscilla told him she thought Pamela was looking for some time alone. "I have a feeling that's the reason she came down here."

A coastal island a short drive from the city, Tybee was large enough to have a town filled with inns and restaurants. Its eastern shore faced the Atlantic, with marshland on the back side of the island. Tybee's slender black and white lighthouse had guided ships into the mouth of the Savannah River since colonial times. Dolphins frolicked offshore, sea turtles nested on Tybee's beaches, and alligators could be seen peeping from the marshes. Fishing, water sports, and biking were big, but lazing on the beach was the number one pastime.

Pamela arrived on Tybee at eleven o'clock and parked her car near Mid Beach, her favorite place on the island. North Beach and South Beach were always more crowded, and being engulfed by hordes of people wasn't what Pamela had in mind. After crossing the boardwalk over the dunes, she removed her shoes and dug her toes in the sand. The murmuring of the surf was like a familiar voice welcoming her. The ever-present flocks of gulls wheeled overhead, streaks of white against the deep blue sky. It struck her that the squawking gulls did sound lonely, as her mother said.

Pamela remained in the same spot for several minutes, soaking in the peaceful scene. She couldn't count the number of times she'd walked this beach. As a toddler, her parents had each held one of her hands as they strolled along with her between them, lifting her into the air when the waves rushed in. Years later, she'd held the hands of a succession of boyfriends. She'd been one of the most popular girls in high school. Where were all those boys now, she asked herself. Scattered to the four winds, she imagined, just as she'd wandered far from home. Sometimes, she wished she'd never left Savannah.

A hundred yards off the shore, a magnificent three-masted schooner sailed past Tybee, headed north toward Hilton Head Island. Its dark blue hull heeled over away from the shoreline, and its beautiful array of crisp white sails stood taut, bowed by the northeasterly wind. Did the people aboard such an extravagant vessel have any worries, Pamela asked herself, or were their lives insulated from the daily cares and woes of ordinary folk. Where had they been and where were they going? Were they were running toward the future or away from the past? In which direction was she running?

Pamela drove back to town around two in the afternoon. She didn't feel like going home yet, so she stopped at Forsyth Park and found a bench beneath a live oak tree, within sight of the splashing white stone fountain. Older men, retirees most likely, shuffled past her bench, and mothers or nannies walked by pushing baby strollers. They all smiled at her, most of them offering some comment about the beauty of the day.

Pamela recalled sitting in Lafayette Square in Washington, across from the White House. She and her friends often ate lunch there in good weather. As far as she could remember, not one person walking past had ever said a pleasant word to them. She wondered what the tipping point was in the size of a city at which friendliness gave way to anonymity.

Thinking of what was waiting for her back in Washington, she wished more than ever that she'd never left Savannah.

Dinner that evening was a quiet affair. Pamela's mother had fixed a fancy spread featuring roasted quail. Pamela picked at her food with a distracted expression.

"Lost your appetite?" Priscilla asked. "You always fancied my quail recipe."

Pamela looked at her mother as if she'd been jolted awake. "Sorry, Mom. I must have been daydreaming." She took a bite. "The quail is heavenly."

Priscilla looked across the table at her husband.

"You can't fool your old dad, young lady," Dr. Johnson said to his daughter. "I can tell something's afoot by the way you've been moping around. You're in love, aren't you?"

Pamela looked out the window. "I'm not sure. Maybe I am."

After dinner, they took their coffee in the living room. The ticking of the grandfather clock in the hallway filled the gaps between the snatches of conversation. When Pamela's father asked her for information about her beau, she only told him it was someone at work. She said things weren't settled between them yet, so she didn't want to go into any details just now. How could she tell him that the man she was thinking of was languishing behind bars?

Shortly before nine o'clock, the telephone on the hall table rang. Priscilla got up to answer it. She came back into the living room and motioned to her daughter. "It's for you, dear. A young man, by the sound of his voice."

"For me?" Pamela said in surprise. "No one but my secretary knows I'm here."

She went into the hallway and picked up the phone. "Hello," she said warily.

"Pam, it's me," said a voice she recognized instantly. "I hope you're sitting down, darlin', because I'm out of jail."

Pamela didn't know whether to laugh, cry, or shout for joy. "Are you serious?"

"As serious as a Baptist preacher on Sunday morning. Inspector Bib let me go this afternoon after I convinced him I wasn't the person he was looking for."

Pamela was stunned into silence.

"You still there, baby?"

"Yes, but I'm having a hard time digesting this. It seems too good to be true." God heard my prayers, she said to herself. God heard my prayers.

"When are you coming back to D.C.?"

"I'll be on the train tomorrow morning," Pamela said, fighting back tears.

"Terrific. I can't wait to see you. We'll make a day of it."

Chapter 23

Saturday

The grounds of Oakwood Cemetery, a woody parcel off Broad Street on the east side of Falls Church, had been in use since the town's first Methodist meetinghouse established a burial site there in 1779. On this tranquil March morning, the cemetery's cherry trees and forsythia bushes provided patches of white, pink, and yellow among the weathered gray tombstones. Soon, dogwoods, redbuds, and azaleas would add fresh hues to the vibrant spring palette.

Archimedes Bib stood beneath a towering oak, looking down at a familiar tombstone. He held a bouquet of daffodils, one of Phyllis's favorite flowers. Since his wife's death, Bib had visited her grave once a month, usually on a Saturday. He'd stood on this same spot more than a hundred times over the past ten years. In good weather, he always brought a bouquet, which he purchased from Py's friend Barbara.

Bib read the inscription on his wife's tombstone, "We'll Meet Again," the title of the song Phyllis had loved, and which meant so much to both of them during the years Bib was away in Europe. It might have seemed like a corny sentiment to some, but Bib's eyes watered every time he read it. It also pained him every time he read the dates of Phyllis's birth and death—a span of thirty-eight years. Even worse was the knowledge of how fleeting their life together as man and wife had been, a mere sixteen years. Those numbers were so unfair.

Bib's name appeared alongside Phyllis's on the tombstone, since he would be buried beside her when the day came. It gave him a strange feeling to see his name and date of birth, with a blank space for the date of his death. It was the most powerful reminder he could think of that our time in this world is finite.

He placed his bouquet in front of Phyllis's tombstone and sat on the nearby granite bench, a seat he'd occupied for untold hours, always trying to remember the good times he'd shared with the only woman besides his mother that he'd ever loved. When his thoughts inevitably turned to grief, he got up and walked over to the graves of his parents. Mary and Joseph Bib had died within six months of each other, and just three years before Phyllis's death. The 1950s had been the cruelest decade of Bib's life.

He took a seat and looked around him. Every one of the hundreds of tombstones he could see had its own story of happiness and grief. Somewhere in Falls Church was the new grave of Joan Smollett, dead for barely two weeks. Was anyone still mourning her, Bib wondered. Even if no one cared any longer, it was his job to bring her justice.

For the past twenty years, that had been Bib's mission—to bring justice to those who'd had their most precious possession—their life—stolen from them. To his credit, Bib had solved nearly every case he'd taken on, but he was dissatisfied with his handling of Joan Smollett's murder. He felt sure he was overlooking something, a passing comment someone had made that seemed insignificant at the time but that could be the key to solving the case.

He began casting his mind back to every conversation he'd had related to the investigation. Suddenly, it came to him. It was such a seemingly inconsequential bit of information that he'd hardly paid attention when he heard it. As the implication of what he recalled dawned on him, he began to understand why he'd overlooked the vital clue. The person it involved appeared to be so far removed from the crime, so lacking in any reason for harming Joan Smollett, that he'd forgotten the first rule of policing—suspect everyone.

Bib returned to his office and telephoned Sergeant Dowden. "Meet me at National Geographic headquarters in half an hour," Bib said. "I'll be waiting for you outside the 17th Street entrance."

"What's up?" Dowden asked.

"We're going to look for an item that I'm all but certain we won't find."

"Pardon me, sir, but isn't that sort of pointless?"

"Maybe, but if we have more luck than we've had so far, it could be worth it."

"Mind telling me what we'll be looking for?"

"A poison dart. A used poison dart."

Before he left police headquarters, Bib telephoned the security office at National Geographic and told the man on duty that he and Sergeant Dowden were coming. Bib suggested that it might be wise to call in Karl Jackson, the chief of security.

Thirty minutes later, Bib, Dowden, and Jackson were going through every nook and cranny of the office Bib had chosen. They searched all the desk drawers and every folder in the filing cabinet. After checking every possible hiding place, they stood looking at each other with resignation. Karl Jackson's scowl seemed to say he thought the effort had been a wild goose chase. He'd much rather have remained at home working in his yard.

"Doesn't look like it's here," Dowden said.

Bib shrugged. "I would have been surprised if it was, but we had to make sure. As you're well aware, Sergeant, killers sometimes hang on to souvenirs."

Bib stared at the line of books on the shelf behind the desk. He stepped closer and examined the titles. He pulled one of the books from the shelf and flipped through the pages. He turned to Sergeant Dowden with a pleased expression.

"Matt, what's the one thing you'd expect to see in every office at National Geographic?"

Dowden glanced around the room. "I don't know. A globe?"

Karl Jackson finally cracked a smile.

"Good guess," Bib said, "but that's not exactly what I had in mind."

"What then?" Dowden asked.

"A dictionary."

Pamela Johnson felt lighthearted as she boarded the north-bound *Champion* on Saturday morning. Riley had been released from jail, so everything was going to be fine. As her train steamed out of the Savannah station, she leaned out the window and waved to her mother and father.

"Bye Mom, Dad. Thanks for everything. I'll call you when I get back to Washington."

Her parents were beaming as they returned her goodbye wave. Pamela's worries seemed to have resolved themselves. She still hadn't told them much about the man whose arrest had unnerved her, only that he was a freelance adventure writer she'd been seeing. When her father asked her how serious things were, Pamela laughed and told them that Xander Riley had a hard time being serious about anything.

As the *Champion* crossed the Savannah River, Johnson took out the copy of *LIFE* magazine she'd brought along but had ignored on the trip south. She turned the pages to find the article on Julie Andrews and was soon wrapped up in the story. By the time the *Champion* pulled into Washington's Union Station, Johnson had read both of her magazines and was halfway through her book.

She grabbed her bag from the overhead rack and almost ran toward the terminal's main hall, where she hoped Riley would be waiting. Emerging from the platform, she scanned the noisy, crowded hall. People were rushing in every direction, and with the announcements of arriving and departing trains over the loudspeakers, it was bedlam.

Somehow, amid the pandemonium, Johnson heard someone shouting her name. Then she spotted Riley waving to her. He had on a leather jacket with the collar turned up, giving him the bad boy look of James Dean in *Rebel Without a Cause*. Johnson ran to him and wrapped him in a furious hug. Her prolonged kiss was every bit as intense.

Riley finally tore her arms away. "Whoa there. I just got my freedom back, so I don't need you squeezing the life out of me."

Johnson gave Riley a perturbed look and poked him in the chest. "You have no idea what you've put me through, bub. Now you're going to show me a good time to make up for it."

Riley grabbed her bag and put his other arm around her waist as they headed for the exit. "Your wish is my command."

"Then I hereby command you to take me to lunch. Somewhere really nice."

"Would the Iron Gate satisfy your majesty?" Riley was thinking of his lunch there with Rebecca Wimberly. The place had atmosphere, and the food was top notch.

"Ooh, would it. I'm going to order the most expensive thing on the menu, and it's your treat."

"Boy, this weekend is gonna cost me."

A few minutes later, they were sitting at a sunlit table on the Iron Gate's brick patio. Johnson ended up settling for a Greek salad and Riley the roasted shrimp, accompanied by a white wine from Santorini. After their waiter poured the wine, Riley raised his glass. "To new beginnings," he said.

Johnson seemed confused. "That's an odd toast. What's the point?"

"The point, my dear, is that I need to reintroduce myself."

"Why would you need to reintroduce yourself? I know who you are."

"No, you knew who I was, but Xander Riley has had to fold up his tent and slink away."

"Meaning?"

"Meaning that the only reason the persistent Inspector Bib released me is because I told him who I really am."

"Who you really are? What are you talking about?"

Riley plunged ahead. "I'm sorry, Pam, but you see, I've been living a bit of a lie."

"Oh no, you're not married are you?"

"It's nothing like that, and please don't get upset, but my name isn't Xander Riley. It's Jacob Stein. I had to tell Bib the truth about my family background and career to convince him I'm not a killer."

"Your family background? I thought you were abandoned on the church steps as a baby."

"Uh-uh. But I am an only child."

Johnson gave him a blank stare. "So your name isn't Xander Riley and you weren't an orphan. Excuse me for asking, but are you really an adventure writer?"

"I'm a writer of sorts. While I can spin a good yarn, I don't always do everything I write about. You see, I'm not much when it comes to actual adventure."

"This is unbelievable. Then you did make up stuff in your story on Ecuador, like Joan Smollett said."

Stein nodded. "But I didn't invent the basic facts. I just embroidered my part in the account."

"You know the magazine will never run your article when they find out."

"I suppose so," Stein said with a glum look.

Johnson took a healthy drink of wine. "What else should I know about you, Mr. Stein?"

"I'm as rich as Richie Rich," Stein said wryly. "Does that cut me any slack?"

"Not with National Geographic, but it does make you interesting. Tell me more."

Stein recounted the story he'd told Inspector Bib. When he finished, Johnson patted his shoulder. "You should catch the next flight to Hollywood. That's where you belong, out there with all the other folks who live in fantasy worlds."

"Tell me one thing, Pam. Does this mean we're through?"

Johnson gave that some consideration. "You may be a fraud, but at least you're a lovable one." She took another gulp of wine. "I don't know what I'm letting myself in for, but I'd hate to see you walk out of my life."

Stein gave her his old rakish grin. "Then let's not get off the carousel." He studied the sunny, cloudless sky. "I've got an idea. Let's visit the National Zoo this afternoon. I'm comfortable with wild animals as long as they're in cages. We can stroll around holding hands like a couple of teenagers."

By the time they reached the zoo, Johnson had regained her lighthearted mood, although she kept glancing at her partner. "Jacob Stein," she said. "There's a fine Irish moniker. Did it come with an emerald green yarmulke? I do like Jacob though. It fits you better than Xander now that I think about it."

"Jacob is all right," Stein said. "It's a lot better than Shlomo. I have a cousin named Shlomo. When I was a kid, I thought his name was short for Slow Motion."

"So tell me, *Jacob*, do you have a coat of many colors? Or perhaps you have many coats of different colors, a whole closetful to suit whichever character you're playing."

"Ouch," Stein said. "Changing the subject, what critters do you want to see first? Snakes?"

"Too scary."

"Apes?"

"Too ugly"

"Ostriches?"

"Too weird."

"Then what, pray tell, tickles your fancy?"

"Let's go see the big cats. They're exquisite—graceful and menacing at the same time. It will give you a chance to see a jaguar for the first time, assuming you made up that tale in your lecture about your nocturnal encounter with one."

"That was a pretty good story, wasn't it? The old gal who asked me that question wanted a thrill, so I gave her one. No harm done."

Johnson pointed to something ahead of them. "There, look," she said. "It's a real, live jaguar."

"I say, they are frightening beasts aren't they? I guarantee you if I saw one of those at night in the jungle it would definitely scare the pee out of me."

A short walk past the jaguar they came to a cage with a black panther pacing inside.

"It's so beautiful," Johnson exclaimed. "And look at those big yellow eyes. They seem to see right through you."

"Did you ever see the old movie *Cat People?*" Stein asked.

"I've never heard of it."

"It's a classic supernatural horror film. It's about a woman who turns into a black panther when she's angry and attacks people. In the end, she frees a black panther in the Central Park Zoo and it kills her. The movie makes you wonder if a person you think you know can be someone altogether different. Kind of like me."

Johnson went silent, and her smile disappeared. "Let's go home, Xander—I mean Jacob. I've seen enough animals."

That night in Johnson's bedroom, they clung to one another with tender familiarity. The darkness and stillness were soothing following a day filled with surprises. Johnson gave Stein a lingering kiss then rolled back over to her side of the bed. She sighed deeply and patted his leg. "At least some things about you haven't changed, my curious friend."

At nine o'clock on the dot, Archimedes Bib received his daughter's weekly telephone call. Bib took Sylvia's calls in his study, where he could relax in his easy chair. Sometimes the calls went on for over an hour. Bib shut the door to ensure their conversations were private, even though the always considerate Amara found some chore to keep her busy in another part of the house on Saturday nights.

"Hi, Pop," Sylvia said when Bib answered the phone. That cheery greeting was like a shot of adrenaline for Bib.

"Hello, Syl," he responded, using the nickname her mother had given her. "How's everyone in sunny California?"

"We're all dandy. Little Charlie got another tooth this week, and Stewart got a promotion at work. But let me give you some even better news. Stewart's company is sending him to Washington for a conference. That means we'll all be coming out to see you. I hope you and Amara can put up with us for a week."

Bib did the rarest of things for him. He whooped with delight. "When are you coming?" he asked eagerly.

"The first week of April. You won't be too tied up with work, will you?"

"No problem there. I'll take annual leave while you're here. The weather should be fine, so we can do whatever you want." Bib hadn't felt this good in ages. He sounded more like a college kid than a tough police inspector.

"I'll start making a list," Sylvia said. "We'll hit the museums on the Mall, and we can take in a play if there's anything interesting. Maybe we can drive over to Great Falls Park. I'm sure the waterfall would fascinate Charlie and Stewart. And of course, I'll want to visit Mom."

Bib's mood changed instantly. "I was out at Oakwood this morning. It was beautiful, with everything in bloom."

"What kind of flowers did you take?"

"Daffodils."

They were both silent for several moments.

"How's Uncle Py?" Sylvia asked. "Still romancing the lovely flower lady?"

"Py's the same as always, the debonair social butterfly. And yes, he and Barbara still make the rounds together."

"Do you think they'll ever get hitched?"

"I doubt it. I think they both like things the way they are. Or at least Py does."

"And how's Amara?"

"She just bought herself a fancy new hat, what with Easter coming up. She and her friends at her church try to outdo each other every year."

Bib savored the sound of Sylvia's laughter, a sound that almost made him cry.

"Are you doing okay?" Sylvia asked.

"No major complaints, although I've spent the past couple of weeks chasing my tail on a case that hit close to home. A woman Py and I went to high school with was murdered at National Geographic headquarters, where she worked. Py and I had recently seen her at our thirtieth annual class reunion."

"Oh my gosh. That's terrible. Was she a friend?"

"Not really, but since our class hasn't lost many members, her death came as a total shock to everyone. Thankfully, we're about to wrap up the case. This morning, we discovered some evidence that appears to establish the killer's identity." Bib paused. "I have to tell you, solving this one isn't as satisfying as other cases I've worked on."

"Why not?"

"Because the suspect seems genuinely nice. I know that I shouldn't let my personal opinions influence the way I feel about an investigation, but I haven't been able to preserve my normal detachment this time. That's why I'm not looking forward to what I'll be doing tomorrow."

"Then you'll be making the arrest?"

"I have to. My job sometimes forces me to do things I don't like, but murder is murder."

Chapter 24

Sunday

Bib put it off for as long as he could, telling himself that most people either slept late on Sunday morning or got up to go to church. He didn't need to hurry anyway. The arrest warrant he'd obtained yesterday wouldn't expire. At ten o'clock, he telephoned Sergeant Dowden and told him he'd pick him up at police headquarters for the short drive they had to make. "We'll get there before twelve in case you-know-who has any lunch plans."

For Bib, the drive south on the George Washington Memorial Parkway was a familiar journey. He remembered driving the road years ago on the way to visit Mount Vernon, where he and Phyllis had taken Sylvia for her tenth birthday. He still marveled that a ten-year-old girl would make such a request. This morning, passenger jets were thundering into the sky as Bib's unmarked black Ford passed National Airport. Out on the broad Potomac River, white-hulled pleasure boats were sailing back and forth like giant swans. It was another relaxing Sunday morning in the nation's capital, although for one person it would be anything but a day of repose.

When Bib reached Alexandria, he double-checked the address he'd written down. He parked in front of a well-kept older building on Queen Street, and he and Sergeant Dowden went inside. On the second floor, Bib knocked on the door of the apartment they sought. He gave Dowden a grim look. Bib had to knock again before they heard someone stirring. When the door swung open, Bib was startled to see Jacob Stein standing inside. Stein was barefoot and wearing a shirt and pair of trousers he'd obviously just thrown on. Stein was equally startled to see Bib.

"Inspector," Stein said. "What brings you out on this glorious Sunday morning?"

Bib was having difficulty getting over the surprise of seeing Stein where he least expected to find him. "May we come in?" he asked.

Stein stepped aside. "Of course."

Hearing their voices, Pamela Johnson appeared from the bedroom. She had on a flowered bathrobe and was in the process of combing her long, tangled hair. She stopped combing when she saw Inspector Bib and Sergeant Dowden standing in her living room.

Johnson threw her hairbrush down and rushed over to Stein, taking his arm as if to retain possession of him. "You're not going to arrest Jacob again are you? Haven't you harassed him enough?"

"We're not here to arrest Mr. Stein," Bib told her. There was a hint of sorrow in his voice. "Miss Johnson, we're going to have to ask you to come with us to police headquarters."

Stein automatically wrapped his arm around Johnson's shoulders. "Just what are you getting at, Inspector?"

"I wasn't aware the two of you are in a relationship," Bib said, "although that doesn't seem material to the business at hand." He heaved a sigh. "Pamela Johnson, we're arresting you for the murder of Mrs. Joan Smollett."

Johnson shrieked and backed away like some hideous monster was after her. "No, no. This isn't possible."

"I'm afraid it is, Miss Johnson," Bib said. "Please get dressed."

Johnson collapsed onto the sofa. Burying her face in her hands, she unleashed a torrent of tears.

"Mr. Stein, perhaps you could help your friend get dressed."

Bib might as well have been speaking Swahili. When Stein grasped what Bib had said, he gave him a pleading look. "May I come with her to the station, Inspector?"

"I'm sorry, but that's not allowed."

Stein knelt beside Johnson and attempted to comfort her. "Don't worry, hon. This has to be another stupid bureaucratic mistake. The police must figure if they keep arresting people, they'll eventually get the right person."

Bib couldn't think of an appropriate response to such an inane suggestion.

Johnson wept all the way to police headquarters. By the time she arrived in the interrogation room, she was all cried out. That was for the best as far as Bib was concerned. He'd tried to interview blubbering women before—and more than a few blubbering men. It was always a useless exercise. Johnson sat across the table from him, staring into space like a zombie. Her hollow, red-rimmed eyes and blank, frozen expression indicated she was struggling to accept what was happening. Sergeant Dowden stood in a corner of the room, huge and silent, the personification of unrelenting justice.

Bib cleared his throat and began. "Miss Johnson, yesterday I recalled a piece of information I'd been given during the interviews we conducted with the staff at National Geographic. At the time, I overlooked that information because it seemed irrelevant, but I was wrong."

Johnson continued staring into space.

"I remembered being told by Peter Nance that you had possession of the artifacts that—let's use his real name—that Jacob Stein used in his two lectures at Constitution Hall. You didn't turn everything over to Explorers Hall until after the lectures. Among those artifacts were a Jivaro blowgun and a quiver full of poison darts. We believe that you used one of those darts to murder Mrs. Smollett. Do you have anything to say in your defense?"

Johnson finally looked at Bib. She knew the time for evasion was over. "There's no point in denying what I did," she said, "but Jacob had nothing to do with it. Lord knows he's committed wholesale fakery with his articles, but he's not a killer."

"I'd already come to that conclusion, Miss Johnson. While Mr. Stein is adept at masquerades, he doesn't seem to be the type of person to take part in a conspiracy to commit murder. That would be too real for a man who prefers playing games.

But surely you must have realized that using a poison dart would implicate him."

"If I'd been thinking straight, I would have. It was only after you arrested him that I saw how foolish I'd been. That's why I was so devastated by the news."

Johnson sat up straighter, resigned to telling Inspector Bib everything he wanted to know. She almost looked forward to getting things off her chest. "You're probably wondering why I remained silent after you arrested Jacob. Please believe me, Inspector. If he had been put on trial, I would have come forward. I was hoping against hope that the case would go unsolved, but I would never have let him suffer for my actions."

"I do believe you, Miss Johnson. Now, please describe what you did on the day of the murder."

"I'd taken one of the poison darts earlier and kept it in my office. On the Sunday when I saw Smollett had come in to work, I pretended that I wanted her advice on a press release I'd written about Jacob's upcoming exhibit. While she leaned over her desk to read the copy, I stabbed her in the neck with the dart. It seemed like someone else was guiding my hand. You should have seen the look on her face. I stood there and watched her die. It didn't take long."

Johnson took a deep breath. "You have no idea how much I hated that loathsome woman."

"Why did you hate her?"

"Because she treated me and everyone else like she was royalty and we were ignorant peasants. After I started working at National Geographic, she began sending me marked-up copies of my press releases, calling attention to alleged flaws in the wording. As I told you before, Inspector, I have a degree in journalism from the University of Georgia. I know how to write, far better than that horrible woman ever could."

"That seems like an awfully thin excuse for committing murder, Miss Johnson. Why didn't you throw away her comments without bothering to look at them? That would have been far less stressful that taking everything to heart."

"Those marked up press releases were the least of Smollett's attacks on me. Once, in a department head meeting in the president's office, I mistakenly used the word 'mute' when I meant to say 'moot.' Smollett laughed out loud and said, 'I suppose a *mute* point would be silent.' I hated going to staff meetings after that. I was always afraid I'd make another gaffe and be mocked in front of everyone by that old hag.

"The final straw came the Friday before…the murder. The woman humiliated me in another staff meeting when I inadvertently mispronounced 'library' as 'lie-berry.' The bitch gave one of her superior little chuckles and said, *'Lie-berry?* Is that some kind of fruit that makes you tell lies?' All the other department heads sitting around the table laughed at me. I've never been so mortified in my entire life. I wanted to jump out the window. When I looked at Joan Smollett's smug, know-it-all face, I knew right then she had to die. I couldn't go on with her constantly hovering over me like some horrid vulture."

"Ah, that explains the page from the dictionary with the word 'library' circled." Bib motioned to Sergeant Dowden, who produced the book they'd taken from the office they'd searched at National Geographic. The book was a Webster's dictionary. Bib plopped the heavy volume on the table and flipped to a place he'd bookmarked.

"This is your dictionary, Miss Johnson. We retrieved it from your office." He turned the open book so she could view where he'd marked. "As you can see, a page has been torn out. A page that would have contained the word 'library.'"

"I bet you were stumped by that. I stuffed the page into her mouth as payback. I wanted to shove her own words down her throat. You don't know how much I've suffered over what I did to her, Inspector Bib. There've been times when I wished I could turn back the clock, but that woman caused so much unhappiness in the lives of those around her."

"As have you, Miss Johnson. As have you."

Johnson's face crumpled, and she began crying once more. Bib waited until she stopped.

"Why did you take the wallet from Mrs. Smollett's purse?"

Johnson sniffed. "To make it look like the killing was tied to a robbery. That was pretty lame, I realize."

"Yes it was."

"What did you do with the murder weapon?"

"I threw it into the Potomac. I took a river cruise one night and dropped it in the water." Johnson's voice grew plaintive. "You have to understand, Inspector. When you hate someone so much, it gives you tunnel vision. They're all that you can think about, and the only way to end the torment is to blot them out."

"I'm no lawyer, Miss Johnson, and I'm not supposed to give suspects legal advice, but perhaps your attorney may decide your best defense is to plead temporary insanity. It certainly seems you weren't in your right mind when you attacked Mrs. Smollett."

"Thank you, Inspector. That means a lot to me."

Bib turned to Dowden. "Sergeant, would you please escort Miss Johnson to her cell."

"Inspector," Johnson said, "all the detective shows say that a prisoner gets to make one phone call. May I make mine?" Her lips began to tremble. "I need to call my parents."

Twenty minutes later, Johnson sat alone in her cell. Once her parents got over the shock of what she had to tell them, they promised to be on the next flight to Washington, and they said they'd hire the best lawyer they could find to defend her.

Johnson shuddered as she looked around the dismal cell. She recalled her lover's description of the oppressive experience of being incarcerated. He hadn't exaggerated anything, although ever since she'd committed the cardinal sin of murder, the weight of what she'd done had been far worse than any penalty society could exact.

Johnson reflected on her interrogation. How strange it was that she'd told Inspector Bib everything she'd wanted to tell a priest but couldn't. The only thing missing was a confessional. Unburdening herself of her secret had given her a measure of relief, even though Bib couldn't offer her forgiveness. Forgiveness seemed beyond her reach. Despite that fact, she knelt beside her bunk and prayed for God's mercy.

That afternoon, Jacob Stein visited Johnson. They sat in the same room where they'd sat when their roles were reversed. Neither of them seemed to know what to say. Johnson was calmer now, having accepted what lay ahead. Her mind had become focused on atonement rather than concealment. She'd even had the crazy notion of becoming a nun once she'd paid her debt to society. Or she could dedicate her life to some other form of service. Maybe join the Peace Corps or work in a soup kitchen. If they ever did let her out of jail.

Johnson laid her hand on Stein's. "I'd never have let you pay for my crime, Jacob. All my fussing and worrying was because of the guilt I felt over your wrongful arrest."

This time, it was his turn to do the crying.

"This is where it all began," Pythagoras Bib said to his brother, "back in 1888." Py looked around the spacious dining room of the Cosmos Club. The prestigious private organization occupied an ornate mansion on Massachusetts Avenue's Embassy Row. "That was when thirty-three prominent explorers, scientists, and scholars decided to form 'a society for the increase and diffusion of geographic knowledge.' They called it the National Geographic Society.

"Of course, that historic event didn't happen in this very building. Back then, the club was located in the old Dolley Madison House, but the inspiration came from the members of the Cosmos Club. Men like Gardiner Greene Hubbard and John Wesley Powell, titans of their age."

"I always enjoy your lecture on National Geographic's beginnings," Archie said.

"Oh, am I repeating myself?"

"A little, but that's all right. I haven't heard the story for several years. It's good to have a refresher course every now and then."

The Bib brothers' Sunday night get-together took place at least once a year in the Cosmos Club. Py was proud to be a member, although he disagreed with the club's policy that women weren't allowed to join. He once joked that the old boys' club should hand out codpieces to new members. The club was as tradition-bound as any gentlemen's club in London, with rooms where members could sip their premium brandy and puff their expensive cigars while reading the newspaper in undisturbed silence.

Archie and Py both wore suits and ties for the occasion, a club requirement for those having dinner. Waiters in crisp white shirts, black ties, black trousers, and black vests circulated about the room, taking orders and serving food. Most of them were older men, with the formal bearing befitting the staff in such an exclusive venue. Archie always felt out of his bailiwick here. He was uncomfortable in a setting where the waiters were better dressed than he was.

After a serious-looking man with a pencil-thin mustache took their order, Py brought up the topic of the evening. "So it was Pamela Johnson," he said.

"It's hard to believe, isn't it," Archie replied. "She struck me as friendly and even-tempered, an unlikely person to commit murder. It proves that you can't always trust your own instincts. You'd think I'd have learned that by now."

"Why did she do it?"

"A buildup of grievances over Joan Smollett's gratuitous criticisms of her work and of trifling things Johnson said in meetings. Twice, Smollett ridiculed her in front of the other department heads, most recently for mispronouncing the word 'library.' Johnson finally snapped over that one. It was the reason she stuffed that page from the dictionary in Smollett's mouth."

"Luckily, most people have a buffer against those sorts of unwarranted attacks," Py said. "Usually, they laugh them off or simply ignore them altogether. Other people are so sensitive that the only recourse they can think of is retaliation. And I'm not talking about mental cases. There are normal, healthy individuals who are stung deeply by malicious criticism.

"You and I both saw examples of that in the Army, most often with young recruits who were doing their best only to be put down by some bully boy who outranked them. You could tell how much it hurt some of those kids. The urge to persecute another person is an aspect of human nature that's difficult to understand. Everyone has their own way of being stupid, and some people are just thoughtlessly cruel. About the only thing you can do is distance yourself from them, if possible."

"That was exactly Pamela Johnson's problem. She couldn't get away from Joan Smollett, and she couldn't stop thinking about her. She reached the point of desperation."

"That's sad. With sufficient provocation, anyone can fall into the abyss of an irrational obsession. Psychologists call them idées fixes. Nasty things, obsessions. They can take over your life and make you do things you wouldn't ordinarily do."

"Like murder someone?"

"Precisely."

"I'm afraid I overstepped my bounds by suggesting that Miss Johnson could consider entering a plea of temporary insanity. I've never done anything like that in twenty years. I must be getting soft."

"You obviously felt there was something different about her case," Py said. "But don't beat yourself up over it. That's the approach any good attorney would take."

Archie waved his hand as if shooing away a fly. "That's enough shop talk. We don't want to spoil our dinner. Besides, I haven't given you the good news."

"What good news?"

"Sylvia's husband will be attending a conference here in Washington during the first week of April, and he's bringing the family."

"That's wonderful. I haven't seen Stewart and Syl since their wedding, and I've never seen the star of the show. Does little Charlie take after his grandfather?"

"I'm relieved to report that he doesn't look a thing like me. Syl proposed making an outing to Great Falls Park. Maybe you and Barbara could join us. We can take a picnic lunch."

"I'm in, but I'll have to check with Barbara to see if she can tear herself away from the flower shop. If she says she can't make it, I'll tell her that I'll have to ask someone else. That should clinch the deal."

"That sounds a lot like coercion," Archie said.

"Let's call it the gentle art of persuasion."

Chapter 25

Monday

There was nothing left for Bib to do but handle the fallout from the events of the weekend. He began at National Geographic by calling on associate editor Vernon Hall. When Bib peered into Hall's office, the man was standing with his back to the door, staring out the window.

"Hello," Bib said in an uncertain tone. "Am I interrupting some deep thoughts?"

Hall turned around with a look of distraction. His hair was tousled, as if he'd been scratching his head, and his owlish eyeglasses were slightly askew. "Oh, good morning, Inspector," Hall said. "I've been expecting you. Please come in."

Bib took a seat in front of Hall's desk. "I assume the reason you've been expecting me is that you've gotten word of what's happened."

Hall plopped down in his chair. "Indeed. Mr. Riley—I mean Mr. Stein—preceded you, Inspector Bib. He stopped by first thing this morning and delivered the most astounding news I've heard in ages. He came clean about his duplicity, and he also told me you arrested Pamela Johnson for the murder of Mrs. Smollett—and that she confessed to the crime. I tell you, Inspector, I feel like I've been hit up both sides of the head with a two-by-four."

"It wasn't his place to tell you about Miss Johnson, Dr. Hall, but since the cat is out of the bag, I'll fill in the details that Mr. Stein wouldn't know."

Hall straightened his glasses and ran a hand over his hair, regaining his professorial look. "Please do."

"Miss Johnson did confess to the murder. She said that Mrs. Smollett had harassed her ever since she took over the Society's public affairs duties. Apparently, Mrs. Smollett critiqued every one of Miss Johnson's press releases, offering unsolicited advice that angered Miss Johnson. Also, Mrs. Smollett reportedly mocked some slight verbal slips Miss Johnson made in meetings, embarrassing her in front of other department heads. The net effect was that Miss Johnson developed an intense hatred of Mrs. Smollett."

"Oh my. It's astonishing that a person's grating personality could drive someone to murder. So Pamela is in jail. That image will take some getting used to. She always seemed like the Belle of the South. Smart, organized, and dedicated to her job."

"I think she truly was all those things—until she succumbed to her obsession with Joan Smollett. You may know that my brother Pythagoras has studied psychology. He emphasizes how easily an obsession can take over a person's life, which it clearly did with Miss Johnson."

Bib's own obsession over his wife's death had certainly taken over his life and could have led to his ruin. He knew he was in no position to pass judgment on anyone who was under great mental stress. His only job was to deal with any criminal consequences, despite how difficult it might be to disregard the circumstances.

"Then Pamela was the one who stole a poison dart."

"That's right. For a week or so, she had possession of the artifacts Stein used in his lectures, and she helped herself to one of the darts. She may not have had murder in mind at the time. It could have been some subliminal urge to defend herself, or maybe she just wanted a souvenir. Of course, those are only guesses."

"It probably doesn't matter much now."

"The prosecuting attorney will likely characterize her theft as proof of premeditation. I don't know why, but I keep looking for explanations that might lessen the stigma of what she did. Silly of me."

"I don't think so, Inspector. It's human nature. Surely even cops have feelings of sympathy from time to time."

"We're not supposed to." Bib scanned the yellow spines of the *National Geographic* magazines on the shelf behind Dr. Hall's desk. "What did Mr. Stein tell you about his creative approach to journalism?"

Hall shook his head over his bizarre meeting with Stein. "After he apologized for his deception, he gave me a cashier's check covering all the payments he's received from National Geographic for his two articles and his lectures."

"He can afford it. Did he mention that he's from an extremely well-to-do family?"

"He didn't."

"After we arrested him, Stein revealed his trickery to me, and he told me all about his family background, which I corroborated. It convinced me that Stein is no killer, so we released him. He's just a rich kid who likes to pretend to be someone more interesting than the heir to a fortune built on selling Chevrolets in Newark, New Jersey."

"That does sound rather prosaic."

Bib recalled what Stein's uncle and Stein himself had told him. "He's also been a mime, a chef, a ghost tour leader, and a blackjack dealer. Who knows what he'll get up to next. None of what he's done for National Geographic is actually illegal, although selling doctored stories while posing as an adventure writer does seem to stretch the bounds of professional ethics."

"His behavior may not have been against the law, but we assuredly feel bamboozled. The strange thing is, Stein went to great lengths to explain that the only falsified part of his latest story was the description of his participation in the expedition to find the Jivaros. He was adamant that none of the facts he included about the Jivaro culture were made up, and he pointed out that Mrs. Smollett had corrected his few small mistakes. He said he drew his information from Jake Plummer's field notes and the *Encyclopaedia Britannica*. Doesn't that beat all. Aside from the photos of him taken in Ecuador, he could have produced the entire article in his bedroom in Newark. So much for adventure."

Hall held up a folder. "In addition to refunding the money we paid him, Stein gave me several documents attesting to the provenance of the Jivaro artifacts he purchased in Quito. He said that since the artifacts were all authentic, National Geographic could continue with the exhibit if we wanted to. He also suggested that we could run the article as a photo story, cutting out any references to him and his phony exploits and giving Jake Plummer the sole credit. Those are radical ideas, but I'll run them by Mr. Grosvenor and our attorneys to get their reactions.

"If it were up to me, I'd take Stein's advice. So much work has gone into this project that it seems a shame to waste it. We've sold a lot of tickets for the exhibit, and it would easy to edit out the mythical Xander Riley from the article, like we do with any other problematic material. Setting Stein's chicanery aside, Plummer's photos of the Jivaros are terrific. They're definitely worth publishing and showcasing in an exhibit."

Bib frowned. "Unfortunately, some unfavorable publicity related to the story will have to come out. There's no way to hide the fact that the weapon used to kill Mrs. Smollett came from the artifacts you'd be featuring in your exhibit. So far, we haven't told the press that Mrs. Smollett was poisoned with curare. This afternoon, however, we'll be announcing that we've obtained a confession from Miss Johnson. Even if we only tell the press that she injected Mrs. Smollett with a lethal substance, the fact that she used one of the Jivaro poison darts will come out in the trial."

"Hmm. I hadn't thought that far ahead. It does complicate things for us, although the connection would no doubt titillate the public in a macabre way. And you have to consider that newspaper accounts of scandals tend to be forgotten in a matter of days, as soon as the next scandal comes along. *National Geographic* articles, on the other hand, stand the test of time. You could almost say they're written for the ages. Anyway, I'm glad I'm not the one who'll have to decide the fate of 'Headhunters of the Amazon.' That will be Mr. Grosvenor's call."

Hall chuckled. "Even if MBG kills the story and the exhibit, Jacob Stein will go down in the annals of the Society. Since we can't call back Mr. Stein's "Treasures of the Orinoco" article that we ran two years ago, his work will mark the only time that *National Geographic* magazine has ever published fiction."

Bib sat in his office at police headquarters attacking the pile of paperwork connected with the Smollett murder. He looked up when he heard a knock on his door. For the second time in two days, Bib was startled to see Jacob Stein.

"Mr. Stein—I didn't expect to see you again so soon. Come in and have a seat."

"Thanks, Inspector. I was in the building visiting Pam, so I thought I'd stop by and ask you if I'm free to leave town."

"Well, let's see. Miss Johnson described how she acquired the dart she used to kill Mrs. Smollett. She simply took one without your knowledge while she had possession of your material. Since that didn't involve you in any way, there doesn't seem to be a reason for you to remain in Washington if you don't want to. If you're needed to testify at her trial, we can always contact you through your Uncle Noah."

"Oh, I'll be back for the trial. I'm not going to abandon Pam. And while I may not have been involved technically in what she did, Inspector, I can't help feeling partially responsible. If I hadn't brought those damned poison darts back from Ecuador, none of this might have happened."

"You don't know that. Miss Johnson may have found some other way of perpetrating her crime."

"Maybe, but I made it easy for her."

Bib's opinion of Jacob Stein was undergoing a revision. "How was Miss Johnson this morning?"

"She seems uncannily peaceful, given the circumstances. Her parents are with her now, so I got to meet them. They seem like nice people. I told them I'd pay for Pam's attorney, whatever the cost."

"That's very generous of you."

"It's the least I can do."

"So what's next in the unconventional life of Jacob Stein?" Bib asked.

"First I'm going home to lick my wounds and sort out my options. After the trial, I may follow some advice Pam gave me. She said I should catch the next plane out to Hollywood, since that was where people who live in make-believe worlds belong. I'd feel at home there, given that Jewish innovators played such an important role in creating Hollywood, from the men who built the studios to the writers, directors, and actors."

"You realize that National Geographic may cancel your article and the exhibit, although Vernon Hall was intrigued by your suggestion about sanitizing the material and going ahead with everything."

"Frankly, I don't care what they do with it. I wish I'd never gone to Ecuador."

"I can understand that," Bib said.

Stein stood up and offered Bib his hand. "So long, then."

Bib stood up as well and shook his hand. "Mazel tov," he said with a wink.

Stein stopped in the doorway and smiled. "If you're ever in Newark again, Inspector, I can get you a good deal on a new Chevrolet." With that, the great imposter was gone.

That night, Bib settled into the easy chair in his study. He'd finally gotten hooked by Harper Lee's novel *To Kill a Mockingbird* and had nearly finished it. The story of the widowed lawyer Atticus Finch had parallels to his own life. Finch's decision to defy the local community by defending a black man falsely accused of raping a white woman drew Bib to the character even more. The fact that Finch's client was unfairly convicted and killed while trying to escape drove home how capricious the law could be.

After Bib read the last page, he laid the book aside and thought of Pamela Johnson, sitting alone in her cell as he relaxed in the comfort of his home. How would the law treat her?

He knew that an attractive young white woman would stand a better chance of earning a light sentence than a black man would in similar circumstances. Even so, Pamela Johnson's life had been stained forever.

Bib chastised himself for the sympathy he felt for Johnson. In taking Joan Smollett's life, she'd committed the type of senseless slaughter that Atticus Finch had warned his daughter about. Joan Smollett may have been more of a squawking crow than a songbird, but as Atticus Finch told Scout, it was a sin to kill a defenseless creature. Young Jacob Stein had felt the weight of that sin when he shot a robin with his new BB gun.

Bib was weary. He vowed to banish all thoughts of right and wrong for the rest of the night. He was no legal or ethical expert. He was just a middle-aged cop, and tomorrow he had to start a new investigation. Someone had broken into the home of a prominent Washington businessman and murdered his wife during a robbery. The police commissioner was already pressing for a quick resolution of the case.

Bib got up from his easy chair. He could hear Amara laughing at the antics of Lucille Ball on *The Lucy Show*, which the good and gentle Jamaican housekeeper watched faithfully every Monday night. As always, the sound of Amara's laughter soothed Bib's mind. He turned out the light in his study. It was time for him to go to bed.

Epilogue

The day that William Price and his wife returned to Baltimore from Palm Springs, Price told Marybeth that he would be initiating divorce proceedings. Marybeth managed to stifle a cry of exultation and said, "If that's what you want, hon." Marybeth was ecstatic over the prospect of gaining her freedom and the financial windfall it entailed. Visions of Parisian sugarplums began dancing in her head. In a motel room across town, Wendy Gibbs awaited word from William Price about their upcoming nuptials, when she'd become Temporary Wife Number Five. Price had already given the busty former cabana girl a substantial down payment for services rendered, and she expected so much more. That night, Marybeth and two of her friends painted the town red.

After rearranging the furniture and redecorating the room to suit her superior taste, Rebecca Wimberly enthroned herself in her new office. It had taken her by surprise when associate editor Vernon Hall made the announcement that she was being tapped to head up the public affairs department. Hall sold the idea to the vainglorious woman by saying that her intelligence and poise made her the ideal person to represent National Geographic before the media. The bedazzled Wimberly even overlooked the fact that the job switch was a lateral move without an increase in salary. She had no inkling that the real reason for her reassignment was to ensure that she'd never be able to retaliate against recently promoted senior editorial researcher Ann Parker.

Having feigned a hangdog look of mourning for as long as he could stand it, Jeffrey Smollett asked Clarissa O'Neill to join him for dinner at Duke Zeibert's. They had a grand time, and afterward, Jeffrey drove Clarissa back to her apartment in his new Austin-Healey 3000, trying to keep his eyes on the road and off her lovely legs. When they stopped, Jeffrey reached behind Clarissa's seat and retrieved a present he'd brought for her, the best of his framed watercolors. Clarissa was so pleased by the beautiful painting that she asked Jeffrey to come up to her apartment and help her hang it. After that memorable night, a romantic Caribbean cruise was definitely within the realm of possibility.

With his tenure as adventure writer Xander Riley at an end, Jacob Stein jettisoned the notion of investigating the wonders of Baghdad, including those tantalizing Iraqi women. On the train ride home to Newark, he picked up a news magazine someone had left behind and began reading an article about China. According to the story, Americans with a talent for acting were being hired to help Chinese companies create the impression that they had important commercial connections in the United States. Pretending to be high-powered executives, the Americans read phony prepared speeches at Chinese business conferences. A familiar gleam came to Stein's eyes, the look of a schoolboy contemplating a clever prank. Hollywood would have to wait. He'd never been to China.

Following his escape from the clutches of Xander Riley-cum-Jacob Stein, Jake Plummer lit out for the territory. Eventually, he pitched up in the Oso Negro Cantina in Tampico, Mexico, where he sat with a sloe-eyed young señorita named Lupe on his lap, a fifth of dark rum within reach on a rickety table, and a half-full glass in his hand. Ritchie Valens was singing "La Bamba" at high volume over the seedy cantina's tinny radio. Plummer lifted his glass to offer a toast to the pseudo adventure writer who'd had his disguise ripped away. "Vaya con Dios, señor Stein, you silly bastard." Plummer knocked back the rest of his drink and gave Lupe a peck on the cheek. He poured himself another shot of rum and smiled. He was thinking about his new assignment for *National Geographic*.

In the first week of April, Inspector Bib met his daughter and her family at National Airport. Bib kissed Sylvia, shook hands with Stewart, and took little Charlie in his arms. Charlie beamed and cooed at him, and when he grasped his grand-dad's long Rumpelstiltskin nose with his plump little hand, short, stooped, homely Archimedes Bib laughed with unconditional happiness.

About the Author

Author of fifteen works of fiction and nonfiction, Paul Martin spent three decades with National Geographic, the last ten years as executive editor of the Society's travel magazine. His writing assignments have taken him around the world. To learn more about his work, visit www.paulmartinbooks.com.

Acknowledgments

I'm indebted to my always supportive sister, Judy Martin, whose encouragement persuaded me to pursue this project. I also thank my former National Geographic colleagues Richard Crum, Cathy Healy, and Scott Stuckey for reviewing my manuscript. I owe my greatest debt of gratitude to the late Robert L. Breeden for making my dream come true by offering me a job at National Geographic. Finally, I want to emphasize that in all my years with the National Geographic Society I never met a single fellow employee who displayed Joan Smollett's abrasive personality or the elitist attitude of Rebecca Wimberly. Those two characters were simply necessary literary devices. My colleagues at National Geographic were uniformly the most accomplished, collegial, engaging group of people I've ever had the privilege to know. They helped make my career with National Geographic the most rewarding period of my life.